Nova checked the ledge—it wasn't more than eight inches wide. Leaning out, she could see, about twenty-five feet to her left, a light from the library where the secret meeting was to take place.

She turned around and leaned her back and head against the wall. She held her hand to her stomach, which was now slowly turning over.

She had to spy on that meeting. Over two months with Jean Paul, and still nothing. If he was innocent and she got caught, her actions would be impossible to justify. Her cover would be blown. But if he was guilty, she couldn't pass up the chance. And if he was guilty and she got caught?

"So don't get caught, Nova," she said sternly to herself. Risking her life was part of the job, especially when the fate of the world depended on whether she got on the ledge or not....

Dear Reader,

Welcome to Silhouette Bombshell, the hottest new line to hit the bookshelves this summer. Who is the Silhouette Bombshell woman? She's the bombshell of the new millennium; she's savvy, sexy and strong. She's just as comfortable in a cocktail dress as she is brandishing blue steel! Now she's being featured in the four thrilling reads we'll be bringing you each month.

What can you expect in a Silhouette Bombshell novel? A high-stakes situation in which the heroine saves the day. She's the kind of woman who always gets her man—and we're not just talking about the bad guy. Take a look at this month's lineup....

From *USA TODAY* bestselling author Lindsay McKenna, we have *Daughter of Destiny,* an action-packed adventure featuring a Native American military pilot on a quest to find the lost ark of her people. Her partner on this dangerous trek? The one man she never thought she'd see again, much less risk her life with!

This month also kicks off ATHENA FORCE, a brand-new twelve-book continuity series featuring friends bonded during their elite training and reunited when one of them is murdered. In *Proof,* by award-winning author Justine Davis, you'll meet a forensic investigator on a mission, and the sexy stranger who may have deadly intentions toward her.

Veteran author Carla Cassidy brings us a babe with an attitude—and a sense of humor. Everyone wants to *Get Blondie* in this story of a smart-mouthed cop and the man she just can't say no to when it comes to dealing out justice.

Finally, be the first to read hot new novelist Judith Leon's *Code Name: Dove,* featuring Nova Blair, the CIA's secret weapon. Nova's mission this time? Seduction.

We hope you enjoy this killer lineup!

Sincerely,

Natashya Wilson
Associate Senior Editor, Silhouette Bombshell

Please address questions and book requests to:
Silhouette Reader Service
U.S.: 3010 Walden Ave., P.O. Box 1325, Buffalo, NY 14269
Canadian: P.O. Box 609, Fort Erie, Ont. L2A 5X3

CODE NAME:
DOVE
JUDITH LEON

Published by Silhouette Books

America's Publisher of Contemporary Romance

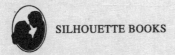 SILHOUETTE BOOKS

ISBN 0-373-51318-6

CODE NAME: DOVE

Visit Silhouette Books at www.eHarlequin.com

Printed in U.S.A.

JUDITH LEON

has made the transition from left-brained scientist to right-brained novelist. Before she began writing fiction some twelve years ago, she was teaching animal behavior and ornithology in the UCLA biology department.

She is the author of several novels and two screenplays. Her epic of the Minoan civilization, *Voice of the Goddess,* published under her married name, Judith Hand, has won numerous awards. Her second epic historical, *The Amazon and the Warrior,* is based on the life of Penthesilea, an Amazon who fought the warrior Achilles in the Trojan War. In all of her stories she writes of strong, bold women; women who are doers and leaders.

An avid camper, classical music fan and birdwatcher, she currently lives in Rancho Bernardo, CA. For more information about the author and her books, see her Web site at www.jhand.com.

No man, or woman, is an island.
This book is dedicated with my profound gratitude
to those colleagues and friends who,
by reading and critiquing *Code Name: Dove,* taught me
priceless, early lessons on the craft of writing.

ACKNOWLEDGMENTS

I am indebted for information on airplanes
or flying, guns, security systems and spy craft to
Rex Anderson, Peter Carroll, Jay Lindsay, Bob Mahon,
Jerome White and Doug Winberg.

The book is dedicated to the following colleagues and
friends who read all or part of very early versions of
Code Name: Dove. To each of you, for your care and
criticism and shared expertise, I am forever beholden:
Shirley Allen, Terry Blain, Drusilla Campbell,
Julie Castiglia, Mark Clements, Chet Cunningham,
Barry Friedman, Phyllis Humphrey, Pete Johnson,
Marian Jones, Janet Kunert, Peggy Lang,
Mary Lou Locke, Bev Miller, Abby Padgett,
Ellen Perkins, Christie Ridgway, Ken Schafer,
Janice Steinberg, Marsha Stone, Jan Tuttle and Tom Utts.

Chapter 1

Valdez, Alaska, 1:00 a.m.
Sunday, May 15

The fishing trawler *Polaris* sliced through heavy drizzle and a calm sea at the mouth of Port Valdez Bay. From the aft deck a man in black peered through the Arctic darkness toward the shore, a tight knot of excitement like a clenched fist in his chest. Along the shore the pipeline terminal lights stood out like diamonds against black velvet.

His face drooped on the right side, its nerves severed by an old wound. He stroked the damp, corpselike cheek and sucked another lungful from his cigarette. In ten minutes they would launch the Zodiacs. He snuffed the cigarette on the heel of his boot, jammed the butt into one of his flack vest pockets and entered the cabin.

Nine pairs of eyes fixed on him. These were The

Founder's elite—Earth's Warriors. Every man here had trained in the special forces of various armies before their dedication to The Founder, but still two faces showed fear: the Nigerian, Kariango, and the Frenchman, "Slow Jack" Soustelle.

"You two look ready to piss your pants," he said in English. "It's time to fix that." He strode to the forward bulkhead, fished out the key on the chain around his neck and opened the locked compartment. He removed a small, gray box that captured the men's attention as though it were a priceless jewel. The Founder's enforcer laid the box on the narrow central table, tilted the lid back and gently plucked the pencil-thin, pale yellow glass ampoule from its foam cushion.

He held it up so the men could see it. "Speed. Strength. Fearlessness. One smell of this and you'll be ten times the men you are now."

He scanned all their faces. "Ready?"

Dark-painted faces nodded. The men gave him grunts of eagerness. Slow Jack said, "Damn right! Bring on the coffee!"

The Founder's enforcer snapped the ampoule's slender neck. There was a slight click, and then the smell of burned coffee quickly diffused through the cabin. He sucked in a deep breath of the drug and felt immediately the flutter of an accelerating pulse. The others followed his example. The drug was altering their bodies, their fight response heightening in a way that made them— short of death itself—invincible. A test bar of steel, half an inch thick, lay on the table. He picked it up and, barehanded, bent it in two. The men murmured. He gestured toward the door. "Get the boats into the water."

Thirteen minutes later he huddled with his men on

stony ground fifty feet up from the shoreline, hidden under starlit darkness and four camouflage thermal blankets. The security system set up by the Alyeska pipeline oil partnership was ridiculously inadequate. A single fence, half a dozen cameras and only a token force of armed security guards. No motion detectors, no dead man's entrance, no slalom barriers. Only a few feet away lay a dead-end cul-de-sac in the road near Loading Berth Five.

The drizzle thickened into cold, pelting sleet. Finally the red security truck appeared. He nudged Wyczek. The two of them shimmied free of the blanket, hugged the ground as they moved apart till they reached the pavement on opposite sides of the cul-de-sac. The truck entered the turnaround and circled. Wyczek rose. The *dummkopf* driver's mouth dropped open in amazement. The man hit the brakes, fumbled at his holstered gun.

The enforcer bolted across the asphalt and, with his bare fist, shattered the window. He grabbed the door, ripped the thing off its hinges and tossed it aside, then pulled his combat knife. The driver turned. The enforcer slid across the seat and rammed his blade under the ribs, up into the man's heart. *"Terra eterna,"* he whispered.

He holstered the knife and then grabbed the driver's twitching body with both fists, yanked it from the truck and threw it like a rag doll to the side of the road. With his men, he piled into the truck bed.

Wyczek leaped into the truck cab and drove them back toward the terminal entrance. They turned right onto an access road to the upper levels, cruised past the Operations complex. The enforcer scanned for signs of danger.

"Still no alarm," Slow Jack muttered.

Wyczek braked to a halt. With Slow Jack, Wyczek and two other soldiers, the enforcer hit the ground running. His Uzi chugging, Wyczek chewed up the Ops Center door. Another Earth Warrior lobbed in a satchel charge packed with C-4 explosive and shrapnel, and the enforcer tossed a matching satchel through a window.

A brief pause, then two quick blasts.

The windows blew outward, the door exploded. The pipeline personnel knew they were here now.

Yellow and red light washed upward into the night. Kariango and Soustelle had blown the microwave antennae linking the Ops Center to the twelve pumping stations. They had cut off the snake's head. No way now could Valdez shut down the flow of oil or alert the outlying stations.

A brief vision of oil spilling across open tundra flashed into his head. *Can't be helped.* He further reassured himself by softly uttering one of The Founder's sayings, "If we must inflict some pain to the body to save it, so be it."

It took only eight more minutes to lay the plastique and the white phosphorus grenades in the walls of the containment dikes. The Alyeska security force finally came to life and under a storm of gunfire, he and his men dashed for the truck. Kariango took a hit in the leg.

Wyczek raced the truck toward the beach. Under fire, all of them piled into the Zodiacs. Two more men took hits before they could get out of firing range. When they were, the enforcer yelled, "Throttle back!" Wyczek slowed to near halt and the enforcer hit the electronic detonator. A roar bounded across the water. Then another.

The sound was impressive, but the sight— Christ!

Hundred-foot-high flames gouged like hungry tongues through the rain, licking the blackness. He clenched his fists. *"Fantastish!"* he whispered. His whole body vibrated. He sat transfixed.

Operation Viper had been executed flawlessly. Within the week he would report to The Founder in triumph. He shook himself and gave Wyczek the signal to get them out of here. As always, in a few hours he and the other men would hit "the pit" when the drug wore off, but the week-long depression was a small price to pay for this kind of thrill.

The Zodiacs streaked into the darkness.

Chapter 2

La Jolla, 7:00 a.m.
Sunday, May 15

"Nova, love. There *is* a Mr. Right for you. Your problem is, you don't try."

Reginald Pennypacker wheezed out his words of criticism between breaths as he and Nova rounded the final curve of the path along the bluff where they ran each morning. First her daily run, then the cougar photos.

They slowed to cool-down speed for the last block, uphill to the white, red-tile-roofed condominium where they each occupied one of the two top-floor units. Nova's lips turned up in a slight smile. Reginald Pennypacker, "Penny" as nearly everyone called him, was the closest thing she had to a best friend and confidant.

She was sorry her refusal to come to his party had him upset, but he'd never know the dark things Nova

Blair had done. *There's never going to be a Mr. Right, because I'll always be Mrs. Wrong.* Murder. Prison. Her work for the Company. No, Penny would never know why all his attempts at matchmaking would fail.

She treasured this spectacular La Jolla coastline. The best part of their run was that it let her gauge the Pacific's waves, smell her breath, feel her mood. Today the great ocean had the blues: flat, gray-blue water sloshed indifferently against the beach. The on-shore breeze carried the stink of seaweed. A perfect day for nitty-gritty slave labor in the darkroom. The magazine photo contest deadline was breathing down her neck. And then, there were the cougars. "I try. I keep my eye out for possibilities."

"If you were *trying,* you'd come Saturday." He used the hem of his red T-shirt to wipe beads of sweat from his forehead. "How *can* you say you can't make my party and still claim to be on the lookout for a man? I told a widowed admiral and a filthy rich, recently divorced trial lawyer you'd be there. They weren't going to come but I promised I'd introduce them to a world-class adventuress photographer. A dazzler with emerald-green eyes and onyx-black hair."

Nova reflected with a photographer's eye on Penny's slender elegance. Thirty-eight. Built like a marathoner. Part Irish and part Afro-American, and fiercely proud of both heritages. He was the owner of La Jolla's most exclusive beauty salon and he'd invited a "select group" of patrons and friends to a bash for his long-time lover's birthday. He smiled. Apparently his temper had cooled. He yanked twice on her ponytail. "You really must show. So I won't look like a fool."

"Why would you tell them I'd be there? You know

how my life works. I might be out of town. In fact, how about you just tell them I am out of town."

A two-brick-high trim bordered the green lawn next to them. Nova purposely stubbed her toe against the trim, did a somersault and landed on her back on the lawn. Alarmed, Penny rushed to kneel beside her. She reached up and, grinning, tugged twice on his earring. "Better yet. Tell them I had a jogging accident and broke my leg."

He shook his head, returned her grin and extended his hand to help her up. "See what I mean? You don't try. You avoid."

I don't avoid. I'm just a realist.

Side by side, they trotted up the three-floor stairwell. At the top they stepped onto the balcony running the length of its west side. From behind four palm trees standing guard on the lawn, a glorious Pacific vista beckoned. They shook out their arms and legs. She took in a lungful of salt air.

"You don't try, but when you make an effort to fancy up, Nova, you're really…well, really mesmerizing. Great legs. Fabulous eyes. That jet-black hair. You should have men hanging around here like bees after nectar."

"Don't be silly, Penny,"

"Don't be falsely modest, Nova." He paused, scanned her face, then looked away. "I watch you. The men buzz around, all right." He fluttered his fingers to mimic busy bees. "But when they zero in to land, you close up your little petals, like you're afraid they're going to steal something."

His words brought a sudden pang, a quick rapier-thrust to her heart. Candido Branco had left no visible scars; her stepfather had always avoided making wounds that would leave traces on her skin. But the scars on her soul were another matter.

Penny planted both hands on the balcony rail. "I've known you nearly twelve years. You've not had one serious attachment. Not since— How many years is it now since the amazing Ramone took off?"

"I'm not pining for Ramone Villalobos. The man did a lot for me. I was—" She started to say, Headed for big trouble, but switched. "He introduced me to travel and photography." She didn't add that he'd also recruited her for the CIA. "Unfortunately, I foolishly thought he loved me when he was just having a good time."

Penny straightened, crossed his arms. "I worry about you now and again, love. Maybe I better shut up, though, before I say something I'll regret."

An eerie feeling raced through her, hot and electric, a feeling that Penny was about to hand her the key to the dark rooms of her past. She felt her pulse quicken at the base of her throat. "No, don't shut up on me." Penny would say words that would explain why she was unable to trust. No. She knew why she couldn't trust any man. But Penny would say words that would tell her how she could trust again and then she'd be free from the past. "Say what you're thinking."

His gaze flicked to her face, apparently checking to see if he should continue. He plunged ahead. "I don't get it. You meet lots of men on the tours you lead. You've never once said you've slept with one. Maybe you just wouldn't tell me that."

He paused, still searching her face. She waited, afraid to interrupt.

"I can't imagine leading the macho, high-adventure

tours you do and not meeting men by the planeload. You think you're honestly open to offers?" He grinned. "You're thirty-three and not getting any younger."

Oddly, as suddenly as the mysterious feeling had hit, it fled; she felt as though she'd taken a six-floor drop in an elevator. Penny didn't have a magic key after all. "I don't know. Maybe not."

"Come to my party Saturday. You can practice opening up and I'll critique your man-baiting techniques."

She threw him a look of mock horror. "That sounds perfectly awful."

Penny turned toward his door, then looked back. "Just say you'll come and deliver a few nice words to the good admiral and the wealthy attorney."

She smiled. "Okay, okay."

"Saturday. At eight."

"I'll be there."

She moved toward her door, but Penny was still plotting. He stopped, his hand on his doorknob. "Wear emerald-green. That skimpy flowy silk that matches your eyes."

"Yes, yes. I promise."

"And I'll do your hair. Something flashy. Black hair can be so dramatic."

Penny hated her ponytail.

"This is going to be a great party." Penny glided toward his door.

As he disappeared into his condo, Nova fished her key from the pouch Velcroed to her wrist. Sitting like a Sphinx on the chaise lounge next to the door, Divinity waited, staring northward along the sweep of the Pacific. Nova scooped up the white Angora, kissed the top of her head. One sapphire-blue and one emerald-green eye stared back. Now here was someone a woman could rely on.

"Hi, sweet thing. Penny insists I need a man. Anyone worthwhile drop by?" She draped the cat over her forearm, unlocked the door, felt a buzz saw of purring on her wrist. As she dropped the key onto the entry table beside the door, the state of the room snagged her attention.

"Diva, dear, our home looks a mess."

Her dark wicker furniture was arranged so dining was done Oriental fashion around a low table in front of the living room picture window. Ten overstuffed green-and-blue lounge cushions reclined in crazy disarray on the carpet or against furniture or walls. Last night's birthday dinner for ten-year-old Maggie had been a hit, especially Nova's own gift: a 3-D video game.

She could almost feel Maggie's small hand in hers. She loved all three of Star's kids. When they called her "Auntie Nova" she felt like putty. But in Maggie she saw her own tender self before fate had set her feet on this…this bizarre life path.

She rearranged the pillows. When they were in place, things felt right. The condominium was the part of the world over which she had absolute control. And keeping things neat, even too neat according to her sister, gave her that sense of control that she had never felt for too many years of her childhood. She retrieved Diva from the couch and, sauntering down the hallway toward the bedrooms, glanced at the telephone answering machine. No messages.

In the master bedroom she spilled Divinity onto the comforter. The cat became a white puff of fur against the pattern of white, green and yellow swirls. A swath of sun suddenly lanced through the bay window. Two quick sets of sit-ups and push-ups, then she stripped. She took her shower hot and steamy.

Toweled but damp, she slipped into her carmine robe. The usual five brush swipes ordered the straight hair that fell to her shoulder blades. Two more straightened her bangs. She picked a pair of red earrings and tilted her head to locate the always difficult hole in her right earlobe. For some unfathomable reason, she always felt incomplete without earrings.

She picked Divinity up as the phone in the diningroom-converted-into-office jangled. The answering machine clicked on. She stepped into the hall. "Hello, Nova. It's Leland. Give me a call. This will be a long trip."

The line went dead.

A bolt of excitement and fear pulled her head up and, unthinking, she stroked too hard. Divinity leaped to the floor, her claws digging into Nova's arm.

Leland Smith managed Cosmos Travel. He was also her Company contact. They had a code. "Hello, it's Smitty" meant "CIA business, call in as soon as possible." "Hello, it's Leland" he'd used only twice before. It meant urgent, she would have to leave now.

"Sorry, love. Didn't mean to scare you."

Her excitement quickly settled to resolve. The grim truth was, the CIA never called unless deaths were involved. The photo contest, the cougars, they all faded to insignificance. "You know how it is when the Company rings. He only says 'Leland' when things are especially bad."

Penny's admiral and lawyer were going to be disappointed. So would Penny. She wasn't going to make the party after all.

Anchorage, 3:15 p.m.
Sunday, May 15

Joseph Cardone pulled his overnighter from under the seat of the passenger in front of him, slung it onto the middle seat and stepped into the DC-10's narrow aisle. The Denver to Anchorage leg of his red-eye from New York held few passengers. As he retrieved his raincoat from the overhead bin, a young, Levi's-clad couple with a toddler in tow edged past and the kid stumbled over the tip of Joe's freshly buffed loafers.

With a quick move, he caught the boy. "Hey, big guy, watch for the bumps," he said, tousling the kid's blond hair. He sometimes wished, like now, that he had more reasons in his life to be around children, but kids and family...his life wouldn't be fair to them.

He strolled forward. One of the stewardesses, Rita Halloran, stood in the galley, puttering with stainless-steel coffee urns. He'd spent the better part of the flight exploring what he and Rita Halloran had in common. Most notably so far, they'd both been born in Corpus Christi, Texas. He smiled. "I'd love not to have to say goodbye, at least not just yet."

It looked as though she might feel the same as he: no professional requirement called for quite that warm a smile. He said, "I have to go on to Fairbanks. The chances are good, though, I'll be back in Anchorage tonight." He shifted his overnighter and coat to the other hand and automatically checked his tie. "Can't be sure I'll be back. But if I can make it, nothin' would make this Texas boy happier than the pleasure of your company this evening."

"The crew stays at the Captain Cook. I'm expected

to join friends for dinner at the Crow's Nest—the restaurant on top. I could get free, though." She paused, eyes sparkling. "If necessary."

He tilted toward her on the balls of his feet. "Think of me as a necessity. Please."

She smiled again. "You got a date, Texas. And by the way, I wouldn't be too confident about catching the flight out of Fairbanks in time, what with this awful pipeline disaster thing. Everything's a mess. Pipeline people and investigators out the gazoo going north and south. The captain says they even caught one of them."

Not good. If the media were already reporting that authorities were holding one of the terrorists, a security breach must have occurred. Joe whipped his pen and a business card, the card that said he was an IBM representative, from his left breast pocket. "Let me have your phone number."

"Honey—" she was writing in large, flowery curves "—you're the best-looking Big Blue representative I've ever had the pleasure of serving." He pocketed the number and then turned toward the arched exit. Rita's soft voice followed him out the door. "I sure will be looking forward to that call."

The Flight Arrival display indicated that his contact's plane should arrive in thirty minutes and was on time. He sauntered to the Alaska Airline's lounge, dropped into a chair, leaned forward with elbows on knees and wished he could shuck the dreads and doubts that clung to him like a cheap, tight-fitting suit. His new partner was female.

Certainly nobody appreciated women more than he. But he had worked his first assignment alone. He'd liked it that way. Then came last night's call. "You'll have a partner. She's highly trained. Very experienced. In fact, when you've been with the Company a while longer you'll learn the Dove is legendary. She has the Deputy Director's full confidence and will be in charge."

The caller had made that very clear. He had a partner. She was senior. A woman, code name Dove, would be in charge.

Once again Joe checked his watch. Ten minutes or so and she should arrive. A man seated opposite seized Joe's attention. Only one side of his face moved. The other side was dead, lifeless.

The flight at the next gate was called and the man rose and disappeared through the loading door.

Joe checked his watch again. Her plane was now late. He stood, paced, sat. If they didn't make the Fairbanks connection, they'd arrive later, finish later and he'd be back in Anchorage too late to see Corpus Christi's Miss Halloran.

He heard the high whine that hovers around big jets on the ground. The twenty-odd people waiting with him stirred. The door to the plane's entry ramp opened. He scanned for "a fair-skinned woman with straight black, Asian hair to her shoulder blades."

He was still seated when a woman matching the description emerged with the first-class passengers. Tall and slender, she wore black slacks and a green silk shirt. And damned if she wasn't wearing black cowboy boots. This was his partner, all right.

He snatched his bag and coat and waded through the emerging passengers.

"I'm Joe Cardone."

His words came out automatically, which was helpful since the thinking part of his brain suffered a brief short circuit. Her face was pretty and feminine, but her eyes were striking. *Like a cat,* his mind said as it jerked back into action. Green eyes with the merest, really no more than a subliminal hint, of almond shape. Twisted jade earrings the color of her shirt framed uncommonly fair skin.

Passengers streamed around Nova as she sized up her new partner. The flight had been long and bumpy, but the excitement of her newest mission hadn't faded.

Agent Joe Cardone was good-looking, but young. Maybe her younger sister's age, twenty-six. And while she might have expected him to be giving her a thorough going-over, too, he seemed to be captured by her eyes. She couldn't resist a slight smile. She extended her hand. "Nova Blair. Glad to meet you, partner."

His grip was warm and firm. He said, "We've got to hustle to make our connection. They've called the flight twice."

"Let's hustle then."

They stooped to pick up her bulging bag at the same moment. She said, "I can handle it."

She caught a frown from the kid, as if he felt she'd rebuked him. *Let's hope Mr. Cardone isn't going to be uncomfortable taking orders from a woman.*

"Yep," he said, a cool edge on his words. "I bet you can handle it just fine."

He spun on his heel and led the way at a fast clip. At the cockpit of their next flight, he paused. "Carrying?" he asked.

She shook her head. "No. You?"

"Never when I'm in my IBM disguise."

"IBM," she said, and smiled. "Interesting cover."

Most seats already held warm bodies. They had a window and a middle seat in row twelve. The aisle seat was already occupied. Her partner shoved his overnighter and coat into the overhead bin, climbed over the man on the aisle, and sat in the window seat.

Nova stashed her things overhead, and slid past the man on the aisle seat and sat in the middle.

Nova listened as her partner quietly flipped through the pages of a magazine. She wondered why they had paired her with someone so young rather than an old hand. She guessed Agent Joe Cardone could not yet have had more than a couple of assignments. Perhaps this was his first.

Fairbanks met them with a light drizzle, a low, leaden sky and a chill wind. They deplaned and hurried across the tarmac, the wind licking up the edges of their overcoats. They had privacy enough now for her to talk freely to him.

"Any other luggage?" he asked right away.

"No," she said. "This is it."

"We're supposed to meet our Company man at city hall. That's where the FBI has set up its Area Command Center. He'll drive us to the hospital."

She frowned. "I don't know when you were in contact last, but I called in from Seattle. I was told the terrorist is in really bad shape. He might not make it."

They entered the main receiving area. From long habit, she did a thorough visual sweep of the room as she continued talking. "Also," she continued, "the Alyeska man may be—probably is—the only survivor from any of the pumping stations. It's questionable whether either will be around much longer. We're to observe the FBI's interrogation, absorb what we can since the ter-

rorist is the hottest lead we have. Apparently there is evidence of foreign involvement, in which case the Company is going to be brought in and they want eyes and
ears here right now. I say we don't waste time picking
up our man. I'll rent a car and get directions. You call
and tell our contact to meet us at the hospital."

She sensed him tense. Just the merest straightening
of his shoulders gave him away. And the slight smile he
offered was stiff. She was quite sure that he wasn't used
to taking orders from a woman—or perhaps might re-
sent it. Only time with him would tell. And whether it
was going to be a problem.

Chapter 3

Nova brought up the car, a Ford Taurus. Within minutes she and Agent Cardone were speeding up Airport Boulevard toward downtown Fairbanks. She'd buckled her seat belt. Her partner hadn't. *The kid's still sure he's going to live forever.*

She snatched a quick sideways glance. He was frowning as he studied the rental agency map. She liked his looks: a broad face with brown, alert eyes set wide apart, dark brown wavy hair. He stood several inches taller than she. Broad shoulders and chest. She usually characterized a man's body by sport type: with Cardone she thought boxer.

He wore the low-key suit associated with an IBM representative, but he carried it with a cool confidence.

There was something flamboyant about him. He put a finger to the map and smiled, and she knew at once it was the movie-star smile that had given her the flashy impression.

"Got it," he said. "The hospital's a few blocks south of this main drag."

Cardone navigated, pointing and saying, "There." At the hospital, an intensified wind propelled needle-like rain as they scurried from the parking lot toward the building entrance. A score of media types paced like hungry cats waiting for a press announcement feeding. Inside, she and Cardone shed their dripping raincoats. Cardone strode to the information desk. She followed.

A gray-haired matron sat waiting patiently to provide assistance to the lost. Nova's partner flashed his Company ID. "We're here to see the two patients brought from Pumping Station No. 6, and I'll just bet you know where they might be."

The matron beamed at Cardone, clearly captivated.

Apparently remembering suddenly that the couple asking directions was on solemn business, the woman smothered her smile. She said, "Isn't all this such a dreadful thing." She pointed to a schematic of the hospital. "You're here, right in the center of this main floor. Take the elevators to your right. Go to the top. Fifth floor. The police and some FBI people are already up there. The nurses' station is just across from the elevators."

"Thanks." Cardone unleashed another dazzling smile.

In the elevator, he punched the Up button. Nova caught her breath when the car took off like a startled racehorse. She had expected the usual hospital elevator—a tired nag. She checked the time. Four-fifteen. Generally a pretty quiet time in most hospitals.

Two uniformed policemen stood guard beside two rooms across from the nurses' station. One man, tall and lanky, leaned against the wall next to his chair, arms crossed. The other, sporting a beefy, bloated face, sat studying a sheet of official-looking paper, presumably the names and descriptions of personnel allowed to see the patients.

Nova scanned the floor. Only one orderly. As she had expected, things were quiet.

Her partner outpaced her. She trailed him to the desk where a nurse in wild purple-and-blue pants and top sat filling in a chart. Both guards caught Nova's attention and smiled. She smiled back.

Cardone flashed his ID. "Who's the physician attending your two special patients?" He cocked his head to indicate the guarded doors.

"Dr. Graywing." The nurse examined the ID carefully.

Cardone continued. "Can we talk to him?"

"*She's* with another patient, but it shouldn't be long. Anyway, you need to check in down the hall." The nurse leaned forward and pointed to her right.

Nova walked with Cardone toward the muted sound of conversation in a room at the far end of the corridor. Three men had commandeered a waiting room near the corridor's end. Institution-issue couches lined the walls, but a table and several straight-backed chairs squatted in the center. One seriously overweight and unshaven man stood in shirtsleeves taking coffee with knock-you-down aroma from a stainless-steel urn. Three sets of eyes examined her and Cardone, but quickly settled on her. "Afternoon, gentlemen," she said.

A blond with a sharp nose, well-cut blue suit and horn-rimmed glasses spoke first. "CIA? Blair and Cardone?"

"Right," Cardone said. "Agent Joe Cardone. And this is my partner, Agent Nova Blair."

The blond shook hands, first with Cardone and then with her, and introduced himself. "David Stivsky, FBI. Been on the case from the get-go."

He introduced the two other men. The hefty man, Jacobson, was a Fairbanks' police lieutenant whose reassuring smile offset several unattractive chins. The other was an Alyeska man, from the office in charge of pipeline security. He was a sandy-haired beanpole named Duncan, and his expression seemed stuck on grim. He flipped open the log, checked their ID's, and entered their names in the record.

"This is one helluva mess," Stivsky said. He twirled one of the straight-backed chairs, sat and rested his arms over the back. "Three pumping stations and the terminal blasted to smithereens. Burning like they're never gonna quit. I gather, since we were told to wait for you two, Langley has hard evidence these guys are foreigners."

"A reasonable assumption," Cardone said in a serious tone.

The men were getting into FBI-CIA turf issues and Nova had zero interest. Instead she asked, "Have you talked to either man yet?"

Stivsky scowled. "No. They were brought in by helicopter about oh-five-hundred. Pumping Station 6 is just north of here. Unfortunately the terrorist is busted all to hell. Been sedated since before arriving here. When he was first brought in, Wiley, the pipeline employee, talked to the doc, but he's also been under sedation since before I made the scene." The scowl deepened. "We've waited to have a go at 'em till you two arrived since waiting also made the doc happy."

She nodded to Cardone. "Let's see if the doctor is finished."

"Is Dr. Graywing free yet?" Nova asked at the nurses' station.

The nurse started to leave the desk. From a room along the opposite corridor, a slender Native American woman with glasses, salt-and-pepper hair and a doctor's white coat entered the hall and bounded in their direction. The nurse pointed and said, "That's her."

Dr. Graywing looked questioningly at Nova and Nova's new partner but addressed her nurse. "So who do we have here?"

After the doctor examined their credentials herself, Nova said, "We'd like to talk to you before we see your patients."

The doctor glanced at her watch. "The pipeline employee is sedated, but should be able to talk in, say, half an hour. I can't let you see the one that's presumed to be a terrorist. He's in critical condition."

"I know that, but still, we have to see him." Nova put a little bite into her words. "As you can imagine, it's urgent."

"You simply can't talk to the terrorist until he's in better shape," she said, lacing her words for the first time with a sharp edge.

The nurse was absorbing their every word. Nova said, "Could we find a more private place?"

Dr. Graywing briskly led them back toward the waiting room. She stopped in front of a door that led to a space hardly larger than a closet. The room held a desk and chair, charts and some posted work schedules. Graywing waved her arm for Nova and Cardone to enter, followed them in, and closed the door. She leaned back against the desk and looked at Cardone with the same charmed sparkle in her eyes that Nova had seen in the woman at the reception desk. "It's a miracle either of these men is alive."

Nova fingered through her purse, extracted her minirecorder and started taping. Graywing saw the recorder and halted. "This won't bother you, will it?" Nova asked.

Graywing shifted position slightly. "Not at all." Again looking at Cardone, she continued. "The presumed terrorist is, as I've explained, in critical condition. He fell down a shaft on the pumping station site. Broken neck. Broken right leg. A concussion. He was unconscious when he arrived and is only barely conscious now." The doctor's brow wrinkled in a sign of minor impatience. "Actually, I've told all of this to your three colleagues down the hall."

Cardone countered with an easy grin. "We appreciate you bringing us up to speed."

"Well…" Graywing took in a deep breath and plunged ahead. "Everyone seems to feel he was left behind because his colleagues couldn't locate him before they took off. As I said, you're not going to get anything out of him for some time. If ever."

Graywing's gaze shifted, met Nova's briefly with a challenge, then went back to Cardone. Nova let the challenge pass—for the moment.

"The pipeline employee—his name is John Wiley—he's in better condition, but he's been sedated. He's the only survivor from any of the three pumping stations." Graywing gave Cardone and then Nova a questioning look. When they said nothing, she continued. "I don't know about the other two stations, but all of the personnel at Number 6 were shot in the head. Really nasty. The medic told me they were almost all in bed. It was as though they'd been put to sleep, then shot. Wiley's alive only because he has a steel plate in his head. The bullet simply grazed it."

"That *is* a break," said her partner.

Dr. Graywing smiled at him. "I presume you're going to question the man, and I want to warn you, he's still very confused—"

Nova cut in. "The FBI has the lead here, Doctor. They'll be in charge of the questioning. We're simply observers, and I'm sure they expect us to keep pretty much out of the way. But if we have questions, I'll be the one asking."

Finally she had Graywing's full and surprised attention. Agent Cardone's lips pulled into a thin line. He crossed his arms and stared at the wall. A notion that the kid might be a bit touchy about his status in their relationship again crossed Nova's mind.

Dr. Graywing's ears flushed pink. "I, yes…well," she stammered. "I stand corrected. Please forgive me, Ms. Blair. Mmm. Let me say, I had a chance to talk to Wiley briefly. He said three things I thought might be of interest." The doctor hesitated.

"Yes," Nova said.

"First, even though it was nearly one in the morning, Wiley was awake, reading in bed in the company residence quarters, when he heard a noise. Then someone ran past the door to his room wearing a gas mask. So the first thing is, it looks like they did use some kind of chemical to incapacitate the workers, all eighteen of them, then took their time going to the rooms to dispatch them one by one before blowing up the place."

Graywing shook her head. Nova shared her feelings. Eighteen men dead at Number 6, shot like cattle. More at the other two stations.

"The second thing Wiley mentioned was burned coffee. The smell was the last thing he remembered."

"That's odd," said Cardone.

Nova said, "Maybe it has something to do with the chemical agent that was used on them." That struck her as plausible and a piece of information possibly useful for forensics. She'd have to make sure they started looking for traces of drugs in Wiley's blood and tissues immediately. "And what was the third thing?"

The doctor opened her mouth. The sound of two gunshots penetrated the small room followed by blood-chilling shrieks.

Chapter 4

Nova beat her partner into the hall. Both guards were sprawled on the hospital's white linoleum floor, blood and tissue splattered on the walls behind where they'd stood.

Bile rushed upward, to burn the back of Nova's throat. She swallowed it down. The acrid scent of gunpowder assaulted her. With their feet pounding in rhythm, she and Cardone reached the reception desk together. Stivsky and company were close behind. The nurse lay facedown over her records, unconscious or dead.

The doors to the two hospital rooms gaped wide. Nova wanted to stop, to check the rooms—the witnesses were priceless—but high-pitched screams still warbled from the mouth of a young volunteer dressed in pink and white. The girl looked with horror into Nova's eyes as she pointed toward the exit door next to the elevator.

Nova was closer to the door than Cardone. She

yanked it open, peered inside the stair shaft to see if anyone was there, then burst onto the landing, Cardone at
her heels. From below came hollow sounds of someone
running down metal stairs. She and Cardone poked their
heads over the handrail. She glimpsed the back of a
dark-haired man dressed in white as he exited from the
stairwell onto the next floor down.

Wordlessly she and Cardone bolted down the steps,
their headlong descent sending metallic echoes clanging up and down.

She trailed Cardone through the fourth-floor door
into the corridor and saw the man in white halfway to
the double doors at the corridor's end, walking fast.
They gave pursuit. Nova guessed that Stivsky would be
on his way to the first floor to secure the exits. The man
in white heard her and Cardone. Without looking back,
he sprinted for the doors, overturning a cart.

"Watch out, idiot!" the surprised orderly yelled.

Side by side she and Cardone streaked after the suspect, avoiding the cart and people hugging the walls. They
barged through the double doors. The corridor diverged.

"Split," they said simultaneously.

Cardone took off to the left. She sprinted right and
burst through the second set of double doors, nearly flattening a pregnant woman against the wall. Rooms lined
the hallway on both sides, but it was unlikely the man
would hide. He wanted out.

Halfway down the hall she passed another stairwell.
The door was just closing. The assailant would be heading for a first-floor exit. An elevator stood four strides
beyond the stairwell. The door yawned, revealing a
skinny, bearded kid. Jeans. Plaid shirt. He moved with
glacial slowness toward the opening. Nova leaped in-

side, shoving the kid out the door with one hand and hitting the first-floor button with the other.

"What the hell!" he protested.

She could have cooked a five-course gourmet dinner in the time it took the door to crawl shut.

Her mind said that if this elevator moved like the one they'd taken up, chances were good, very good, she would descend faster than the bastard could run. She flexed the fingers of her right hand, wishing her gun was nestled in it. Unfortunately the Walther was at home, snugly tucked under her mattress.

At last. A final moan from the elevator and a slight bounce. The doors retracted with agonizing slowness. She bounded into the hall and from inside the stairwell heard a clanging of running feet. *Good!* She was ahead of him.

The stairwell door flew open. The man in white bolted into the hall twelve feet away and headed right for her. His hands were empty: apparently he'd holstered his gun. He looked as big as a pro linebacker. *I've thrown bigger many times,* she told herself.

Upstairs he hadn't seen her. He'd probably think she was just a civilian in his way. She set her feet, bent her knees. He swept past. She grabbed his right wrist, twisted it out and back, letting his momentum add to the force that should bring him to the floor in a hammerlock.

He pivoted on his right foot with the direction of her movement and with his left fist, delivered a forward punch. She dodged it, but his arm wrenched free.

Now he faced her—stubby black hair, amazed dark eyes, thick lips open. She was clearly an unexpected obstacle in his path to the exit. He followed up with a smooth, left-footed roundhouse kick. Right at her face.

She blocked it—barely. His foot slid off her shoulder. Cold prickles raced up her back. He was equally skilled—and much stronger. Sure, he was bigger, but there was something abnormal in his strength.

Before he could set his left foot squarely, Nova lunged and grabbed his left wrist. She wouldn't get another chance. Kicking out at his right foot, she prayed he'd go down.

The unstoppable bulk anticipated her. He finessed her kick and used his weight as leverage to twist his wrist free. He planted his left foot, swiveled his back to her and, with his right foot, back-kicked her in the solar plexus. She felt as if she'd been hit by a rocket. Breath whooshed out from her lips. Pain streaking through her belly, arms flailing, she lifted astonishingly, unnaturally, high off the floor as if in a Kung Fu movie, and flew backward toward the wall.

Chapter 5

Heart pounding like a jackhammer, Joe rammed open the double doors. The fourth-floor corridor was empty: no terrorist, no civilians. Logic argued that his new partner had drawn the full house and was this instant on the hot trail.

Still, there must be exits leading outside that had to be checked. And sure enough, three-quarters of the way to the hallway end he found a stairwell and an elevator—coming up. He sucked in his breath, flattened against the wall, slammed the stairwell door open. Nothing in sight. No sounds. He pounded his fist against the wall.

He swiveled to backtrack and Jacobson crashed into him. Stabilizing the Fairbanks' detective, Joe muttered, "Bastard went out the other wing."

Still furious he'd been dealt a busted flush, he sprinted to where he and his new partner had split up,

Jacobson lumbering behind him. At the other wing's stairwell they galloped down, two and three steps at a time. Agent Nova Blair lay stretched flat on her back on the ground-floor corridor, those big eyes closed. As he'd feared, no sign of a terrorist.

Three panicked civilians and Duncan, the Alyeska man from pipeline security, clustered around her. God, she looked so fragile. A halo of red blood framed a fan of black hair spread over ivory linoleum.

Duncan looked up at Joe from a kneeling position beside her with frightened eyes. He said, "Stivsky's gone after him."

"Blair…?" Joe snapped. The rest of his question stuck in his suddenly dry throat.

Duncan read his mind. "Just unconscious."

Relief muddled with fear and anger. Joe felt his jaw muscles tightening. He was going to be taking orders from a part-time agent. Whatever her talent might be, it wasn't capturing terrorists.

Duncan could take care of Nova Blair. Joe waved for Jacobson to follow. Together they bolted toward the exit.

Outside, two hospital security men ran with guns drawn through what was now a light rain toward a part of the parking area hidden behind the hospital wing's shoulder. A burst of gunfire erupted from the same direction. With Jacobson at his heels, Joe dashed after the guards. He skidded around the corner, heard another triple burst of fire.

A couple hundred feet away, the FBI man, Stivsky, gun drawn, squatted behind a yellow school bus, peeking around its fender. Stivsky waved to the guards, indicating they should flank the target left and right. The terrorist fired again, another triple round. Joe took off to the left, Jacobson close behind him.

Stivsky shouted, "Keep him pinned down. I radioed for backup. I located him behind the big blue van."

Cardone and Jacobson found cover at opposite ends of a black Cadillac. The lieutenant gave him a look of amazement. "Shit, man," he muttered, "you've got no weapon."

"Afraid not. But our friend doesn't know it. I can still draw fire. Let's get closer."

Jacobson nodded. Together they raced another fifty feet fast and low. A quick burst from the terrorist's automatic riddled the air. A bright green Plymouth provided cover. Joe clenched his teeth, wryly cursing his misfortune that IBM reps weren't required by law to travel armed.

He figured that by ducking and dodging in a 180-degree loop, he and Jacobson could get behind the mark. But why had the SOB stopped running? Stivsky had it right; he was holed up behind a big blue van. Where was his transportation or his pickup man?

With Jacobson, Joe moved again. When they'd circled ninety degrees and only five cars separated them from the terrorist, Joe spotted the tops of heads and the gun hands of three men in plainclothes sticking out from behind an unmarked car.

They were local police. Maybe FBI. Whoever. The SOB hadn't fled because their car blocked the exit. Joe whipped out his ID folder, flopped it open. The fine, cold drizzle pearled drops on the plastic cover. Peeking over the Plymouth's fender, he aimed the folder in the direction of the three plainclothes men, waved it in the air. "Police," he bellowed.

The assassin let loose another triple burst. A bullet zinged past Joe's left ear just as he turtled his head behind the fender. The dampness on his brow wasn't just rain; his underarms were hot and wet. He bellowed again, in the direction of the plainclothes types who'd squatted out of sight. "He's one of the terrorists. Keep him pinned down."

The terrorist fired off a single round. Stivsky yelled, slowly and in clear words, "This is the FBI. You cannot get away. Throw out your weapon, raise your hands and walk out so we can see you."

Silence.

"I don't like it," Joe muttered. "Let's try drawing fire again."

Jacobson nodded.

They rose and scuttled two cars closer to the bull's-eye of their deadly little circle.

Joe put his head against the ground, scanned under the blue van and found what he was expecting. The man was sprawled flat on the ground. It might be a trick. He sorely doubted it.

Stivsky gave the order and they all rushed the van. With Stivsky's gun trained on the prone man, Joe felt for a pulse at the base of the man's neck. The guy was dead. But no bullet wound anywhere. The autopsy would probably find cyanide or some other quick way out. So much for an interrogation. The FBI lab boys could get information out of him in other ways. If he had a record. If the organization he belonged to wasn't all that professional. All in all, however, not a good day for the good guys.

A dark silence was receding; sound was filtering back to Nova. She trembled with terror. *Please, don't hurt me.* Her eyes pinched tight to blot out the hated face, she struggled to pull into a fetal position. She should protect her stomach. Her stepfather, Candido, was very likely to kick again. The effort brought a wave of nausea.

"You probably shouldn't move."

That wasn't right. The voice—a man's—was soft like Candido Branco's but it was full of concern, not lust, not anger. She felt, instead, her father's presence. The man who had loved her, whom she had adored and who had died so unfairly. Way too soon, and in a stupid, meaningless accident.

Nova forced her eyes open. Saw pale yellow walls. But not her father. She saw the face of the Alyeska man.

A great sadness of loss tightened her chest—through the years that crushing weight had caught her many times and she was always unprepared for it. She would never stop missing her father.

And then suddenly relief washed over her in a warm flood. The terror wasn't real. Childhood fears could be pushed again to the depth of her mind.

She sat up and the Alyeska—what was his name? Yes, Duncan—scooted so he could support her back.

"Do you feel dizzy?" a male attendant in white asked her.

Her struggle with the assailant flashed in front of her in all its violence. God in heaven, she'd blown it! She looked at Duncan. "Where is he?"

"Who?"

"The assassin!"

"He ran out that way." Duncan pointed down the hall to her right. "Stivsky and Jacobson and your partner went after him."

The throbbing at the back of her head was growing hard to ignore. She put her hand to it. Mistake. Her palm came away covered with blood. Her skin crawled.

The attendant put a heavy hand on her shoulder. "You should sit a bit longer. Are you sure you don't feel dizzy? Someone's getting a nurse and a wheelchair."

Sitting like a slaughtered lamb with an audience to observe her humiliation was unbearable. She put her bloodied hand to the floor, pulled her legs under her till she was on all fours and, feeling like a defeated prize-fighter, began to rise. The attendant and Duncan rushed to take an arm each. A wave of dizziness left her swaying.

She clenched her fists. The dizziness receded, but the pain in her psyche did not. God help her, she'd blown it. The others simply had to catch the assassin. She'd still have to face her failure, but at least the Company would have a critical lead. The worst thing she could imagine now was that the assassin had killed both witnesses and then escaped.

Maybe I was overconfident. Maybe afraid. Her psyche took another blow. It was true. There at that critical moment, fear had ruined her concentration. But the man had been so strangely, weirdly strong.

A woman handed her a white towel. "For your head," she said. Nova put the towel to the throbbing spot, then checked for damage. There had to be blood all over the back of her head, and a generous smear of bright red indicated she was still bleeding. A nurse arrived, pushing a wheelchair. "Let me take a look at that," she said in a cheery voice as she took the towel from Nova's hand. "Mmm. We're going to need stitches. Come along, sit down, and I'll take you to the emergency room."

"First I need to check what's happened upstairs." Nova pressed the elevator button.

The nurse frowned. "You need to come to the ER with me. A doctor must check you out. You can't just start wandering around."

The lady in white was missing the point. "I'm still on the job. First I have to check upstairs. Duncan, you explain to her."

Most of her spectators had wandered off. Only the male attendant, Duncan and the nurse stood gaping at her as though she were a sideshow freak. Mercifully, anger finally kicked in and pushed out her anguish. No use lamenting what she couldn't change.

What she could hope was that he'd failed. And hopefully she'd find the witnesses still alive.

At the fifth-floor nurses' station, a rain-drenched Joe was handed a towel by three nurses who informed him that both the terrorist and pipeline employee were dead, as were the two guards, that the desk nurse had merely been knocked unconscious, that the candy striper would probably never recover from what she'd seen, and that his partner was having her head stapled by Dr. Graywing in the third room down the hall, on his left.

He thanked them, gave them a warm smile, then headed down the hall.

When he knocked on the door, Graywing called, "Come in."

Nova Blair sat on an examining table, her back to the door and her head tilted slightly down so the long hair draped her face. Dr. Graywing was daubing the back of Blair's head with gauze.

At the sight of the wound, his anger rekindled. He was angry that by bad fortune Nova Blair had been the one to pursue the assassin. "Legendary," his phone contact had said. Legendary for what? He moved to the other side of the room so he could see their faces.

"The assassin's dead," he said. "Suicide capsule I'd guess."

His partner didn't say anything.

Graywing shook her head and said, "Ghastly."

"How's your head?" he said to Blair.

Without moving she said, "It's nothing."

Graywing clucked. "Not so. It is a deep, two-inch long scalp wound. She insists she won't remain here for observation, but I've told her for the next twenty-four hours she must look out for signs of concussion. Drowsiness or nausea."

"How'd it happen?"

Blair shrugged. "I took the elevator and managed to beat him to the first floor, but I couldn't hold him." She spoke softly, her answer dragging like a whipped dog. Very unlike the confident woman he'd met a couple of hours ago.

"I suppose he just barged right past you?"

Nova Blair raised her chin slowly. She straightened her shoulders and her hair fell back from her face. "There was a bit more to it than that." Her eyes had taken on a glacial, emerald chill.

He stuck his hands into his soggy suit pockets. "Sorry. I didn't mean that quite like it sounded."

"Yes, you did. Exactly like it sounded." She lowered her head again and Graywing clamped another staple. A sickening sound. He was glad he couldn't see what the doctor was doing. His partner said, almost as if to herself, "There was something bizarre about him. I've never felt that kind of strength in any man."

A loud silence followed, as if the room was holding its breath. Agent Blair finally broke it. "You were telling us, Dr. Graywing, before we heard the screams, that there were three things Wiley said. First, that the terrorists had gas masks. Second, that Wiley smelled burning coffee. We'd like to hear the third. Agent Cardone, you'll find my recorder inside my purse, on top. What was the third thing, Dr. Graywing?"

The doctor let her gloved hands hover in the air a moment, obviously thinking, while Joe found and started the recorder. After a brief pause the doctor plunged ahead, stapling as she talked. "It was the oddest part. I regret very much he can't tell you himself, because I'm not absolutely sure I remember exactly how he put it."

Joe said, "Do your best."

"Well, Wiley said when he was a kid he loved dinosaurs. He'd memorized most of their names. He said he swore that when the man in the gas mask ran past his door he yelled out the name of a dinosaur. Terratornis. You're stapled," she finally said.

Nova raised her head, twisted around and the look of puzzlement on her face matched his own feelings perfectly. "A dinosaur name?" she repeated.

"That's what Wiley said. He said he thought Terratornis was a kind of dinosaur, and he was sure that was what the man yelled out."

"Well, it's as good a lead as we've got," Blair said. She stood and faced him with a new confidence in her eyes and said, "Let's see what headquarters has to say about all this."

Chapter 6

Langley, Virginia, 4:30 p.m.
May 16

After passing innumerable security checks with Agent Cardone beside her, Nova made it to the seventh floor of the modern white complex in Langley—the heart of the CIA. In a very few minutes she and Cardone would meet the Deputy Director of Operations.

"Price's office is to the right," Nova said.

"How's your head?" Cardone asked with obvious concern. "Your hair does a great job of covering the staples."

"Doing just fine, thanks." Although her head still throbbed where the wound was, Nova felt sharp and focused.

Everyone knew Claiton Price's secretary, Cleo Jackson, by sight—always a colorfully dressed black butterfly in a field of blue, black and gray moths. She swept around her desk and hugged Nova. "It's been such a long time since I've seen you, girl." She held Nova at arm's length. "As lovely as ever."

Nova hugged Cleo again. Their friendship had formed during six months when Nova had done her CIA training.

"I saw the photos you did for *Maximum Extreme*," Cleo added. "The ones of the guy sky-surfing. Woman, it looks positively crazy. Skydiving is bad enough. Trying to surf the wind is just…"

"Just great fun."

"Would you ever let that sweet niece of yours do it?"

"Maggie?" Nova envisioned Maggie leaping from a plane, her heart pounding, her imagination soaring at the enormous great fall ahead, her skyboard stuck to her boots. "Maggie's a lot like me, Cleo. She'll do what she wants to do, whether it would scare the daylights out of me to have her do it or not."

"Well then, I just hope neither of you gets splattered onto some farmer's field."

Cleo finally seemed to notice Nova's partner. "Agent Cardone?"

"Right," he said. Nova could only imagine what Joe Cardone might be thinking. He'd probably never before been anywhere near the DDO's office, and he must be wondering why a contract agent was close friends with the top dog's secretary.

Cleo pulled her smiling lips into a serious line. "The Deputy Director is expecting you both. I'm sorry, my dear, that once again when we meet it's over bad news. How long do you think they will keep you today after you leave here? Could we find time for coffee?"

Nova looked at Joe. "We should know our schedule pretty soon, shouldn't we?"

Claiton M. Price sat in his chrome-and-black-leather swivel chair with his back to the office door.

Price stood, circled the desk and stuck out his hand to her.

Nova smiled, took the DDO's hand, and shook it. It was a firm, cordial and hearty handshake.

"It's a true delight and pleasure to see you again," he said to her.

Price then shook hands with Cardone. "Good to meet you, Agent Cardone. I understand you prefer Joe rather than Joseph."

"Yes, sir. A pleasure to meet you, sir."

Price retraced his path and eased into his chair. She heard the leather creak. "Please, sit," he said indicating the pair of chairs in front of his desk. "I understand you'll be debriefed later about Fairbanks. What I want to do now is put you into the broad picture with respect to Operation Jacaranda. Our government is facing a formidable threat to our sovereignty. To be a bit more precise, four of the Big Five nations are being blackmailed.

"In general, here's the situation," Price continued. "Over a year ago, a Transoceanic jetliner crashed in the Pacific. You may have read that no cause was determined. What hasn't been reported is that a madman—he's thought to be part of a larger terrorist organization—somehow incapacitated the crew and the plane crashed because it ran out of fuel. We know because a fax the President received almost simultaneously said the plane was downed as an attention-getter."

"How many people on board?" she asked.

"Three hundred and sixty."

The number stamped itself into Nova's brain as if delivered with a branding iron. Three hundred and sixty innocent people had perished. In every project she accepted for the Company, real people had been affected. Not some governmental agency or because of some theoretical governmental need.

Price leaned back and laced his fingers together. For a moment he studied her carefully. The man knew very well what it would take to involve her. She felt her new partner shift in his seat, as if impatient to get on to the details.

Finally, Price continued. "The author of the letter—he calls himself The Founder—has sent other faxes to the President stating irrational demands. The first was that the President must lobby Congress to pass a bill introduced by Senator Legnett to shift the country entirely from gas-driven to electricity-driven cars. You are familiar with the bill in question?"

She nodded. So did Cardone.

"The Founder threatened that if this bill didn't pass, other planes would go down."

Cardone leaned forward. "As I recall, the Transoceanic flight was lost last August. And in late September—or was it early October?—a spate of plane crashes occurred."

"Quite correct. It was in September. Within two weeks, two good-size liners and nineteen smaller planes crashed. We believe all, except seven of the smaller crashes, were caused by The Founder."

For a moment, Nova couldn't breathe. The room had fallen deathly silent. She looked at Cardone and found him looking back at her. To her knowledge, the magnitude of this kind of devastation on a repeated basis was unprecedented.

Price continued. "This bastard informed the President that the air crashes were 'just punishment.' After its first defeat, Senator Legnett reintroduced the legislation and it also didn't pass on a second vote."

"I remember the vote," she said.

"After that second negative vote, through an astonishing piece of luck, authorities at Glen Canyon Dam in Arizona found a bomb in time to prevent the dam from being blown all over the northern Arizona desert. The Founder—or as he is affectionately addressed by most agents tasked to stop him, The Fucker—claimed responsibility."

"Is Senator Legnett implicated?" she asked.

"Not yet. Though you can be sure the intelligence community now knows more than God does about Senator Legnett."

Price frowned, then added, "Britain, Germany and France are dealing with similar threats. To date the Japanese remain untouched. Most likely The Founder simply can't place operatives in Japan. There seems to be no end to the demands. The most recent is that President McBride increase our donation to UN family planning programs from three hundred and thirty million to two billion dollars per year."

"Extraordinary," Cardone said, shaking his head. "This madman doesn't want money. He doesn't want his terrorist brethren released. He doesn't want the government to give North Dakota and Utah back to the Native Americans or for all Protestants to leave Ireland. He wants Americans to drive fuel-conserving cars and promote birth control?"

"Quite so. To put it bluntly, The Founder states that he feels the world is woefully fucked up, and he is going to unfuck it. Which brings us to your assignment—Operation Jacaranda. There's a young German politician, Jean Paul König. He's riding the crest of the resurgent German ecology movement. He once belonged to the Greens, but he's now the foremost proponent of his own aggressive brand of ecological politics. Six days ago, a Company contact in East Germany was found dead. Cause undetermined. But she had passed a message suggesting that König's German Homeland Party was in some way involved in an 'accident' at one of the French nuclear plants. Need I say, one of The Founder's faxes referred to this 'accident.'

"There's not a breath of serious scandal in König's dossier and the man certainly isn't alone in objecting to nuclear power, so a connection between König, the plant accident and The Founder must be considered unlikely. But since our asset's report is presently the only real lead we have, we must pursue it full-throttle.

"Nova, we want you to get close to König. You and Joe can make contact as a team. A writer and photographer. You utilize your genuine, and may I say formidable, photographic skills. We've arranged for it to appear as if you two have been working together for several years. Joe works for you, Nova, as your assistant. He also writes articles built around your photos."

"Isn't it more usual that a writer would hire a photographer?" Cardone interjected, his tone stiff. "Shouldn't she be working for me?"

Surprised that Cardone would dare to challenge Price himself, Nova stared at the agent. Apparently he had been so intent he hadn't thought before speaking.

Clearly a strong emotion had been running his mouth—most likely ambition. And then there was also that thing about her being a woman. Maybe that was it. Or just that her performance in Fairbanks had certainly left a whole lot to be desired.

"You need to keep in mind that our analysts believe the way to this man is through Nova," Price said to Cardone, his voice having taken on a decidedly chilly tone.

She turned her attention back to Price. Cardone, she noted, had the good sense to remain silent.

"Wait, are you suggesting that I seduce him?" she asked, the steel in her voice leaving no doubt as to her feelings on the subject. "You know, I don't do seduction."

"Charm him, Nova. As only you can do," Price said, capitulating. "This is your great gift. That way you have of winning trust. How far you take it will, of course, be up to you."

Price shifted his gaze to Cardone and added, "We want König's attention on Nova. Our psych analysts feel that if anything can disarm König, it's a woman with genuine talent, such as her photography. And what Nova has in addition is a seeming fragility that disarms the susceptible male. And our psych profilers are convinced König is susceptible."

Cardone turned to face her, giving her a thorough inspection, head to toe. She could almost feel him touching her—not undressing her, as men often did with their eyes when she took the time to dress up and look nice—but tracing her face and clothes as though trying to discover the magic she possessed that Price seemed to be talking about.

She was her usual self, the self that Penny said she wore to make herself invisible. Very little makeup and plain black slacks and a forest green shirt. But Penny was right. When she got dressed up, some strange chemistry happened between her and most men she met. And if getting next to this König was the assignment, dressing up would certainly be part of the strategy. She smiled. Her new partner was in for a big surprise.

Cardone, who couldn't know her thoughts, smiled back in a way that said he was resolved to play his part in this charade whether he believed Price's estimation of her or not.

Price continued his lecture to her partner. "While you may think it more natural for the journalist to hire a photographer, world-class photographers often work the other direction. That's what we see here, Agent Cardone. Keep in mind also that you were selected in part because when you dress appropriately, you can pass as much younger than you are. We want this.

"And by the way, I've already had our research people check out that lead, Terratornis. It's not a dinosaur. It's an extinct giant vulture."

Odd, she thought. Why in the world would a terrorist group be yelling the name of an extinct giant bird when they were blowing up the pipeline?

"Both of you will be worked hard for the next eight days to bring you on-line with Operation Jacaranda, at a place not far from here," Price said, interrupting her thoughts. "Your contact in the field will be the chief of station in Berlin, Martin Davidson."

Price informed them about their briefing later in the afternoon and then dismissed them.

Chapter 7

The Founder's Compound

For over an hour The Founder's enforcer, Franz Maurus, had studied the Earth's Warriors recruitment reports. Since his return from Alaska he'd noticed that the number of dedications was falling dangerously behind schedule. He rubbed his dead cheek. The problem wasn't recruitment. It was the dedication process. He rang Singh's laboratory.

When the Indian scientist picked up, Maurus said, "I'm coming to the laboratory."

He strode across his office and into the underground hallway that connected the office to Singh's lab. He found Singh standing between two rows of laboratory benches, the small glass-enclosed experimental chamber behind him. Sitting in the chamber, bound to a straight-backed chair, was a young woman Maurus didn't recognize.

Singh said, "I trust your trip was successful, Herr Maurus."

Despite his general disgust for the forty-year-old scientist, Maurus usually experienced the thin, balding Indian's singsong accent as soothing. Now, however, the soft words merely irritated. Again out of habit Maurus stroked his limp cheek. "I am reviewing the buildup of fighting manpower. We are behind schedule."

"Yes. There is a problem. But it's not serious."

"From the moment of the first public demonstration of The Founder's power, any delay in our plans is serious. We are being hunted now, by every powerful agency in the world. We must move swiftly. Why have dedications with the Loyalty Inducer fallen off?"

Singh inhaled a breath. His thin hands fluttered nervously at his sides. "The Loyalty Inducer is unique among our suite of drugs. You see, unlike sleep and fear and so forth, loyalty is a higher cognitive process. Our more primitive inducers, the Sleep Inducer for example, can affect any subject, but the Loyalty Inducer functions only on persons strongly sympathetic to the person on whom they will be imprinted."

"I don't like what I hear. Neither will The Founder. What about the Fight Inducer? The drug is critical for my commando operations. All of the damned drugs are critical to everything we do. Does this 'small problem' happen often?"

Singh gave him the obsequious smile that played more than a small part in fomenting Maurus's loathing of the man. "Transition from producing small quantities of the drugs for experiments to a larger scale must inevitably entail some difficulties."

The Indian scientist wrung his hands. The enforcer knew he superficially scared Singh, but Singh knew his value only too well. Fifteen years ago, this brilliant nonentity had developed and offered The Founder the first drug—the Sleep Inducer—and the promise of many related drugs tailored to regulate human behavior. The drugs were not only capable of bending people's minds and wills, what made them particularly useful—and frightening—was that they had the astonishing ability to be delivered to the brain through the nasal passages. One inhalation and the subject, or victim, succumbed. In return, for fifteen years Maurus had, at The Founder's direction, supplied Dr. Sanjiv Singh with his "recreation"—little boys.

Maurus noticed that the girl in the chamber hadn't moved so much as an eyebrow. He nodded toward the girl. "Who the hell is she and what's wrong with her?"

"Ah. She is Helmut's latest girl. He finished with her and I asked if I could use her. I've just tested my latest drug on her. The first human test. I call it a Pacification Inducer. Seems to have worked perfectly."

"Why doesn't she move?"

"The drug is essentially a permanent, chemically induced lobotomy. She will live and carry out all basic functions, but she no longer has any will."

"A damn vegetable!"

"Yes. Quite right. Quite useful as a threat or blackmail weapon, don't you think?"

Maurus rubbed his dead cheek. "You're a scary man, Singh."

Chapter 8

Berlin, 3:30 p.m.

With the naval aviator dash Nova had come to expect, Cardone zipped their rental car off the Messendamm and into the parking facilities of Berlin's International Congress Center—a white, steel-and-concrete mammoth. The beautifully cut suit he'd worn when she'd met him had been replaced by a casual look, at the moment consisting of blue sneakers, baggy brown slacks and a red, open-necked pullover from L.L. Bean. He looked remarkably young. He could pass for twenty-one or two.

At four o'clock, Jean Paul König would speak to a sold-out crowd of thousands and for the first time she'd see her mark in person. Yesterday, within an hour of their arrival in Germany, they had met at a safe house with Martin Davidson—code name Cupid—to review strategy.

"Just like chumming for fish," their chief of station had said. Davidson was as round all over as his code name suggested, but he would never put one in mind of a sweet cherub; more like a Swiss banker: conservatively subdued, with gold-rimmed glasses and eyes that conveyed no emotion. "We scatter tempting stuff in front of König to get his attention, first Nova and then the idea of a photo piece on his pet project."

Cardone knew exactly where to go, having spent part of yesterday scouting the congress center's halls and conference chambers.

They stepped inside to find the massive space already three-quarters full. A young woman with a doll's rosy cheeks and Delft-blue eyes stuck a brochure in Nova's hand. The girl said to Joe, "Your tickets?" She was giving him that same sparkly look Nova had seen over and over from women in the handsome Texan's presence.

"Just follow me," the girl said as she led them to their row. She reluctantly left only after a parting smile to Cardone.

Nova could not stop a grin. "Do you *always* have that effect on women?"

He shrugged and grinned back. "Not always. I haven't had that effect on you."

They took their seats and she noted with approval that he began what appeared to be a professional scrutiny of the crowd: he'd be looking for anything unusual, any familiar faces, especially, known terrorists or sympathizers.

Electricity rippled through the room. This was an audience holding its collective breath, waiting for the magician to make the beheaded beauty reappear.

She skimmed the flashy brochure. In the past ten days she'd studied many similar materials from the König camp. Her appraisal was that his ideas sounded too idealistic. According to the Company's analysts, what made König controversial—and exciting— weren't his views per se, but the radical rate at which he proposed to make changes.

Cardone asked in a half whisper, "Feel the excitement?"

"Absolutely. These folks are dying to pounce on something."

Four men and a woman sat on the stage. None was König. A slender, slightly stooped man—Detlev Kleitman—rose and proceeded to the lectern. Kleitman, as head of König's German Homeland Party, was also strongly suspect. Other teams were doubtless pursuing Kleitman in whatever way Company strategists felt most likely to succeed.

Kleitman waited with palms down on the lectern till the hum of conversation subsided. After introducing the program and the VIPs, he took a deep breath and, with a dramatic pause, introduced the main attraction. "I present with great pleasure the rising star of the German Homeland Party, the next Governor of Bavaria, Jean Paul König." The audience burst into applause and from stage right König strode to the podium. He shook hands with Kleitman, then eased into his presentation.

Nova raised opera glasses and studied the face of the man she'd been sent to dissect. She possessed every shred of information the Company had on his life. She'd memorized his psychological profile. But success would only be hers when, beyond these facts, she learned the hidden desires that were the essence of the man, and found a way she could fulfill some of those desires for him.

König had short blond hair, light eyebrows, and deeply set eyes. "Glacial blue" according to his file. His nose was straight and sharp, his jawline square and strong. The Company's psychological profilers had described Jean Paul König as a man with the message of a saint, the speaking skills of a demagogue and the looks of a movie superstar.

Nova was already becoming comfortable with German again, and König made listening pure pleasure. He spoke in flawless High German, the words rolling out of his mouth and into and around the room. Cardone, she noted, watched the crowd, not König. Logical, since Cardone didn't understand much more of German than *danke schön* and *gesundheit*. But very soon, even Cardone's eyes fixed on the tall presence in the center of the stage. The rhythm of König's speech, the lithe way he moved, the occasional turning of his side to the audience, the grace of his hand as he lifted it to accent a point, all compelled attention. She couldn't pull her gaze away.

Nova raised the opera glasses to view his face again and a light shiver slipped down her sides.

When he finished, five thousand charmed souls burst into applause. Several dozen people near the front stood. An irregular wave rippled through the auditorium as others rose to their feet, straining to see and clapping as a waving König finally left the stage.

"Can you feel that?" she said to Cardone.

"How could anyone miss it? The place is electrified."

"I can see why the Company figures he's guaranteed to win in Bavaria."

Cardone gave her a grim smile. "I can see why they say he could eventually be chancellor. I can see why they say he's one of the most popular figures in the European Community. I can see how if this guy is who we think he is, we better stop him."

"Now," Nova agreed.

At seven in the evening Nova heard the expected knock on her door. They would soon attempt their first meeting with König. She slipped on her high heels, crossed the wooden floor to the door and opened it.

Cardone looked stunned, then dramatically grabbed his chest over his heart. "My God, Blair! You look—well."

She had wondered what his response would be when he saw her all dressed up. In front of him, wearing regal crimson trimmed with black, stood a woman of utmost sophistication. At least, that was the intended effect. With the help of an agent who specialized in disguises, Nova had brought clothes, makeup and jewelry—including the beautiful swarovski crystal chandelier earrings she had on—to create an image few men would be able to resist.

"I heard all those tales in Virginia about a woman who could become any man's most addictive fantasy."

She grinned. "Ready for battle."

He bowed. "I pity the enemy."

At five after eight, she walked beside Cardone into the Hotel Intercontinental Palace. The two of them were now, as planned, only slightly late. With her hand resting lightly on his arm, they strolled through the lobby and down a brilliantly lit, golden-carpeted corridor. Every eye turned in their direction.

"Fancy place," Cardone said. "But maybe fancy like this is old hat for you?"

She let the question pass. "It really is beautiful, isn't it? I love crystal. I love light."

The doors to the ballroom stood open. Their planners had assumed the banquet would not begin on schedule and, true to human nature, a number of couples and foursomes continued to filter in.

"I'll wait," she said. "See if König's arrived."

Nova detected just the slightest hesitation from her partner. Perhaps she had been too abrupt. Men could be so damned sensitive when a woman spoke firmly or ordered rather than asked. Cardone had seemed uncomfortable from the beginning with her, but she had thought they were past that now. Apparently not.

The space vibrated with the hum of over three hundred people with nothing to do but talk. Waiters were pouring water and slapping down silver trays of butter.

The long head table dominated the room's opposite end. Joe spotted König, one seat off center, his attractive blond wife, Ilse, to his right and the slightly stooped German Homeland Party president, Detlev Kleitman, to his left.

He returned to Blair's side. She pivoted in his direction and the scarlet gown flared around her ankles with the elegance of a matador's cape. His heartbeat did a neat flip. Her hair was down but pulled back over one ear and long, dangling crystal earrings swayed and glittered in the artificial light. His thought, ice cascade against black silk.

He imagined himself starting to unzip her gown. They were together in a darkened room in front of a fireplace and soft music was playing. What might be this beautiful woman's favorite music—

What the heck was he doing unzipping her dress! My god. They were partners in a dangerous game. And she had never once hinted at any sexual interest in him.

"König's there," he said. "He's seated at the head table at the opposite end of the room."

With Cardone at her side, Nova entered the ballroom. She felt a grim exhilaration. König *must* grant her an interview. Fleeting panic rushed through her as a tumult of thoughts bombarded her. Could she do this right, say the right thing, *be* the right woman for this mission? But just as quickly as the logical fears had quizzed her, they were gone. She had years of experience charming men. This was not going to be any different, even if he was a mass murderer. She would succeed again.

Her hand on her partner's arm, she strolled to the center of the ballroom. They turned and aimed for the head table down what suddenly felt oddly like a church aisle.

Heads turned to look at them. After a promenade that seemed the length of the coast from La Jolla to Los Angeles, they reached their destination. Jean Paul König had been talking to Detlev Kleitman but he turned his piercing blue gaze toward her. She quickly looked away, but as Cardone pulled out her chair and she glided onto it, she sensed König's appraising gaze touch her skin.

The waiters started the first course: pâté de foie gras. Introductions at their table commenced in German. She and Cardone stuck to English. Cardone did an admirable job of engaging the woman to his right—a white-haired matron having passable English—in small talk. Nova chatted with the man to her left, the editor-in-chief of *Der Zeitgeist*.

Eventually waiters delivered the main course. The editor's attention shifted to his plate. Nova, who had never taken her attention completely from the head table, used the lull to scrutinize König's wife. Ilsa König had a distant look, as though her body was present but her mind was somewhere else. Nova had read that the couple had married when quite young and had two sons. Their marriage was no longer close, if it ever had been, according to the Company profile. But König was faithful to his wife. Always skeptical of that bit of info, Nova was even more so now after seeing the living man in action. König, in her opinion, could have virtually any woman he wanted.

The Company's psychological profilers had said the key to ensnaring him lay in deciphering the reason for his strange fidelity to his wife despite their tepid union. If Nova could, the profilers were confident König was emotionally ripe for the picking. Nova wasn't in the business of breaking up marriages. Or sleeping with her marks. But Price had reminded her that this man could be a terrorist and thousands of lives were at stake. And resting on her shoulders.

Cardone leaned in close and whispered in her ear. "König's wife looks bored out of her mind."

Nova snapped out of her thoughts and focused on the task at hand. "From the look on her face, I suspect you're going to be the most exciting thing in her whole evening."

"Listen, a beautiful woman tied into that kind of marriage will be easy to please." Cardone flashed her a grin, then added, "I don't know if I told you. I'm a great dancer."

So terribly confident the young agent was. "I'd love to make an independent judgment. Before we leave tonight, a long twirl around the floor is a must. Okay?"

Cardone started to answer but a waiter materialized behind König and handed the politician a note. Horrified that König might be called away, Nova stared while her heart thumped over speed bumps. König read the note, said something to Kleitman and something even briefer to his wife, then rose and left, following the waiter.

"Uh, oh," Cardone muttered. "What the hell will we do if—"

"He'll come back," she said calmly. "Think positively."

She started counting every second while stirring food around her plate. She believed absolutely in the power of positive thinking. It was what had gotten her through the darkest days and hours of her life. But, if König had been called away, that was beyond their control. Positive thinking wasn't going to bring him back, but it would help them think of a Plan B, rather than focus on their frustration and negative energy.

Mercifully he reappeared and took his seat.

She heard Cardone exhale slowly. She felt her heart rate settle as she suffered through several brief speeches. Finally, Kleitman announced that dancing would begin. Waiters folded back a paneled partition and an orchestra began to play a waltz.

She and Cardone were prepared to approach the Königs at the head table if necessary, but Nova knew a move that forward ran a tremendous risk of offending. Minutes ticked by. König and Kleitman seemed deep into some subject.

"I wonder what can be so important," Cardone said, his impatience obvious. "König is supposed to like to dance."

Nova watched as König turned to his wife. The pair rose and König escorted her to the dance floor.

Without speaking, Cardone pulled out Nova's chair. She settled her hand in his and they slowly wove their way to the edge of the swirling mass of dancers. She and Cardone stepped onto the parquet floor and he swept her into his arms. In spite of her fixation on what she would say to König, Nova was caught by her nearness to Cardone. His hands were large and strong but he held her gently. Through the dress she felt heat from his palm in the small of her back. He was, after all, a great-looking guy. Serious-faced, he sailed them into the rhythm of the music. He wasn't a bad dancer, and made it easy for her to follow his lead as she homed in on König. Cardone guided them next to the Königs, then let her go, tapped König on the shoulder and addressed him in English.

"Mr. König, I'd be honored if you would allow me a dance with your wife."

König's wife spoke English, although not as well as her husband. She smiled at Cardone. König frowned. But Isla König let go of her husband, and she and Cardone began to dance.

Nova's quarry turned, gave her a wry smile, acknowledging the inevitable, and held out his arms. Her skin alive with electricity, Nova stepped toward him, nodded in a silent greeting and moved into his embrace.

König swept her skillfully across the floor as they explored how to make two bodies move as one. Nova looked up at him. His eyes surprised her. They were a cool blue, but they radiated amusement and charm that easily made up for the lack of superficial warmth. The frown was now completely gone. She was surprised at the sense of well-being emanating from him.

Pitching her voice low and making sure she caught his gaze squarely, she delivered her rehearsed opening slowly in English. "You must forgive my partner." She paused, waiting for him to take the lead.

"He isn't your husband?"

"Oh, no."

"And why is it I must forgive your partner?"

"He's had a great day professionally and decided your wife is the most lovely woman in the room and no matter how much nerve it took, he was going to ask to dance with her."

Nova focused on König's body, on matching her every movement to his. He must be made to feel, with strong impact, a harmony between them.

"Your partner is mistaken. It's true my wife is lovely, but I believe I am presently graced with the room's most beautiful woman."

She chuckled, remembering to keep her voice low. "You're kind."

König's hand tightened slightly on her waist. Probably an involuntary response, or maybe a good sign that he was intrigued. He said, "Somehow I'm sure you must be told often that you're beautiful."

They glided through several more turns with König watching a point in the air over her shoulder. Then the penetrating blue eyes found hers again. "Your accent is American. Are you living in Berlin?"

"No. We arrived yesterday."

Intentionally, Nova stumbled out of rhythm, sagged against him and clutched him tightly. "Oh, dear."

He stopped and, courteously supporting her, searched her face. "Are you all right?"

"Just embarrassed. Could we move off the dance floor? Just for a moment."

"Of course." He slipped a supporting hand under her arm and she clung tightly as they navigated between the swirling dancers and off the parquet.

She put one hand to her temple while retaining a good grip with the other on Jean Paul König's arm. "Just a bit of dizziness." She looked into his eyes and smiled. "I've had a slight ear infection. I thought I was over it."

His look was one of sincere concern. He filled the silence with "You say you and the young man are partners. What is your business?"

"Not a business, really. I'm a freelance photographer. Joe's the team's writing half."

"And you are here to photograph something?"

"Yes. A week or two more here in Germany should wrap it up."

"Sounds intriguing." He encouraged her with a nod.

"It has to do with GATT agricultural subsidies."

König's brow wrinkled in an appropriately baffled response. Like a good angler, she waited to let his curiosity tickle his mind. "And just how does the raging debate on the General Agreement on Trade and Tariffs come to interest a photographer?"

"I assure you, only through a very indirect route. A year ago a newspaper article left me feeling as though I was about to be robbed. The article was about the GATT agreements and how much land the European Community countries might lose to urbanization at the upcoming Brussels meeting."

Interest flashed in the blue eyes. "Not a very photogenic subject I should think."

"My obsession is nature. I found myself very upset over what my government wants, what Europeans want and what I think would be the best for Mother Nature." Nova had carefully prepared this line to make him feel at once that their interests were aligned.

"And what do you think?" he asked.

"That's partly what our project is about. To let me see for myself. We'll do a photo essay on what the country-side and farmlands look like now and then juxtapose them with examples of what Europeans might end up with if this agreement goes through."

"Have you drawn your conclusion yet?"

"I think European farmers can't begin to compete with Americans and other countries. But is the solution to abandon them and industrialize? If the EC gives an-other inch, any trace of a European pastoral way of life is finished."

He gave her a single approving nod. "My thoughts exactly."

Yes, indeed. Of course they were his thoughts, exactly.

The waltz was over, the music stopped. Bad timing. She felt a tightening of alarm in her chest. König must not escape just yet. His gaze flicked through the thicket of bodies on the floor. Cardone was positioned so König could see that his wife was happy. The orchestra began a two-step. Cardone swept Ilse König into another dance.

Nova grasped the opportunity. "My dizziness is gone."

"Good." He raised his free hand, palm up in invitation.

They stepped back onto the dance floor and slipped into the new rhythm. König leaned away a bit and said, "What is it exactly you'll do while you're here?"

"Joe's so pleased because he's arranged for me to meet with your agricultural minister. Mr. Meyer can give me a rundown on endangered scenic spots."

König snorted. "I'm not very impressed with your choice for a source." Rudolph Meyer was a thorn in König's side, a man the CIA knew König detested.

She feigned surprise. "I was informed Meyer would be the best source I could get."

He returned with evident sarcasm. "I'm sure your informant was well-intentioned."

She resisted the urge to mention her goals again, to in any way seem to be rushing him. He had to be the one to lead. She felt him relax as they swayed to the music. His eyes sought hers and the corners of his mouth turned up in a smile so engaging it made her want to blush like a schoolgirl. She kept her head and smiled warmly back.

She hoped he'd pull her closer, preferably to feel her body against his. He didn't. But he did the next best thing. He said, "When do you meet with Meyer?"

"Tomorrow."

"I, too, am deeply concerned about the GATT talks. I have ideas of my own I could suggest. If that would be useful to you."

He'd struck the line. Now to lure him in.

He frowned. "Unfortunately, I return to Munich tomorrow."

"If you could find time for us, Joe and I will gladly fly to Munich."

"That's a long trip and I'm not sure how much time I could—"

"We would gladly come." She paused, trying not to sound too desperate. "This would be very important to us."

"Call my headquarters, then. I'll ask my secretary to try to find room for you."

She didn't want to seem too eager. "And are you quite sure I won't be imposing? The campaign must put incredible demands on your time."

"No, no. The GATT agreements are a major concern.

I'd like to express the views of a conservation group with which I'm affiliated. Are you familiar with Earth Alliance?"

She nodded and said in a tone crafted to carry profound sincerity, "They think like I do."

"Then come to Munich. I believe we'll be helping each other."

König turned his attention once more to the music. She kept her mind on making Jean Paul König feel like he'd never had a better time dancing in his life.

The music stopped. König's "thank you" was no more than a slight formal bow and an equally slight smile. Not good. He immediately turned and began to make his way toward his wife and Cardone. He didn't take her arm.

His dossier stated that he didn't womanize so she wasn't expecting him to be an easy catch. Although this was Europe, not America where extramarital sex was much more scandalous, even the appearance of an affair could still be a risky, potentially fatal mistake for a politician. But if König's sex drive was, in fact, low or, heaven forbid, virtually nonexistent, the Langley game planners would have to devise some other way to get close to him. An agent with all the training and beauty in the world wouldn't do it.

She glanced at König's face. Beside her walked an impressively handsome man with a charming smile—who was suspected of killing innocents with cold-blooded regularity. If that was true, she'd do whatever it took to get close to the man. And crush him before he had the chance to hurt another man, woman or child.

A new waltz started just as they joined Ilse König and Joe. Nods and murmured "thank-yous" were exchanged.

Cardone swept her into his arms and maneuvered her away from König and his wife. "Well?" he said.

"You dance very well."

"Blair!"

She grinned. "You can call his appointments secretary tomorrow. He's looking forward to telling me everything Meyer doesn't know."

"Terrific! That was fast!"

A sudden urge to hug Cardone surprised her. She throttled it.

She was just excited that they'd achieved their first objective. She also noted, a touch annoyed, that Cardone's shocked amazement wasn't altogether flattering. Had he not expected her to succeed? She had, and within the next week she would start the hard work of convincing König he wanted to take the bait, that he couldn't, in fact, be without her.

Chapter 9

On Friday morning after the banquet, Joe telephoned König's secretary. The woman scheduled them for Monday afternoon. That same morning he flew with Nova to Bonn for their meeting with Meyer. Their chief of station, Davidson, had reserved two rooms in a modest pension.

After an anticipated unremarkable Meyer interview, Joe filled the remaining hours of Friday and Saturday with jogging, working out and rereading profiles on activist ecology movements. Several times he found himself wondering what Nova Blair was up to. In fact, she managed to invade his thoughts too much.

On Saturday evening, he knocked at her door. She was picking up her purse, hungry for some local food. When she opened the door, he gave her that inviting Cardone grin.

"How about something to eat?" he asked.

"I was just going to do exactly that."

They bought Weisswurst and rolls from a corner vendor and, with two beers to complement the sausages, retreated to the pension. The two days of waiting for their appointment with König had bored her to distraction. Joe's presence brought life into her room. She ran him once again through the correct moves of a photographer's assistant. She'd already discovered he was a fast learner and exceedingly careful with details. They finished at ten-thirty. "Look, let's get out awhile," she said. "I'd love a cappuccino."

"I'm game."

The closest the first two bars could come to cappuccino was Irish coffee. "I really want cappuccino," she said. When the third bar also couldn't do cappuccino she said, "Would you mind if we try one more?"

He shook his head and lifted his eyebrows, as if he thought her an obsessive nut, but nevertheless smiled and opened the door for them to exit.

Finally they got lucky in the restaurant of a small hotel.

It was fun to draw him out about his life. About flight training. About his parents' home in Puerto Rico. About his love for Texas. He was witty and forthright—at least, he seemed to be telling straight stories.

Joe was thoroughly enjoying his partner's company. But suddenly he realized that *she* was leading him. He was telling all, she nothing. His admiration for her skill at making a man want to talk hitched up several notches. "You mentioned you knew the diplomatic world. Anything you can talk about, or is all your experience tied up with Company business?"

"No. Not business. I'm a diplomat's daughter. We

lived in Germany for a while. And in Italy. And in Saudi Arabia. My father met my mother when he was ambassador to the People's Republic of China."

A very unbusiness-like image of Nova Blair in the red gown popped into his head. He was doing his level best to think of her as simply his partner, but the woman was a stunner. She now regularly used makeup in addition to lipstick, with remarkable results. Without it she was pleasantly attractive, but could blend in, especially if she wore casual clothing and that nothing ponytail. But fully made up, there was no way this woman could escape attention. "An American ambassador? Would I know of him?"

For Nova the conversation was taking a much too personal turn. But still, oddly, she found herself wanting to share with Cardone. "Not likely," she said. "He was ambassador for Great Britain. I was born in China. My dad was English and Black-Irish. He fell head over heels for my mother in Beijing. She's half Chinese and half English." A vivid memory of her father lifting her into his arms and swinging her in a great circle at her sixth birthday party caused her throat to tighten. She swallowed hard.

"Ah. That explains the green eyes, fair skin and straight black hair."

"Right."

"I notice that you keep saying, 'was.'"

She couldn't speak. She shook her head, felt her big multicolored earrings—parrots in a hoop—swaying against her neck. Tears threatened. She blinked them back—successfully. "He died when I was twelve." She waved for the bartender and asked for the check.

"I apologize if my question brought up sad memories."

"It's nothing."

They said nothing further as he paid the check and they were quickly on their way back to the hotel.

After leaving his partner at her door, Joe headed for his own room, kicking himself that he'd made her unhappy. That sure hadn't been his intention. And he'd learned virtually nothing personal about her. Nova Blair was way ahead of him on information gathering, easily three to one.

Sunday they flew to Munich and checked into a pension not far from Marienplatz. Nova divulged that she only slept three hours a night.

"So what will you do while I'm catching ZZZs?"

All she did was shrug. Getting personal information out of his new partner was like trying to pry open a clam. And he hadn't yet learned the secret.

He didn't sleep much himself. He now looked forward with galloping impatience to finally engaging König.

At one-thirty Monday he knocked on her door. What would she be wearing? *You've been told that you're going to see a pro in action here.*

She looked every bit a professional, but like a businesswoman, not remotely seductive. A fascinating, lovely woman. A blue wool sheath draped her body so the curves of her breasts and hips were just suggested then rose in a turtleneck that said business, not pleasure. Her hair was down, touching her shoulder blades. Blue and green ceramic earrings matched her eyes and the outfit.

What weird history would lead a woman of Blair's intelligence and background to work for the Company? Was she an excitement junkie? He said, "You look great."

She waved him into the room, apparently eager to be on her way to their meeting with her target. "Thanks. I'm ready. I just need a moment."

"If I was König, Nova, getting my attention would be about as difficult as forcing coke on a junkie."

She chuckled. Joe did have such a dramatic way of describing things.

"And I bet you could stock a gymnasium-size boutique with your earring collection."

She was reaching into the closet for her black overcoat, her back turned to him, when he said, "König's a handsome guy. Should be a pleasure to seduce him."

She stopped for half a beat, then removed the coat from the hanger and pivoted slowly, draping the coat over her arm. A chill tickled the back of her neck.

"If you think in those terms, Cardone, you're speaking for yourself. My job is to get close to him and gain his confidence, not to seduce him. And most surely not for my pleasure. For me, what I do for the Compny is strictly business."

His smile vanished. He clearly knew he'd stepped over an important line.

"I see Jean Paul König as nothing more, or less, than a man who may be responsible for hundreds of deaths."

"I—I've a good feeling about this meeting. And if I presumed, and clearly I did, I apologize, Nova."

Yes, he was sorry. Genuinely. But still, what a huge gap there was between how she saw the world and Joe's vision of it.

Chapter 10

Cardone held the door as Nova climbed into the back seat of the taxi she'd ordered. While the cabbie maneuvered northward through the Munich traffic, she mulled her partner's comment. *Should be a pleasure to seduce him.*

Sex was only a physical act to her now. She'd concluded this long ago and out of desperate necessity. It was a sad conclusion, especially to learn it as a child. But she never let herself feel the emotions that came with sex. Not after her stepfather destroyed any chance for her to see the act as one of love.

But would she even have to go so far as to seduce König, as Cardone seemed to assume? Strangely, she didn't come up with no. Still, she felt irritated that he would imagine her gaining pleasure if she did.

The taxi stopped in front of the building housing

König's campaign headquarters. A southeasterly wind was driving elephantine cumulus clouds toward the Bavarian Alps. They headed for the building's ground-floor entry and took the elevator to the sixth floor. Campaign posters plastered the hallway leading to König's office.

König's secretary sat behind a sleek black desk. She was perhaps twenty-five, petite, blond, with gentle brown eyes. No cold reception here. She smiled warmly. *"Guten Morgen."*

"My name is Nova Blair. This is Joe Cardone. We have an appointment." Her stomach felt as though a ball of snakes roiled in it in tight little circles.

"Mr. König is expecting you." The secretary's English was quite polished. Joe unleashed one of his better smiles; the secretary's attention shifted to him. "If you would please make yourselves comfortable, he will only be a few moments more." A slender finger directed them toward a modern-looking gray couch and chairs.

After discovering the secretary's name was Ellen Nöe, Cardone began thumbing through a magazine. Green plants softened the room's essential utility. On a table in front of the single large window stood an almost violent sculpture. Of darkly veined gray marble, the sculpture was about five feet long and portrayed six wolves bringing down a deer. The table had been carefully chosen to display the valuable piece. Nova rose and went to Ellen Nöe's desk. "I like the sculpture," she said to the secretary.

"Interesting, no?"

"Seems an odd thing to have in his campaign headquarters, though."

"Wait until you see the piece in his office. Next to his

conservation work, I sometimes think Herr König's sculpture collection is his greatest passion."

Before Nova could ask the sculptor's name, one of two doors behind the secretary's desk opened and König's campaign manager, Peter Grund, barged out. He made a quick, clinical appraisal of Nova's body, then dismissed her as he handed a sheaf of letters to the secretary. "They're signed. Make sure they all go out this morning."

The portly Peter Grund in the CIA photos looked nothing like her stepfather, but Grund's voice and bearing recreated Candido Francisco Branco's arrogance in detail. She could imagine Grund grabbing her by the hair, twisting her face to look into his and saying, "You love me don't you?" Nova despised him at once.

Careful, she warned herself. Her briefers had proposed, as one of many possibilities, that Grund was the mastermind and Jean Paul König merely his pawn. Her instincts immediately charged off in that direction. She could imagine Grund doing almost anything.

Grund retreated to his office.

A green light flashed on the secretary's intercom. "Mr. König will see you now."

She and Cardone met König halfway into his office. He shook hands with Joe and then took hers. She hoped his hold might linger a bit longer than one might expect. It didn't.

He gestured toward four low-slung upholstered armchairs pulled up to a low coffee table occupying the left half of the room. In German, König said, "I think we'll be more comfortable over here."

"Neither Joe or I speak German," she replied in English, which was true for Cardone, but not for her. Her German was nearly flawless.

"Ah, forgive me," he said, switching to English. "I had suggested that we might be more comfortable at the coffee table."

In the corner behind the table and chairs stood two five-foot-high, white-marble polar bears on a pedestal, apparently carved from a single enormous slab, their bodies locked in combat. The claws, fearsomely long, were of black onyx.

Cardone said, "Nature. Red in tooth and claw. You could paint names on them. Consumerism and Conservation."

König laughed and clapped Cardone on the shoulder.

Nova stepped to the piece. "May I?" she asked.

"Of course."

She ran her hand over a huge paw and traced her forefinger under one of the black claws. She fought a shiver. The raking feel of it lingered even after she took her hand away. The statue's ferocity seemed ominously symbolic.

König said, "Coffee? Or tea perhaps?"

She and Cardone declined and the three of them eased into the chairs. "Let me summarize our interview with Rudolph Meyer," she began. She tried to monopolize König's eye contact, but his attention tended to wander. He crossed his legs away from her, a classic body-language barrier. This was not a male on the prowl.

Cardone said, "I have the impression from Meyer that the Europeans are going to try to hang together on this GATT thing. They're not going to, as Meyer put it, 'buckle under to the Americans.'"

König became animated. He uncrossed his legs. "The impression you received from Mr. Meyer is, I am confident, absurdly weak. We both belong to the German

Homeland Party, but we differ substantially on what will keep the EC from ecological disaster. Mr. Meyer is far too willing to compromise. The EC is not going to try to reject further weakening of our agricultural subsidies. The EC *will* reject the US pressure to."

"The vote is coming up soon," Nova said. "What if things don't go as you hope?"

König's brow creased, he crossed his legs again. "I may not be able to control this vote, this time. But the German Homeland Party is going to make major gains this next election. We are the spirit of the people."

Nova leaned toward him and put all the sincerity she could muster into her voice. "Joe and I, we know you're right. But can the people avoid the siren call of cheaper goods? Even to save a sentimentally valued lifestyle? I'm afraid the average citizen wants cheap produce even more."

König's gaze bored into her. "I believe with all my heart, Ms. Blair, that you're wrong. Europeans already subsidize relatively uncompetitive farms. And why? Because they're stupid? No. Because they want to drive from their homes and visit the countryside."

He looked at her with an intensity that actually left her feeling unable to deny him, made her want to follow. His power was scary.

"People long for stability," he continued. "And quality of life. But time's running out. Birth rates out of proportion to resources doom sixty thousand children a day on this planet to death. This is obscenity. And to expect the old power structure to make changes is like expecting a wolf to chew off its foot to free itself before it even feels the pain of the trap."

She shook her head. "The trap?"

"The current world power structure derives its power from the status quo. Those who sit at the top will never willingly sever even one of their precious limbs of acquisition. Only if their own deaths were imminent—the trap so evident they knew they had to chew off a leg or they would die—would they change anything."

His gaze was on her but his eyes, snapping with anger, seemed to be seeing somewhere else. "Strong action is needed. We're all like the proverbial frog in the pot. Raise the water's temperature slowly enough and a frog sits calmly and boils to death. Its sense organs aren't able to tell it the water is becoming deadly. Human affairs will only change when the people have a leader who can raise the warning convincingly and then offer new ways to live."

"And you believe that's what the German Homeland Party and you, their candidate, have to offer? A clear and convincing warning?"

"Absolutely."

"Do you think you'll win Bavaria?"

"Absolutely." König leaned back. "You know, the wicked tragedy, truly wicked, is that technologies to achieve immediate results, even utopia if we wished, are already available."

"I agree," she said, trying to sound convincingly in total agreement with him. "And by using the media, and working together, I'd like to be a part of bringing your vision to people. May I show you some of my work? Things I've done over the last month." She placed her attaché case on the table and spread out the European photos. König didn't lean in when she did. Bad sign.

Her palms started to sweat. Only after she slid back in her chair did he uncross his legs, bend forward, and finger through the pictures.

"Quite remarkable. Excellent, really." He relaxed again into his chair. "Very sensitive work." His cool blue eyes met hers and seemed to warm a fraction. It was the first time she felt a sincere personal reaction to her.

She responded with a faintly intimate smile. "We believe, we fervently hope, your campaign and this election will be historic. Something much bigger than just Bavaria or even Germany. I believe you can change the world. We've budgeted to be in Europe much of this summer on this photo shoot. And I think you have provided us with the right direction and inspiration. We'd like permission to tag along with your campaign. We'd do a photo essay on the German Homeland Party. On you. That could be one of our angles."

König frowned. "I don't know about that."

She had to sway him. "May I show you some other pieces?"

He nodded.

From the second envelope she pulled out the five photos of children. "I also work part-time as a tour guide. The company arranges adventure tours to some pretty exotic places, and I've had opportunities to work in some very primitive settings."

Again König waited for her to set the pictures on the coffee table and slide back into her seat. He then picked them up and studied each carefully.

Her mouth felt parched. She thought about asking for water, but caught herself, realizing it would be disastrous to break the mood.

For the longest time König said nothing. Finally he returned to a picture of a Brazilian boy in a patch of butterflies.

She said, "I think Joe and I could do a terrific

piece. I have connections with several top news magazines. Most importantly, we believe in what you want to accomplish."

"My campaign manager is the person who arranges this sort of thing. Frankly, I'm not sure how he'd view having the two of you underfoot."

Cardone jumped in. "Like Nova says, we have our own funding that will last easily through to the election. We wouldn't be a financial burden. How about a trial period? How about convincing Mr. Grund to let us accompany you for two weeks? If it doesn't work out, he can bounce us then."

König nodded. Like everyone else they had met thus far when she was with Cardone, König liked her partner. "Fine," König said. "We will try it for two weeks."

König stood. She and Cardone also rose. König shook her partner's hand, then reached for hers. She would let her hand linger in his as her eyes lingered on his face. She must make that magnetic connection.

König's gaze held steady, but his handshake was brief to the point of being obvious.

Once again she had the disturbing thought that the intelligence guys at CIA headquarters in Langley, Virginia, had it wrong. Maybe König wasn't vulnerable to a woman at all, intelligent, talented, or otherwise. Maybe, contrary to what they had dug up, he was homosexual.

She and Cardone rode the elevator in silence to the ground floor. Nova mentally reviewed the interview. Soon she would debrief with Cupid.

Conclusion number one: Jean Paul König was a committed man. Possibly obsessive. He'd said, with a glitter in those cool eyes, that strong action was needed. Just how strong did he mean? Did "strong" include a little blackmail and mass murder?

Conclusion number two: gaining Jean Paul König's confidence wasn't going to be easy.

Chapter 11

Cologne, Germany

At eight in the evening, a black Mercedes-Benz taxi delivered Nova and Jean Paul König to Cologne's finest French restaurant.

For more than two weeks she and Cardone had been with the König campaign and she'd never missed an opportunity to get near Jean Paul at campaign affairs, but this meeting over an evening dinner was the best opportunity she'd had to get close to him.

The husky, bald-headed bodyguard—Klaus Wyczek, an addition to the campaign entourage since a death threat to König a week ago—stepped from the front seat passenger side and opened Nova's door. Wyczek compensated for his lack of hair on top with a Vandyke to cover his weak chin. In her experience thus far, a feral look of suspicion mixed with cunning never left his face. Wyczek paid the cabbie. König joined her on the sidewalk.

Time had become a knife tip never removed from her back. According to Cupid, in only three days The Founder's next punishment would be delivered. She was working hard, but she couldn't help but worry that they were sniffing down an entirely barren path.

The June air was warm against her skin, the evening beautiful, the setting romantic. She had only to smother jitters that attacked whenever her mind sidetracked to the fact that she was unarmed, had no backup and, if all went well, would eventually be alone with a suspected terrorist and his linebacker-size bodyguard.

The maître d' greeted König effusively, then led them to adjacent tables along one wall. Flickering on the center of every table was a large candle, which created the perfect intimate setting.

Unfortunately, Wyczek took the table next to theirs. Nova sat opposite to Jean Paul, putting her back to Wyczek so he wouldn't distract her with his watchful brooding gaze.

The maître d' backed away and a blond waiter with a gold stud in each earlobe and his nose took his place. She and König ordered Cinzano.

"I've been wondering," Jean Paul asked, "why is Mr. Cardone not with us? Shouldn't I discuss textual changes with him since he is your team's writer?"

Nova had figured Jean Paul would inquire about this, and planned to use it to her advantage. "We had a deadline for a piece we have coming out next month for an outdoor adventure magazine. We agreed he should finish it tonight. And the fact is, we write the text together since much of the articles feature in-depth captions. He does first drafts and finishes, but I always have input. So whatever needs to be changed, you can tell me."

He smiled, perhaps pleased they were justifiably alone. They studied their menus. Having picked her choice, she laid the menu aside. When König did likewise, she said, "I've been looking forward to your comments on the article."

He shook his head. "My schedule this week has been horrendous. This was the only time my secretary could manage for us. I've looked forward all day to enjoying your company."

She felt another rush of the satisfaction she'd felt this morning when his secretary had divulged where and when this meeting would occur. This evening hour was not, in fact, the only time they could have met. Ellen Nöe had indicated König could just as well have picked eight o'clock tomorrow morning.

The waiter returned with drinks. Jean Paul smiled, a warm one that put a friendly, confiding twinkle in his eyes. "You know, during our dinner we'll have to be extremely discreet. Peter is always concerned about my appearing in public with any woman other than my wife. And he specifically warned me, from the first day you came to my office, that I should be careful with you. He knows a beautiful woman can invite scandal."

"That's a campaign manager's duty, isn't it? To keep you focused on the job. Why did he relent and allow you out with me tonight?"

"I simply told him there wasn't another time and that I wanted to insist on some changes in the article." Jean Paul chuckled. "I promised I'd be careful."

"Changes? Nothing serious I hope." She feigned concern, but she was still reveling in the fact that this was the first time the man had laughed in her presence. He was letting himself relax around her. A very good sign.

"No, no. Mere suggestions. Nuances about the spirit of the German Homeland movement that perhaps only insiders would feel didn't ring true."

From her evening bag, Nova quickly withdrew a pen and pad. "I'm ready."

She jotted down his ideas, making sure to make eye contact often. Davidson would see to it the changes were made before Cardone submitted the final product tomorrow to *Der Stern*. The Company would ensure that this article made a huge splash. The König campaign was going to find Blair and Cardone a first-rate team of publicity-getters.

König ordered himself a second drink. Another positive sign he was letting down his guard.

They both ordered coq au vin, a shared taste that she filed into memory. Chilled salads of ingeniously sliced cabbage, beet, radish and squash appeared at once. Wyczek's food arrived at the same time. She leaned close to Jean Paul and lowered her voice. "I hope you won't be offended, but I don't much like the looks of your sour-faced bodyguard."

Jean Paul smiled. "It is unpleasant to have someone tagging along everywhere. He practically never speaks, though, so he's not personally annoying. In any event, I knew this time would eventually come, and if I win the Bavarian election, it will get seriously worse. Klaus does look like something you wouldn't want to meet alone in the dark, but there are none better at what he does. I find that reassuring."

"When I learned about the death threat, I was terribly worried." She would have faked concern if necessary, but it wasn't. She squeezed her glass so hard she was surprised she didn't break it. Jean Paul was so compelling a force that for the fiftieth time she forced herself to focus: *Evil hearts can inhabit beautiful bodies. I'm going to destroy this pretty man if, in fact, he is rotten at the core.*

She set the glass down and glanced from under her lashes at his face. A strong sensual tug stunned her. She blinked several times. Took a deep breath. *Be very careful,* whispered an urgent inner voice.

The waiter whisked their dishes away and scooped crumbs from the linen cloth. Still surprised at the sudden sexual rush she'd just felt, she lurched into another topic. "This article is just the beginning, Jean Paul. You've seen a sample now of what we can do. Have you decided about Joe and me? Can we stay and follow your campaign trail?"

He leaned back and interlaced his strong, long fingers together. He seemed to be studying her face. Sizing her up.

"I've discussed your proposal with Peter and with the publicity people." A smile turned up the corners of his mouth. "Although Peter warned me about appearing too publicly with you—and by the way, don't ever tell him I told you this—he was as impressed with your work as I was. At first I was skeptical. Peter even more so. But we're sold."

Her relief no doubt put a great deal of dazzle into the smile she gave him. "We're grateful. And I assure you, you won't be disappointed."

The waiter glided up and asked in German, "Would madam care for some dessert? Perhaps coffee?" The buzz of voices in the room had decreased. Most of the tables were empty. The height of the evening had passed.

To reinforce the impression she'd been trying to give him that she had little knowledge of German, she looked blankly to König.

"He wants to know if you'd like dessert or coffee," he translated courteously.

"If they have it, I'd love cappuccino."

"Two cappuccinos," Jean Paul told the young man, who disappeared and returned in remarkably short time. As they sipped their coffee, Nova explained to Jean Paul what she and Joe would do during the campaign, up to and through election night.

"Your plans sound fine. As we go along, you can refine them with publicity and scheduling. I wonder, though... This project can't occupy your days completely, can it?"

As if doing so unconsciously, she slowly unfastened the button at the neck of her blouse. "We've also been working on the text for a coffee-table book on children. The pictures I showed you?"

He nodded. "I remember them well."

"That, plus your campaign, will keep us more than occupied."

Jean Paul's eyes followed her fingers. Fortunately, Wyczek couldn't see her hands.

Jean Paul's attention returned to her face. She moved her eyes to her cappuccino, took another sip, set the cup down, absently undid the second button, then casually picked up the pad from the table and put it back in her purse. Was she going to try to actually seduce him? Her body seemed to be outracing her conscious intentions.

As if feeling too warm, she spread the blouse's lapels, then returned her gaze to König. He quickly shifted his gaze from her breasts to her eyes.

He finished his cappuccino, then he gave her a questioning look. "Shall we?"

Once outside, the bodyguard started to hail a taxi. Nova handed her lightweight wool cape to Jean Paul and, as he helped her pull it around her shoulders, said, "Jean Paul, I very much need a walk. Could I impose upon you?"

"Of course. My pleasure. Which way?"

The bodyguard spoke, a rough voice, and in German said, "A walk might be dangerous."

Jean Paul's reply, also in German, was that this was an unplanned walk late at night. No assassin would be able to anticipate it. He didn't consider it risky.

The guard set his jaw but acquiesced.

Nova asked, "Does he think it will be too dangerous? Perhaps it's not a good idea after all."

"He is concerned. But I disagree that it's dangerous. And I, too, would enjoy a walk. So again, which way?"

Company research indicated König had seldom been to Cologne. Even this trip was merely a political drop-in. He'd have no idea which way to go. Nova, on the other hand, had been well briefed. "East. Just a few blocks from here is the river. We'll go down through the Altermarkt. My guidebook says it dates back to the Middle Ages."

They turned. Would he take her arm? It would be a natural move. Neutral. A move that could be interpreted as innocent yet would signal his willingness for contact.

Jean Paul tucked his hands into his suit pockets.

They fell into matching steps, Wyczek plodding

along ten paces behind. Very romantic, she bemoaned silently. *So intimate. Almost as bad as trying to charm a man with his mother breathing down your neck.*

"You know," Jean Paul said, "we've talked all evening about me or the campaign. Tell me about you. Do you have family?"

She explained truthfully that she had a mother and sister, and that her father had died in a plane crash when she was twelve. She left out the fact that her father had been an ambassador to Great Britain at the time. It didn't matter that she divulged her childhood since the CIA had incorporated this part of it into her history. Without breaking the rhythm they'd fallen into, König turned his body and gazed at her. "How very sad for you. And for your mother and sister. How did it happen?"

"We were living in Rome. He was coming to join us for vacation on Capri, and the small sea plane coming out from Rome crashed into the Mediterranean."

They were strolling past remarkable old buildings—Gothic and eighteenth century—but Jean Paul's attention never wavered from her.

"My mother has not been well for years." The truth was, her mom lived in a nursing home close to both her and her sister in California. But because of Nova's hectic life, she didn't get to see her mom as often as her sister did. Besides, she knew her mom still felt guilty for bringing Candido Branco into their lives, and seeing Nova only reminded her of their tragic past.

A landscaped parklike area ran along the Rhine embankment. The full-moon reflection shimmered on the face of the river's slow current. A cargo vessel lumbered north, perhaps bound for Holland and the North Sea. Nova was keenly aware that Jean Paul still hadn't touched her. She imagined she could hear Peter Grund warning, "Keep those hands in your pockets!"

And she disturbingly wanted Jean Paul to touch her. Jean Paul the man, not the mark.

At a railing overlooking the riverbank, they stopped. She leaned both hands against the rail and feigned an intense study of the black water and the moon glow quivering on it.

"Have you never married?" he finally asked.

"I'm afraid I'm either too picky or too busy." She shook her head. "My sister thinks I'm too compulsively neat for any man to tolerate. I also know I love my work and that it keeps me uprooted. It's difficult for a relationship to grow."

König faced her, leaned one elbow against the railing. Instantly she was acutely aware of Wyczek, leaning against the same railing, not more than twenty feet away.

"I enjoyed dinner this evening," Jean Paul said softly. He had lowered his voice. Jean Paul's voice was one of his great gifts. He moved crowds with his voice when he spoke forcefully. Now, as he spoke intimately, his voice was almost hypnotic.

"I did, too."

"The walk was also pleasant," he said, "but I think I should put Klaus to bed."

She turned away from the river. "How do we get home?"

"Let's see if Klaus can flag a cab. Or we may have to walk back to the cabstand."

Traffic was light. Jean Paul took her arm and a bizarre mixture of pleasure and revulsion raised gooseflesh along her sides. Charming a man who might well be a monster brought revulsion. But the pleasure he'd kindled in but a few brief moments by such slight gestures—a softly spoken sentence, a touch on the arm—that, too, was alarming. She would tell Davidson they must not, under any circumstances, underestimate König's power to evoke emotion—the weapon of the demagogue—even in the most skeptical subject.

Wyczek fell in behind but Jean Paul waved him to join them. "See if you can find a cab," he told the guard in German. Nova had learned in the past few weeks that Jean Paul insisted on taking cabs and mass transit when possible. He felt having a car and driver was too extravagant and that taking mass transit was more environmentally sound.

Within minutes, a cab Wyczek flagged down stopped in front of her modest hotel. She bet herself that Jean Paul König was too much the gentleman to simply drop her off. He'd see her inside.

She won her bet. And then, as they stood waiting for the elevator, he instructed Wyczek to wait in the small lobby. The guard frowned—the first expression she'd seen break his stony face—but he obeyed.

Might Jean Paul be willing to stay the night, right now? Should she encourage him?

The fourth-floor hallway was deserted. Again Jean Paul took her arm. A turning point loomed. Her strategy planned for no more than an intimate evening to create a bond. But things seemed to be moving fast beyond that modest goal.

At her door he took her hand, looked deeply into her eyes and said, "A wonderful evening, Nova." His tone was courteous. The evening was over. "I hope we can do it again sometime." He gave her hand a continental kiss.

She forced out a smile and nodded, then slid her key

into the lock. In the doorway, her hand still on the knob, she turned and said with all the warmth she could command, "I'm going to be looking forward to another evening."

Jean Paul nodded, turned and retreated down the hall. Nova closed the door and sagged against it. Her pulse beat strongly against a lump in her constricted throat as she fought disappointment and fear of failure. *What is wrong with this man!*

And what's happening to me?

She'd actually been ready to give herself to him for the night of his life and he'd settled for a kiss of her hand!

Brooding would accomplish nothing. From her suitcase she fetched the minirecorder. Insomnia—a reality she'd finally accepted gratefully in her late twenties— allowed her to live the equivalent of two lives. In her teens and the troubled years behind prison bars, she'd considered the long nights a curse. What do you do when everyone else you know is sleeping? Then she'd discovered serious reading, languages and bodybuilding. Her nights had transformed swiftly and beautifully from curse to gift.

She dictated the evening's events for Davidson. During sit-ups she began to think the CIA's strategists might have to adopt a different approach. So much effort had been spent on inserting her, she doubted they would try another woman, but that option would be discussed. The thought that some other woman might be called on to achieve what she could not shoved a booster shot of competitive vigor into her last two sit-ups.

She rolled to her stomach for push-ups and thought of Joe. Maybe in the morning he'd tell her that unlike her evening, his had been a success. Into the wee hours, she read a new Russian novel. She was adding Russian to her suite of languages.

Nova folded her *London Times* as she spotted Cardone heading toward the small round table she'd commandeered. His tray held coffee, a bowl of fruit and the same chocolate-covered pastry she'd chosen.

Over the clink of silverware and coffee cups he said, *"Guten Morgen."*

"'Morning, Joe," she returned in English. Even though he was picking up German rather quickly, she didn't want to break their cover of speaking in English.

She waited for him to empty the tray and set it aside before telling him the bad news. The Founder had sent another set of instructions. According to Cupid, the targeted event was an international meeting on deforestation in Denmark, in mid-July. The terrorist demanded the countries involved in the meeting grant forgiveness of foreign debt in return for certain preservation measures instituted by several Third World nations. The President of the United States's position was that giving in to yet another demented demand would put the American economy into a panic-generating nosedive.

But if the U.S. didn't give in there would surely be more deaths. She took a bite of pastry.

After he had taken his first hit of coffee he asked, "So what did you find out last night?"

This grilling was going to be uncomfortable—but unavoidable. She shrugged. She hoped she was doing a good poker-face hiding of the disappointment she felt. He was expecting progress, he was hungry for progress, just as hungry as she was.

He frowned. "My dinner with Ellen went fine, but after dating for nearly two weeks that has included shows, dinners and finally a lot of conversation in bed, I've concluded she's simply an outstanding secretary. I don't think she has a devious bone in her body."

Nova dropped her gaze toward her tray, a mental image jolting her—of Cardone naked in bed with Ellen Nöe, their bodies pressed close, legs entwined and his lips brushing Ellen's cheek. The thought bothered her for no definable reason. Just as it was her job to get close to Jean Paul, Joe was to get as close as possible to Ellen. Perhaps because jumping into bed with Jean Paul was still her last resort.

"And the office?" she asked.

She looked at Cardone again and found him studying her intently with his dark brown eyes as if he cared what she might think about him seducing the secretary.

"A complete nothing," he said, breaking his study of her and picking up his coffee. "Breaking in was easy, a sure sign nothing would be there. And there wasn't. I went through everything. Grund's stuff. All the mailing and publicity files. Nothing but campaign junk. So, how's the bonding with König working?"

He sounded pushy. Demanding. Well, The Founder was ready to attack again and what real progress could she report? Nothing.

"The walk went well. Jean Paul even ditched Wyczek briefly to accompany me to my hotel room door."

"So he asked you out again?"

"No."

"No! Nova, you need to work it a little more aggressively. We need to get some results!"

"I know what I'm doing!" she snapped at him. "I can handle this!"

"Can you? What does that mean? You've been all over and around him for over two weeks. Then you have an intimate dinner. Did you get any sense at all that he wanted more than a murmured good-night?"

Unspoken but hanging in the air was his disclosure that he'd gotten very close indeed to Ellen. Nova wanted to clarify his target wasn't married or running for political office so was a little easier to get to. "I suppose the ladies' man is sure he could win over any quarry in less than a week."

"Well—" He struggled with some words that didn't come out. For a long, painful moment the silence between them seemed louder than the clinking and talk buzzing around them at other tables.

Cardone scrubbed the five o'clock shadow that was more than likely on its twelfth hour and took a sip of his coffee. He sat the cup down and gave her a weary look that seemed to say he was sorry for jumping on her. They were both clearly tired and frustrated with their progress, or lack thereof.

"Look," he said, "Ellen isn't running for a political office. Peter Grund couldn't care less whether Ellen sees me after work. Don't think I'm making any kind of comparison. I'm not."

He waited. She had quickly hidden the hurt look. But he'd seen it and he regretted having caused it. He finished his coffee. She finished hers. He offered her a smile. "We don't want to be late."

They rose and made their way toward the door. The freeze coming off Nova Blair made him feel like he was swimming beside an iceberg in an Arctic sea. Davidson was going to be even less pleased than he was himself with her lack of progress. He felt more than a little bit sorry for her.

Chapter 12

The Founder's Compound

After three firm raps on his study door, his wife strode in, uninvited. She never respected his privacy. Casting him an irritated look, she said, "The results from last month's sales in Hong Kong have come in. I want you to look through them. They are distressingly low. Something is wrong there."

"All right."

"Now. Not tomorrow."

He sat quietly. After a long pause, she turned and left.

He stood and slipped his hand behind the rosewood panel and pressed the hidden button. The disguised elevator door from his study to the underground corridors slid silently open. He stepped in and pressed Down.

His hands, he noted with amusement, were trembling. He licked his lips, knew he was wearing a crooked smile. It was always like this when he had a new model: his excitement recreated his teenage anticipation of first sex, an act he'd shared with a whore. The door opened. He stepped into the corridor and headed for his sculpting studio.

Disciplining this excitement was important; loss of control of himself or the model would show in his work. Twice the relationship between artist and subject had spiraled too quickly beyond anger and pain into fear, submission and a plea for death. The resulting sculptures had lacked animation. He had destroyed them. This time the model was a woman, delivered only an hour ago. Maurus, his dedicated associate, selected and procured all of the special subjects, unimportant people, unlikely to be missed, or if missed, their disappearance wouldn't be aggressively explored.

He opened the door and heard her handcuffs clink against the metal posts of the bed as she twisted in an attempt to see who was there. He took slow breaths. The two tables in the middle of the room held his tools. He forced his gaze to linger there a moment.

Finally again in command, everything felt right. He walked to the bed.

Her eyes went wide, probably because of his appearance. He would certainly not be what she was expecting. She said in English, "Who the fuck are you? You can't keep me here!" She was wearing jeans and a pink T-shirt, perhaps twenty-seven or eight in age. An American by her accent. She had short curly brown hair and was lean. A lean body; he liked that in his models.

"I said, you can't keep me here. I'll be missed."

"I don't think so. In any case, no one can find you. I have done this many times."

"What do you want with me?"

He felt she would do very well. It would take time to break her, and the slow disintegration of a defiant will created the very best material. He stepped to the three video cameras mounted on tripods and switched them on, then turned back to the girl. "You are going to be the model for my next sculpture."

He removed the prod from a drawer. Her gaze fastened onto it. "This is a cattle prod. I will use it to control you as I train you to do whatever I ask. Whenever you disobey, I'll stun you with it. You'll be paralyzed for a short period, and it will hurt terribly afterward. Do you understand?"

"Fuck you!"

He laughed. "Oh, not right away."

Chapter 13

Augsburg, Germany

Their lookout walked through the door leading from the lobby of the Hotel Winterpalast into the bar, signaled by rubbing his thumb against his nose, and disappeared into the men's room. Nova had dressed with casual but stunning in mind, in white slacks and matching white silk shell top.

Cardone wore a yellow shirt with rolled-up sleeves that looked great against his tanned skin, showed off his impressive biceps and cleverly reinforced his air of youth. He bellowed, impatient and loud, "Why can't I get another drink?" He waved his hand toward the waiter.

Nearly five weeks had passed now, and Nova still had failed to make any noticeable headway with Jean Paul.

She'd spent countless hours in his presence taking photos or lending a helping hand with campaign chores. Last week she'd accompanied him to a wedding to take publicity photos. Afterward, over punch and wedding cake, they'd traded confidences in a corner for nearly two hours. All apparently to no avail.

Jean Paul was like no case she'd ever worked. He was inspiring. He seemed without guile. She had to keep reminding herself that, if he was The Founder, the punishments he decreed involved the horrible deaths of innocents. Think con man, she reminded herself frequently to guard against his immense charm.

Then, the day before yesterday, in his office, something seemed to have changed. She had gone ostensibly to get his opinion on some photos. But the first thing he'd said was, "That color of green is beautiful on you. A perfect complement to your eyes."

For a moment the air molecules between them had seemed to vibrate against her chest. She discovered she was holding her breath. She'd said, "I'm surprised you'd notice. I don't think I've ever met a man more involved in his work and nothing else."

A small pause—two beats of her heart—and he'd said, "You're a woman quite impossible to overlook under any circumstances."

She had thought he might ask her for another dinner, was certain the invitation was coming. But Peter Grund interrupted. She was certain he'd done it on purpose and she'd wanted to take an ax to the campaign manager.

To put the worst face on it, which Cupid had done later that evening, it was possible the change in König was because he may somehow have smelled the scent of bloodhound on her rather than perfume. But her feminine instincts were telling her that Jean Paul was slowly falling for her. And now the plan tonight was for her and Cardone to push the envelope.

Nova leaned toward Cardone and spoke in a soothing tone, loud enough for those nearby to hear. "I think we ought to call it a night." All conversation for thirty feet on either side of them had crawled to a halt. The waiter, a look of disgust on his pinched face, stood flat-footed, eyes narrowed on her partner.

"I been waitin' for 'nother drink ten minutes. The service sucks!"

Nova sent the waiter a silent plea for understanding. She looked back at Cardone. "Why don't we try someplace else?"

"Great. Lezz do that. The waiter puzz his fingers in our drinks anyway."

Joe shoved himself to his feet and swayed slightly, just enough to be convincing. He reached into his pocket and extracted a money clip. After riffling through the bills a moment, he shoved them into her hands. "You pay. Lezz get the hell outta here."

He launched himself unsteadily toward the door leading from the bar into the hotel's main lobby. She scanned the check and put down enough money to cover it and tip the waiter generously for the insults he'd endured for the past ten minutes.

In the lobby, her partner slumped into a brocade wing-backed chair in a conversation island in the center of the room, a strategically prominent location. Within seconds König, fresh from a campaign dinner and surrounded by several local businessmen and the new movie star rage, Gunter Heglund, entered the lobby from the hotel dining room.

She approached Cardone. He straightened and bellowed, "For the cos' of the liquor here, should get damn good service."

She feared he might overdo it: the marbled walls and floors of the lobby, though covered with tapestries and area rugs, bounced his voice into every corner. A couple passing by shrank away from them, anger in the man's face and pity for Nova in the woman's. Nova didn't dare risk a look to see how König reacted.

Cardone struggled and stood. She put an arm under his elbow. He shook her off. "I'm all right. Don't try and mother me all the time."

"Good evening, Ms. Blair. Mr. Cardone."

She turned to find Jean Paul, with his shadow, Wyczek. The other men were already halfway out the brass-and-glass front entry, the paparazzi for once dogging Heglund not Jean Paul. "Herr König," she said, eyes wide with surprise.

"Well. Mr. König. A good, good evenin'." Cardone extended his hand and swayed slightly.

König shook it, warmly she thought, then looked at her. "I gather you two have been enjoying Augsburg's nightlife. Or are you staying here?" As he stood gazing into her eyes, no more than two feet away, stiffness crept over Jean Paul. His jaw muscles tightened. She had the odd feeling he wanted to touch her.

"No. Not here. And I'm afraid our evening has gotten a bit out of hand."

Joe Cardone swayed like a redwood about to go down. "Shii—" he muttered softly, collapsing into the chair. His head hit the back and his eyes closed.

Jean Paul eyed Cardone. He smiled disapprovingly and looked back at her. She grinned and shook her head.

"The kid's overdone it a bit. Please don't get the wrong impression."

"What's the occasion?"

"I haven't the slightest idea. I only know he received a letter and went into a nosedive. I suspect woman troubles." She shook her head again.

"Can we help you manage him to your hotel?"

"I hate to be a bother. But I would be extremely grateful."

König signaled to Wyczek. They hoisted her partner. As they helped him up, he muttered, "I'm okay. No problem."

"Right," König said in a lightly amused tone. "Don't worry. We're just helping you to your room." To Nova he said, "Have the doorman fetch my limo."

She barely registered that he'd hired a limo tonight, then hurried, looking back only once to see König and Wyczek with Cardone shuffling between them out a side door of the hotel.

König, Wyczek, and the driver tucked Joe into the center of the rear seat. She jumped in so that she and Jean Paul flanked Cardone. They traveled the short distance to her hotel in silence.

With Nova leading, the male trio struggled through the tiny lobby into the elevator and finally to the door of the agent's room. She fetched the key from his pocket and let them all in, and from a wall switch flicked on the floor lamp. A cozy light flooded the space.

The room was small and unpretentious, done in a homey, Bavarian-country style. Thick white comforters lay on two twin beds. König and Wyczek removed Cardone's jacket and shoes and stretched him out on one of the beds. Wyczek threw the down coverlet over the lower half of his body. "That should keep him until morning," König said. "I imagine he'll have a nasty hangover tomorrow."

Probably not even if he really had been drinking, she thought. Cardone could handle his liquor from what she'd seen in their time together.

She captured Jean Paul's gaze again. This was easy to do; his eyes seemed to be all over her. "I can't thank you enough. If there is anything I can do for you…anything…"

Wyczek the Faithful had gone into the hall, just outside the door.

Jean Paul spoke almost in a whisper. "You are very beautiful."

She let the silence wait for a moment. "I think, Jean Paul, we'd better let him sleep."

"I do want something." He hesitated. A muscle at the corner of his lower jaw jumped. "I want to stay here. Tonight. With you."

She bit her lip, then slowly turned her back to him. "I'm not sure what to say."

With two steps he was behind her. The aftershave that evoked the image of high mountains and crisp air clung to his jacket and skin. Warm hands touched her arms. He turned her to face him. Beneath his touch, her bare arms raised into goose bumps. Odd, she thought, as if detached from her body.

"I'm obsessed with you, Nova. The way you talk. The way you move. Always pulling at me. You must know this. I want to spend the night with you."

She shook herself loose, stepped sideways away from him and out of Wyczek's view. She also suddenly wished Joe wasn't hearing their every word. "Think what you're saying, Jean Paul. You're married. A prominent politician." She chuckled cynically. "Think what Peter would say."

"Peter Grund can go to hell. I've been miserable for weeks, and I no longer care what he thinks." He shook his head. "Perhaps I'm doing this badly. Perhaps you don't want to spend the night with me. I can understand. You need only say so."

She laced her fingers together and then unlaced them. She would take her time so her words would have weight. Finally she faced him full-on again. "Just the opposite. I've lived the last weeks with the fantasy that you'd do what you're doing now."

He kissed her. At first she pushed against his arms. He mustn't think her foolish enough to enter into such a relationship easily.

Jean Paul simply held her harder. And when his tongue sought to penetrate her lips she let her physical self go. His body seemed to quiver and his excitement telegraphed to her. She pressed against him and took his tongue eagerly. He wrapped a hand in her hair and the force of his kiss became painful. She felt as though a gate within him had been opened and a great flood of passion surged through him to her.

Wrenching away, she moved to the other side of the room, but still out of Wyczek's view.

"I can't do this, Jean Paul," she said, words mentally rehearsed many times for just such a moment. "Spending the night with you will simply make everything worse. I care too much for you already. And besides, it's dangerous for you."

He followed, and when he stood next to her he said nothing. He touched her hair. He touched her lips. He brushed his hand over her cheek. "For the love of God, don't say no to me. I can see to it that no one will know. Let's go to your room. Now." He took her hand. "Yes?" he asked. The cool blue eyes were begging.

She hesitated, contemplating the proposition that in moments she would be utterly alone with him for the first time. She ran her tongue over her lips. Then without unlocking her gaze from his eyes, she gave him her hand.

Coming up from the lobby, she had let Jean Paul know that her room was adjacent to Cardone's. Jean Paul stopped at her door. He turned to Wyczek. "You may meet me below in this lobby at seven o'clock tomorrow morning."

The hulking guard seemed to put down roots into the floor. Only after a very long moment did he nod his head in a stiff Germanic salute. He then strode off, his heavy body coaxing the inn's pine floorboards to creak with every step.

She asked, "Can you trust him?"

"If Wyczek's discretion wasn't trustworthy, he'd be out of work in short order."

She took her key from her shoulder bag and let them in. Like Cardone's, her room was small and cozy. But unlike his, hers had a large double bed and a private bath.

They would have this night together. She must convince this man to let her into his life. To trust her so that she could spy on him. She would begin by letting him lead her, but when they made love again and yet again, she would find out his secret desires. He would find her at first almost shy, but finally abandoned—if that pleased him.

Jean Paul turned out to be as unskilled as a schoolboy. He undressed her awkwardly, and when she began to remove his clothes, it had to be in haste. He could scarcely wait.

Afterward he said, "I am sorry. I've disappointed you, haven't I?"

She rushed to assure him. "Don't be foolish. It was wonderful."

But the truth was his performance could qualify as a disappointment in many respects. She was confident now that the CIA files were right about his restricted sex life—surprised but confident. She traced the vertical line beside his mouth, then ran her hand over his smooth chest.

He stroked her arm. "I've thought of you so often. I dream of you. "

"I can't believe I'm here with you. It amazes me when you say you've dreamed of me. I had no idea you felt remotely the way I do." This was a lie, yet not a lie. Her attraction to him, the affection she often felt toward him, was both powerful and real. Everything she said with Jean Paul, everything she did, seemed to be double-edged.

For a long while they lay in the bed, sharing warmth and caresses, their hands exploring. When she thought he was ready again, she rose on one elbow and let her hair spill over his chest. She started with a kiss on the lips, one hand caressing his face, but her kissing and touching and licking moved lower and lower.

Only when she began to move still lower did he resist. She heard him suck in his breath and then hold her head as if to prevent her. But she persisted, and almost immediately he surrendered. He moaned softly and the sounds of pleasure continued intermittently as she took him up and up into rapture and out of his own control.

Playing him, she eased off and he grabbed her head, "My God. My God. Please." She began again. When his hands finally dug into the flesh of her shoulders, his strangled groan was followed by repeated shudders.

She waited a few moments then said, "Wait," as she backed off the bed. From the bathroom she fetched a warm wet cloth.

"Feels wonderful," he murmured. He was more in control of himself again. He pulled her down to a kiss and soon thrust his tongue into her mouth. When she finally pulled away she stretched herself along the length of his body, sliding one leg over his thighs.

He hugged her and wrapped his hand to cradle her head and nudge it back to look at her. "You will never know what you mean to me."

"Tell me."

"I can't."

"Try."

"I can't, Nova. Just know that this night—this night is for me very special."

"And for me, Jean Paul."

"What we are doing is totally irresponsible of me. I have done everything I could to keep you out of my thoughts, but nothing worked." He laughed softly. "You know, Peter has warned me about you. A number of times."

She trailed her fingers down his side. "Of course."

"What you may not appreciate, but he does, is that I have never—never—done anything like this before. It will worry Peter no end when he finds out."

She pushed away from him and sat up. "When Peter finds out? Surely you won't tell him. And you said Wyczek was reliable."

"Of course he is. But I will tell Peter. From this moment, Nova, I don't intend to spend any more nights away from you than necessary. As long as you'll stay with me. And we can't manage that unless Peter knows.

Peter may not like this, but he is absolutely trustworthy. It's your partner I worry about."

Her heart, still beating strongly, actually trip-hammered in her ears. This was sweet success indeed. She hugged him gently, then pretended reluctance. "We have to think this through very carefully. I know my partner. We're close. We've shared confidences. He'd never betray us. But what you're saying is scary."

"Why should you be afraid?"

"My God! Aren't you afraid? A night is one thing. But to be together often? What if other people find out? You'd be courting political disaster."

She stretched alongside him again, her palm spread over his nipple; she felt the hard, tight bud in the center of her hand. He rose on his elbow and when he kissed her, she felt from him the longing of a man afraid to lose contact with the first water he's tasted after walking barefoot across a desert.

When he finally pulled away again he said, "For myself, I already made that decision. Before I asked you to let me stay. I don't care about the risk. And Peter is clever. Other politicians do this all the time. Clever Peter should be able to help us."

His blue eyes searched every feature of her face. He fingered and tousled her bangs. He touched and traced the lines of her ears. He studied her eyes and then her mouth. He seemed to eat her up. "I fear I may be in love with you, Nova."

Deep in her chest she felt a pang of alarm. She squeezed his arm, soft compared to the rock-hard biceps she'd once, by accident, felt in Joe's arm. "Don't say that, Jean Paul. It's too soon. You can't mean it."

She broke from his embrace and sat up on the side

of the bed, shocked at the speed at which Jean Paul seemed to be moving. That he should be professing love this soon was extraordinary. Who was conning whom?

Still, she must let herself go, let her mind adjust quickly, let this character she played move from attraction to passion. "I don't want you to say love, Jean Paul. You'll make me believe it."

"If what I feel isn't love, maybe it's obsession. Whatever it is, it won't let me rest."

She put fire in her eyes. "You're married, Jean Paul. I'm doing something crazy here, too. I'm falling in love with a married man. I detest the very idea. It's pointless. Crazy. Something only a stupid woman would let happen to her."

"You love me?"

"I didn't say that."

"You said you're falling in love with a married man." He smiled crookedly. "At least I may take hope from that, may I not?"

She shook her head. "I didn't mean to say I love you. Only that I feel myself…have been feeling myself…losing control around you."

He took her by the arms and used his eyes to capture hers. "I pray to God that what you say you mean. I'm not going to tell you the old cliché that my wife doesn't love me. But I will tell you this. There is not now and never has been any passion between my wife and me." A slight flush of red blotted the skin of his neck. "She would never have done to me what you just did."

Foolish woman.

"I've needed someone like you—I've needed you—all my life. Since forever. And now you're here. I decided last week at the wedding. I'm not going to let you slip away."

"What you're suggesting we do is just plain crazy."

"Yes. But I accept the risk."

"You want me with you. As often as we can arrange it."

"Yes. Every night possible."

She smiled up at him. "Kiss me again, then. Make me not afraid."

He rained kisses on her lips. She enjoyed them for a while. Then she took his head in her hands and directed him to her throat. He held her arms tightly, his fingers digging in painfully like a tightening vise, as if he were desperately afraid she'd flee.

Soon his mouth found her mouth again and she let him enjoy her for a while. But then she took his head and forced it downward. She forced him to a breast and when he took it, he moaned over and over.

She sighed. To her surprise, her nipples tingled. Her hands never stopped moving over his hair and face and shoulders. She talked to him in whispers.

She forced his head farther down. He kissed and licked her belly, but tentatively, as if he were unsure of himself. His lack of experience wasn't to be believed, yet it was evident; he took little initiative, but everything she encouraged he did.

Finally she pushed his head still lower, his straight blond hair soft in her hands. "Please do it for me, Jean Paul," she whispered. "Please."

He tried.

"No," she said. "Higher." Suddenly it was good.

Shock. "Oh, yes." A burning iron stabbed from the place he touched to the pit of her stomach. Her breathing, shallow now. A dark spiral was coming for her. Wrapping around her. Lifting her. Her fingers clenched and tightened in his hair. His tongue. Yes. Yes! *Oh my God!*

Spasms racked her.

When she opened her eyes, Jean Paul was studying her face. "Beautiful," was all he said.

Chapter 14

Fear radiated from the warmth Nova felt in her belly. She shook. She wanted to leap from the bed, but she made herself laugh softly. "Yes. Beautiful."

"I mean you," Jean Paul said.

"And I meant you."

He laughed, his wonderful, warm laugh.

She couldn't stay in this bed, so close beside him. Not another second. *Must have space, for at least a moment,* said her mind in a frightening and unfamiliar near panic. It wasn't the smart thing to do, but she had to get up.

"I'll be right back." She kissed him, then fled into the bathroom and closed the door.

For a moment she leaned against the bathroom door, her legs threatening to buckle under her. *Must hurry. Shouldn't be away from him too long.*

She turned on the cold water and threw two handfuls

into her face. Not since Ramone—how many years ago?
It was dangerous in the extreme for her ever to be moved
by a man, to ever lose control. She grabbed the towel
and rubbed it hard over her face. She closed her eyes and
took three deep breaths.

Shock was needed. She conjured. There was Candido
Branco and he was undressing her. Nova held the picture steady until, as if she'd heard an audible click in her
head, her composure returned.

She wiped her face and took several breaths more.
Finally the fear drained away. Determination and resolve stuck a steel rod up her back. She replaced the
towel and hurried back to König's arms.

She stretched beside him and cuddled close, her head
on his arm. Amazingly they slept; she wasn't sure how
long, but König was looking at her when she woke.

"I have a dead man's arm," he said with an apolo-
getic smile.

She sat up quickly and began massaging his forearm
and hand. "You should have awakened me."

"I like watching you sleep."

Her stomach growled. She giggled. "I'm famished."

"I think we can safely say I've burned off all my dinner." With a finger he traced the tip of a breast, then
kissed it.

She said, "I have a tin of cookies and some coffee.
Shall I heat water?"

"Wonderful."

She threw on her silk traveling robe and set her cof-
feemaker to heat water. Jean Paul disappeared into the
bathroom, then reappeared with a large white towel
wrapped around his waist. He grabbed her from behind,
lifted her and tossed her face first onto the rumpled

sheets. Next he straddled her back, then he rolled her over to face him and kissed her again. He moved beside her and began toying with her face, tracing her eyebrows, her jawline. "Does this annoy you?"

He took the tip of her robe's belt and stretched it across her forehead. "Your eyes are a fabulous color. The robe is the same. Exactly. What is the color, in English? In German it is *smaragdgrün*."

"In English, people usually say emerald."

"Are they contact lenses? Don't be offended, but I've wondered very often."

She laughed. "No. They're not contacts."

He put the belt down and let his hand sweep over the material. He opened her gown and his gaze followed his fingers as he trailed them over her belly. "Tell me something about yourself," she said. She moved the pillows under her head to be comfortable.

"What kind of something?"

"Oh, anything. I just want to hear your voice. Maybe tell me about how and why you got involved in Earth Alliance. I think it's your great love."

He shifted to lie beside her, propped on an elbow, his hand still playing over her belly. "My father was a professor of biology. He loved nature. All our vacations were spent somewhere out-of-doors. He died when I was twenty-three, but he'd had a powerful influence on me."

"But why Earth Alliance? Don't you lose supporters by your close association with a group that advocates spiking trees?" She put her finger to his lip. "And why so much passion from you? I've interviewed lots of people now, all of whom tell me you're like a man obsessed."

In a long caress, he moved his hand over one breast

and up her throat and then caught her chin. "It's you I'm obsessed with."

She smiled and stroked his arm. "You're avoiding my question."

The tiny lines at the corners of his eyes crinkled. His hair was mussed and a loose strand fell over a forehead creased in thought. His body pleased her. It wasn't heavily muscled. He had no time for the vanities or practicalities of the kind of workout regime she maintained. Or Joe for that matter. It was a marathon runner's body, just not so hard.

"Something very profound happened to me on the last trip I ever took with my father. We went to Alaska. I don't know if you've ever been there?"

A cold chill raced up from the base of her spine and fanned over her ribs. He might be very surprised to learn just how recently she'd been to Alaska, and why. Or would he? Once again fear triggered the thought that perhaps König was playing a devious game of his own.

She slammed the door to her mind on that idea. In this physically and emotionally exposed situation it could paralyze her. "I have," she said. "I've led several tours there and done a lot of photography."

"Do you know Denali park, then?"

"Of course."

"Then you know it is true wilderness. No trails, no maps, no helpful signposts, no campsites. The rangers warn you to make noise in dense vegetation so you don't surprise the very real bears who can and have killed people."

König kept his voice low. It was, after all, the early hours of the morning and he was in bed in a hotel with a woman who was not his wife. But his speech grew animated.

She chuckled. "I had a friend who insisted that real wilderness was a place where there lives an animal dangerous enough to kill you." That was Ramone talking.

Jean Paul smiled. "Your friend and I would agree. From childhood, I had known about so-called wilderness, from Germany or the Alps. We even took a safari to Africa. But when my father took me to Denali, something profound happened."

He sat up and crossed his legs. "My father made me camp for a day and a night alone. I experienced a great many emotions. But the feeling that outlasted all others was anger. I love Germany, but there is absolutely nothing wild here. To experience unity with the planet, I had to go halfway around the world."

The muscle at the angle of Jean Paul's jaw tightened and jumped. He clenched his right hand. His eyes remained on her face but he was talking at her now. His vision had turned inward. "Look how the oil companies are eating up Alaska and trashing it."

The inward-searching eyes grew cold. No warming smile, no amused wrinkles at the corners of his eyes. This was exactly how The Founder might speak. Here was love of nature, but also rage. An imagined arctic breath on her half-bare arms raised goose bumps.

"If we don't learn to treasure quality rather than quantity, this generation will leave only dregs. And I've discovered that, by a quirk of fate, I've an almost uncanny ability to persuade. I have two sons, you know. I simply have to do what I am able to do."

Abruptly he seemed to sense his intensity was out of

place, or perhaps that it left him too exposed. He shrugged. "As I say, a simple story."

She sat up, saw that the water was boiling. "Tea or coffee?" she asked.

"Tea."

She handed him the tin of cookies and he sat cross-legged on the bed and watched her dip bags for two cups of Earl Grey, known to be his favorite. She joined him. "If I had my druthers, this would be cappuccino."

"You like cappuccino? I will buy you a portable maker."

They sipped quietly. Then, praying she sounded sufficiently casual, she said, "I know Earth Alliance embraces ecosabotage. What I don't know is how far it should go. Did you read in today's paper that someone blew up a coal-burning power plant in England? Twenty-five people died."

He nodded but said nothing.

Cupid, her chief of station for Operation Jacaranda, had explained what the newspapers had not: the plant's destruction had been The Founder's punishment for the British parliament's contrary vote on a measure to severely curb gas consumption. "The article hints that ecoterrorists blew it up."

"Those plants are perfect examples of things that have to go."

"But, Jean Paul, over twenty people were killed."

"That is a tragedy. A terrible thing. Whoever's responsible must be insane. Nevertheless, the plant is better gone."

She strained to judge his tone, his mood. She sensed nothing extraordinary. Neither victory nor much sympathy. *Careful,* she thought. "Who could do such a thing?"

He unfolded his legs and stood. "Why do you ask— and with such an intense look?"

Was he suspicious? Was she pushing too hard? She was searching for just the right response when he said, "I couldn't even guess who did it. This morning Peter Grund and I talked about the situation at length. Also with Detlev. You've met Detlev, haven't you?"

She nodded. Detlev Kleitman, Earth Alliance's president, another prime suspect. Jean Paul, as chairman of the organization's board of directors, talked with him regularly.

Without prompting, Jean Paul continued. "The newspaper reports are contradictory. Some say the Brits have no leads. Some claim the Brits received blackmail letters from an ecoterrorist. We've had reporters and supporters calling. Some Alliance supporters suggested we put out a policy statement as a timely denial, and we decided this morning to do just that. So, in a way, the plant's destruction is good publicity for us."

"But, Jean Paul. What a dreadful way to get publicity."

"Certainly. But no opportunity to stress the urgency of our message should be lost."

The Founder's next deadline, mid-July, was less than a month away. She burned to press Jean Paul further, but he'd finished with that subject. To ask more now would most definitely have an unnatural feel.

At six-thirty they awakened. Jean Paul showered and while he dressed they discussed again their decision to defy fate. Jean Paul was resolute. Combing back his still damp hair, he said, "I'll call you when I've worked things out. I'll tell Peter what I want. I'll arrange a way for you to come this evening to my hotel room."

At seven, he left by the back stairs, having explained

that he would go through the front to meet Wyczek in the lobby.

What had she learned for Cupid? Had Jean Paul sounded truly grieved at the loss of life at the English power plant? That really was the big question, wasn't it? And she wasn't sure of the answer.

Chapter 15

Munich

Nova padded naked into the bathroom to prepare for Jean Paul's arrival. The Hotel Bavaria had once been a mill. Beautifully converted now, its impeccable service included utmost discretion, a most valuable asset: Jean Paul could come and go without attracting notice. Last night he'd slept at his home; this night, as he'd done for over a month, he'd sleep again with her.

Operation Jacaranda's planners had decided she and Cardone needed to expand the scope of their information gathering to include the Earth Alliance organization. Soon she would learn if Jean Paul had convinced the Earth Alliance board of directors to let her do a photo-essay on them.

She was eager for Jean Paul's arrival. He seemed

head over heels in love with her and was always thoughtful and tender. But she needed to stay sharp— and be on guard. She was here to spy, not fall in love with the enemy.

She reminded herself of that as she slid on skimpy black lace panties and bra set and pulled on her robe. For earrings, she selected emerald studs. In eight practiced minutes she applied makeup to appear as though she was wearing none. And no perfume. Her skin still smelled of lilac from her bath.

She glanced at the clock: 7:50. Right on schedule. She was ready ten minutes before he'd said he would arrive. She took a deep breath and visualized Jean Paul saying Yes to the Earth Alliance project, then began to read her novel.

Hearing Jean Paul's key in the lock, Nova shifted her mind into high gear and sat the paperback on the night table.

The big double bed was placed so it was the first thing seen when the door opened. She went to its foot, sat facing the door, leaned back on the palms of her hands and spread her legs, ever so slightly. Jean Paul stepped into the room. He smiled, shook his head and, never taking his eyes from her, quickly closed the door. "Shameless creature. You're a bad influence on me, Nova Blair."

She smiled. "Why, whatever are you referring to?" She inched her legs further apart.

He held a bouquet of sweet peas. He laid them on the highboy by the door and in three long strides stood over her. He knelt between her legs, leaned close and slid his hands over her robe to her waist. "My incomparable emerald," he said, his voice husky.

She leaned forward and, holding his head, kissed him hard on the mouth.

"With…with my wife…" He hesitated and searched her eyes. An empty, unsatisfied, haunted look reached out to her from those eyes. "With my wife, I've always had the feeling that nothing was being given. You give me everything."

His hands felt hot. She slid her fingers under his light jacket and he quickly shrugged out of it. She loosened his tie, pulled it free and tossed it after his jacket. Within a few heartbeats they were naked on the bed's light down comforter. Soon his voice and body told her she'd pleased him again.

Afterward he held her tight, and she decided to take advantage of the afterglow of their lovemaking to try to nudge more information from him. "You brought me flowers again."

"It's a poor substitute for what I really want to do. I want the election to be over. I want a divorce. I want to be free to take you out into the world, into a field of flowers and watch you pick them."

Her conscience flinched, as if he'd lashed it with a strap. *What if he isn't guilty?*

But, her conscience countered, *what if he is?* "We have to be patient." She laid her hand along the side of his jaw. "I become more convinced every day that nothing must interfere with your destiny." He seemed poised to protest but she sat up and swung her legs off the bed. "I'll put the flowers in water."

She returned to the bedroom feeling calmer and put the sweet peas on the table in front of three draped windows. She hopped onto the bed, grabbed Jean Paul around the waist, pulled him down, then entwined their legs. "How did it go with the Earth Alliance board about the photo essay? Did you ask?"

"I talked to Detlev and two others whose opinions matter. They like the idea. And why not? Free publicity should probably never be turned down. Their main concern is who will publish it. And if you would do it only in English, seeing that neither you nor Joe speaks German."

She explained her thoughts on publishers. Claiming her ideas were deplorably provincial, she solicited Jean Paul's suggestions. "We can settle all this later," he finally said. "The good news is the board likes the idea."

She hugged him. "Yes. Good news." She kissed him and her hand wandered over his skin to particularly intimate places.

"I know what you're thinking, Ms. Blair," he said, grinning. "But I did more talking than eating at lunch. I'm hungry. Could you take pity and agree to order dinner first?"

She returned his grin. "I'm another starved soul. I'm lusting for the broiled chicken. What are you lusting for?"

He kissed the back of her neck. Hot breath fanned her skin as he whispered, "Whatever you have, I want."

She laughed. While she ordered, he shrugged on one of the hotel's white terry robes. When she put down the phone, the corners of his mouth twitched impishly. "Let me massage your back." She opened her arms. He untied her belt, then slipped the robe from her shoulders and led her back to the bed.

The massage was good. Her mind drifted away from Jean Paul, away from her job, her worries. Then he interrupted her voyage. "Peter has arranged an important reception for me here in Munich. On the fifteenth. At the home of Manfred Wagner. Do you know of him?"

"No." Her voice was still lazy with the drug of relaxation. Actually she knew Wagner was one of Earth Alliance's major financial backers and a prime suspect.

"He's one of our most prominent industrialists. I've arranged for you to come. You and Joe. I am sorry, but I will be there with my wife. Will that bother you?"

Thinking how to reply, she said, "This feels wonderful." Jean Paul waited, his hands kneading her flesh. She continued. "I haven't had to see you and your wife together. I'm not sure how I'll feel. I try not to think of your wife, Jean Paul, because when I do, I feel like someone sticks a dull knife in me."

His hands halted. "I am so sorry to hurt you even this much." He paused a moment. "I feel bad about Ilse. I truly believe in fidelity. But we married too young, in my case mostly at my mother's insistence. I was young and a fool, and I don't think Ilse knew me, either. The ecology movement has become my life. And until you, it was sufficient."

"I'm beginning to understand that," she said. "I'll do whatever you ask me to do."

"I don't want to ask anything that will hurt you."

"Perhaps it isn't necessary for me to attend."

"I'd like you to, though. Especially now that you will be doing the article. All the people will be supporters of my campaign or of Earth Alliance. I want you to meet them. Especially Helmut Hass. A great man. He's one of my staunchest financial backers."

Nova rolled onto her back and looked up at him. The CIA's files contained no report of any person named Hass. Somehow the contributions of this important donor had been disguised. Cupid would relish this bit of information, a genuine fresh bone for the intelligence dogs to worry. "I want to go, then."

He moved off her and sat cross-legged again. "The reception will be formal. The red gown you wore the evening we first met would be fine."

"I use all special occasions as an excuse to spend money. I'll surprise you."

A soft knock on the door interrupted. She scrambled for her robe and fled to the bathroom. Jean Paul let the serving man in. She waited in the bathroom until the food had been laid out, the man tipped and the door closed.

They sat at the table. Jean Paul poured the wine, Zellarschwartzekatz. The chicken, spiced with dill, was cooked to tender perfection.

"I also have some bad news, at least for us," he said, buttering a roll. "Peter and I have been invited by Helmut Hass to be houseguests for a week in August. He has a secluded home seventy miles outside Munich. He wants to discuss strategy for my campaign and for Earth Alliance. He insists there be no distractions, so I won't be taking Ilse. So, it certainly wouldn't be wise to take you, either."

Using a sip of the wine, she calmly washed down the bite of roll suddenly jammed in her throat. No way was Jean Paul going to get out of her sight for an entire week. "How can you leave the campaign—and me—for a week?"

"Because he has asked me. He is a critical supporter. I simply can't say no. Peter agrees we are early enough in the campaign that my being away will pose no problem."

"Jean Paul—"

"Actually, this invitation is an honor. Helmut's home

is beautiful. He's entertained some of the most important people in the world, Nova. EC leaders, United
Nations representatives, any number of your own leg-
islators and media executives. And he argued, perhaps
correctly, that I could use some relaxation."

But Jean Paul thrived on a schedule that would kill
an ordinary man. There had to be more here. And the
Company knew nothing about any connection between
this man and Jean Paul.

"A week is too much, Jean Paul. Please."

He placed his fork on his plate and seemed to shrink
two inches. "I don't want to be away from you. I did
suggest that two or three days would be better. But Hass
insisted. And frankly, when I tried to back out, Peter
very nearly had a heart attack."

"Then take me, too."

He shook his head. "We can't successfully use your
work on the campaign as a cover for our affair in the
man's own home. He will know, Nova."

A prickling fear swept under her skin. The stakes in
this mission of seduction had suddenly skyrocketed.
She couldn't let him be away from her that long. She
had to push. That was her duty.

"If you truly love me," she said, "and we're going to
be together after the campaign, you may as well tell him
the truth now. Tell him you feel you must be honest because you respect him. You're a great persuader. You can
make him understand."

The blue eyes fixed on hers. "I love you. More than
my life."

Did he mean it? Every fiber of her being told her he
meant it, but he was undeniably a very great persuader.
But so was she. "And I love you."

Chapter 16

Munich

The Mercedes-Benz taxi wove its way along Königinstrasse with the English Garden on their right. Nova's attention wandered to the filigreed beauty of streetlight flooding through the shadowy trees. She and Cardone had spent days preparing for this evening, and in a few minutes, when they arrived at the Wagners' home, she would face high stress again. The taxi passed the American consulate and turned into a neighborhood of stately old mansions.

The mid-July summit on deforestation had occurred and the votes had not gone as The Founder had ordered. Nova stewed, every minute, in a kind of slow agony. Any show of frivolity or gaiety, especially with Jean Paul, required impressive acting. A punishment for the "incorrect vote" would soon fall, and once again Nova could do nothing.

Worst of all, Peter Grund was dead set against her going to Hass's Bavarian home. So far, none of her arguments had moved Jean Paul.

The cabbie swung right into a drive. Two armed guards stood at a wrought-iron gate. The German chancellor was expected to attend the reception, which explained the heavy-duty security. She and Joe showed invitations; the guards waved the taxi through.

Manfred Wagner's home was a two-story affair crafted from gray stone blocks. Light flooded into the darkness from all the downstairs windows. The front sat back a hundred feet from a ten-foot wall that separated the spacious grounds from the public world, and old oaks gave the mansion shelter from the street traffic.

Joe paid the fare. A breeze ruffled the leaves of the trees. The August evening lingered softly on her shoulders, left bare by the low cut of the white silk gown, a body-hugging eye-catcher slit to the knee on one side.

Cardone took her arm, gave her a conspiratorial smile, and they proceeded up the steps. Two more guards waited, one with a hand-held metal detector. She opened her small evening bag for inspection. Joe fetched out then retrieved the contents of his pockets. They passed the scrutiny of the metal detector, innocent as lambs when it came to any heavy metal. She carried only a small tape recorder designed to function as a pen. Joe's miniature camera was built into a pocket currency converter.

Their host and hostess waited not far inside. After the customary exchange of pleasantries, Manfred Wagner introduced them to the next arriving couple.

Wealth was on display everywhere: from chande-
liers to vases to rugs to furniture. Two spectacular bird
paintings faced each other on the foyer walls. Manfred
Wagner, the house said, was a very wealthy man.

Cardone's target was Ilse König. Jean Paul's wife
rarely attended public functions, preferring an exceptionally private life revolving around her children, her
show horses and select friends. The evening offered an
uncommon opportunity to question her. Having danced
with her once before, Cardone would start from that
shared encounter. Nova would chat with Manfred Wagner and meet Helmut Hass.

This morning Jean Paul had assured her that Hass
spoke English, which of course she already knew.
"You're going to be very surprised," he'd also said. She
knew Jean Paul expected her to be surprised that Hass
was an albino.

The foyer bisected the house and ran straight from
the entry to a stairway that offered curved steps, left and
right, to the second floor. The light elegance of Mozart
reached them from somewhere at the other end of the
mansion. She said, "Let's find a drink."

Cardone steered her toward the dining room, detour-
ing them deftly around the chatting social clusters of el-
egantly dressed people. She forced herself to smile at
Peter Grund and his wife. While the bartender poured
their drinks, she searched for Jean Paul. Cupid had provided a sketch of the house interior layout with details
of the ground floor, but a smart spy always does her own
verification. "Let's do a little on-site recon before we
split up," she suggested.

"Roger that."

She led and they backtracked. Directly across the

foyer lay the living room, also packed with people. The music grew louder. Still no Jean Paul or Ilsa.

Beyond, at the far end of the east wing, lay a room with a curved and glassed-in outer wall. An honest-to-god music room. A gilded baby-grand piano, looking very Louis XV, graced one end. In a semicircle sat the tuxedo-clad string quartet now playing Handel's *Water Music*.

Further along, the hall spilled into a long, narrow room, also filled with people. Jean Paul dominated its center. With him were the German chancellor, Wilhelm Gottfried, Earth Alliance's Detlev Kleitman and a tall, pale man with white hair. Surely, Hass.

Cardone gave her hand a squeeze. "I'll keep looking for the missus." He drifted away.

Jean Paul should pick the time and circumstances for introductions. To occupy herself, Nova studied the room. More bird paintings covered its walls. Hung nearest to her was a brilliant cluster of six small works. The birds' iridescent feathers leaped off the canvas: blues, greens, yellows and reds. She leaned in close. A David Andrews had done the little beauties.

She checked Jean Paul again. He smiled and he beckoned. She straightened her shoulders. Things were about to get interesting.

The chancellor was speaking in German. This short man with the world-famous bulbous nose radiated sincerity. Even in an age of the television image, power still sometimes came in small, odd packages. "My visit to Prague is coming up soon, Detlev," the chancellor said. "I am quite sure a meeting with at least one environmental delegation has been scheduled. But check with my office." His eyes swiveled to Nova.

Jean Paul spoke in English. "Nova Blair, I would

like you to meet several gentlemen. Gentlemen, Miss Blair is a photographer. You may have seen some of her work on our campaign recently in *Der Stern.*"

She shifted her drink to her left hand.

Jean Paul looked first to Wilhelm Gottfried. "Chancellor Gottfried."

The chancellor peered at her over his famous glasses and nose. "My pleasure, Miss Blair. I hope you are enjoying Bavarian hospitality and Germany in general."

"Thoroughly, Mr. Chancellor."

After lifting her hand to deliver a continental kiss, he said, "It is a quite uncommon first name, is it not? Nova?"

"Yes. I think so."

The chancellor swept his eyes around their circle and said, "You must excuse me. I'm afraid I have another engagement and I ought to speak to our hostess." He warmed Nova with another smile. "It has been a pleasure meeting you, Miss Nova Blair."

The men nodded an acknowledgment and the chancellor headed for the foyer. Two heavies wearing earpieces unstuck themselves from the wall to follow him.

Jean Paul completed the introductions. "Of course you have already met Detlev Kleitman." Kleitman nodded but did not extend his hand.

"And this is Helmut Hass, a highly valued friend."

The albino extended his hand. His black tuxedo underscored his pale skin. He was attractive: his face had good strong lines and his starkly white hair waved back from a tall forehead. Nevertheless, she felt a cold shock wave come off the tall, spindly figure. He didn't seem real, but from another species. *A white praying mantis.*

"Delighted to meet such a lovely woman," Hass said. A cold blue-and-pink gaze seemed to slice under her skin. "Jean Paul tells me you and your partner will be doing an article on the Earth Alliance. I applaud your efforts."

As the four of them exchanged pleasantries, she couldn't help thinking that the oddly attractive albino certainly bore an unfortunate name. After all, in German the word "hass" meant hate.

Finally the White Praying Mantis said, "Please excuse me. I should talk with several other people whom I will not see again for some months. I shall look forward to seeing you and Peter in Bavaria, Jean Paul." He nodded his head on his slender neck, then, accompanied by Detlev Kleitman, moved with giraffe-like grace to a group standing near the door leading into the foyer.

I absolutely must go with Jean Paul to Hass's home, she decided.

According to Cupid, Hass was an extremely wealthy pharmaceutical manufacturer who was, in most respects, a recluse. Not that he didn't come out of his big complex in the countryside now and then.

Suddenly Jean Paul bent close. "You are especially lovely this evening," he said. "And the dress—*extraordinaire.*"

"Be careful, Jean Paul. We shouldn't even be seen standing here alone. Go on and socialize. I'll have you to myself later."

She started to move away. He caught her arm. "Wait. You always have a pen. I need to borrow it." He took her evening bag and opened it. "And the notepad, too? I'll have them back to you within the hour."

Her fingers itched to snatch the pen, an act tantamount to announcing she had something to hide. She hesitated, momentarily paralyzed. He didn't wait for her

reply, just smiled and squeezed her arm as he returned
her bag then turned to the man behind him, a face she
didn't recognize. To cover her confusion, she headed for
the foyer, passing Kleitman and Hass and two others.

Just outside the "bird room" door, a florid-faced
young man intercepted her, saying in German, "Please,
do you have the time?"

She shook her head. *"Keine Deutsch,"* she replied in
a dreadful accent.

"Excuse me," he said, again in German, then disappeared into the room behind her.

Wyczek came down the hall. He, too, nodded but
didn't smile as he passed and followed the young man
into the bird room. She heard his rough voice say, "Excuse me, sir. The meeting will be in fifteen minutes. In
the library."

A meeting? Jean Paul hadn't mentioned a meeting.
Maybe that's why he'd wanted the pen and pad. Certainly the potential for something significant was great
because most of these people were Earth Alliance supporters, from all over Germany. Her favorite suspect,
Grund, was even here.

The reception provided perfect cover for an insider
get-together. She flicked open her evening bag and
checked her watch. Ten-thirty.

She stared at the open bag, now bereft of the tape recorder disguised as pen. This could be a tremendous opportunity. She snapped the bag closed.

Wyczek had said "the library." The library was somewhere on the second floor. The stairway lay to her right.
Maybe she could retrieve the pen and plant it. She
glanced back into the room, searching for either Jean
Paul or Cardone. She found neither. Wyczek had said

"fifteen minutes." Time was short. She should try to find the library.

She sat her glass on a credenza, lifted the hem of her gown and climbed the staircase, affecting an "I know what I'm doing" air. A wide hallway bisected the upstairs. Nova opened the door to the first room on the northwest side. "Just admiring the decor," she'd claim if someone caught her. The room was dark. She flicked on the light. An unoccupied guest bedroom. She flicked the light off and moved on.

Next, a bathroom connecting the first room with another bedroom. The last room was yet another, smaller bedroom. At its far end she glimpsed a door opening into another bathroom. Definitely not a library.

She turned to the other side of the hall. Two floor lamps lit the room in the southwest corner with warm light. One mullioned window of four panels would let in daylight. In the room's center two rectangular tables sat parallel to each other with four chairs around them, and the walls had hundreds of built-in drawers reminiscent of map cases. A strange room, with a slightly oily petroleum smell. But still no library.

The next room she hit paydirt. Bookcases lined three of the walls. On the fourth were two four-paneled windows. On the room's left side was a mahogany partner's desk and in the room's center were four wing-backed chairs surrounding a coffee table. Side chairs stood in the corners.

The room provided no place to hide. She checked the hall again. No one. No sounds. She entered, closed the door and ran to the windows. They were shut.

They appeared to be of the same age as the house, but weren't. The mansion had been remodeled: the windows were double-paned thermal glass. The panels opened outward with a crank. Outside and slightly below the window ran a narrow ledge.

I just might be able to do it.

She unlatched the window panel farthest to the right and cranked it slightly open, then scurried back to the door. Squaring her shoulders, she opened the door boldly, and stepped into the hall. Still deserted.

She sprinted back to the odd little room and shut the door behind her. The door had a lock. She snapped it closed.

She turned toward the windows. If she turned the lights off, one of the guards at the front door or gate might notice. On the other hand, leave them on and she could be seen at the window and would have to abandon her plan. With no further hesitation, she clicked off the floor lamps, hurried to the window, unlocked it and cranked open the far left pane. The window swung out to the left, so even if she were to climb onto the ledge, she was going to have to close the pane almost shut again to maneuver past it.

She looked for the guards. They were gone, presumably with the chancellor.

She checked the ledge again and cold fingers tightened on her stomach. The ledge wasn't more than eight or nine inches wide. Leaning out she could see that about twenty-five feet to her left, light from the library flooded into the darkness. But three-quarters of the way to the library window, a decorative granite slab protruded outward several inches from the building face. *I'd have to work around it.*

She straightened, turned around and leaned her back and head against the wall. She held her hand to her stomach, which was now slowly turning over.

If at all possible, she should do it. Over two months with Jean Paul, and still nothing. If he was innocent and she got caught, her actions would be impossible to justify. Her credibility would be irreparably damaged. But what lasting difference would it make? If he was innocent. But if he was guilty, she simply couldn't pass up this chance. And if he was guilty and she got caught?

"So don't get caught," she said.

Again she surveyed the ledge. It was walkable, just barely, if she didn't let herself get psyched out by the height. Which, she assured herself, was no big thing. *It's only two stories.*

Sprawling oaks protecting the house from the road made certain she couldn't be seen from the street. The loop-around driveway didn't extend this far, so even if late guests arrived, they *probably* wouldn't notice the lady clinging to the east wing's second-floor ledge. And no guards were to be seen.

The immediate problem was her gown. She looked down at the white silk. No way could she inch down that ledge in a tight, floor-length dress. How about pulling the hem up, twisting it in a bunch, stuffing it down the low-cut front? But the material would wrinkle. How would she explain that?

She scanned the room. Maybe she could find a way to tie the dress hitched halfway up her legs? Or around her waist? She snicked open the evening bag and checked her watch's luminous dial. Five minutes or less before the meeting should start.

She dashed to the closest bank of drawers and pulled one open. Even in her agitated state, stunned delight momentarily halted her. Ten nests of white cotton filled the drawer and each nest held four incredibly azure-blue eggs. She opened the drawer in the next row over.

More beautiful eggs, these perfectly round with a deep black background and white splotches. Manfred Wagner was a bird egg collector.

Fascinating, but it doesn't solve your problem, she told herself.

She looked down at the dress again. Not only did she have a problem with securing it so it wouldn't trip her up, the rough stone would catch and damage it. It would get filthy. She had to shuck the dress. And what did she have under? Nothing but panty hose and high heels.

The panty hose had to come off, too: the stone would rip them to shreds. That left her stark naked. *Think. Think!* It must already be a quarter to eleven. The meeting, if the participants were on time, was starting.

She ran to the door and unlocked it. She pressed her ear to the wooden panel and could hear nothing in the hall. Her mouth felt as though it was stuffed with cotton from one of the egg nests. If she were caught running around up here— But it just wouldn't work to go out on that ledge naked.

She opened the door a crack, peeked into the hall, dashed across it into the small bedroom and yanked open the closet door. Not one stitch of clothing! Nothing but empty hangers.

In the adjacent bathroom she grabbed the largest towel, which lay folded over the edge of the tub. She combed frantically through every drawer: hairpins, scissors, tweezers, combs and a brush, extra towels and washcloths. Not one safety pin.

"My kingdom for a safety pin!"

A rush of panic warmed the skin of her throat. "Stay cool, Nova."

Again she checked the hall, then, towel in hand, dashed back to the egg room, locking the door behind her. It took a second for her eyes to adjust to the room's dim light, then she went to the table, kicked off her shoes, unzipped the gown, stepped out of it and draped it over the nearest chair.

Chapter 17

Nova peeled out of her panty hose and draped them alongside the gown. She slid the dark green towel across her back, under her arms, wrapped it around her chest just above her breasts, then twisted and tucked in one corner. The towel's lower edge covered her hips with several inches to spare.

When examined again, the ledge was still only a miserly nine inches wide. "Nova, my dear, this is no worse than that little challenge in Tibet."

She'd done Tibet with a vicious wind whipping her back and her face caressing the sheer, seemingly featureless cliff, and she had survived. Here she had only to deal with the ledge's narrowness and one short section of protruding decorative block. Instinct said to go with what had worked before, face to the wall.

Check time. The luminous watch dial read ten-fifty, already five minutes past meeting start time.

She dragged a chair to the open window, climbed onto it, backed through the window onto the ledge. Oh, God. The stone protrusion blocked her view of the library window itself, but no light came from the room. Someone had apparently closed the drapes. *But please not the window.*

Lack of illumination from the library was actually a plus; light gushed from all windows on the lower floor, so the building's upper half was now cast, by contrast, into deep shadow.

Her toes wanted to curl too tightly. She sucked in a deep breath. "Relax," she crooned to herself. With her right hand, she pushed at the open windowpane that had to be nearly closed in order for her to edge past. *But not too hard.*

If she pushed hard, her mind would play tricks: she would feel as if the block wall was pushing back. She'd overcompensate and cling too tightly, tense up till she became little more than a frozen decoration on the outside of Manfred Wagner's house.

The pane moved easily. She left the opening just wide enough to slip her fingertips back inside. *You're in your living room, practicing, and Diva is watching. See yourself sliding effortlessly down to that window.*

She slid one step to her right. The imagery was working.

She reached the vertical slab. Hugging the wall with only the gentlest embrace, she estimated the slab's size: two feet wide and jutting out from the building face about the same width as the ledge. Maybe eight inches.

With her right toes she traced the line of the ledge. Now, she thought. *Shift weight onto your right foot.*

The wall started pushing.

She stopped dead in place, her weight evenly distributed, her hands and right cheek flat against the wall. *Don't push back!*

Her palms and soles were suddenly wet enough to finger-paint the cool stones. A bead of sweat tickled as it ran from her armpit down her right side. "Don't stop moving."

She shifted her hips and forced her weight fully onto her right foot. Again she pictured the ledge running across her living room floor: she eased herself around the protruding stone, but the towel caught on the rough corner of the slab.

Don't stop moving!

The towel pulled tight.

Just when she was certain the towel would be pulled off, the material escaped the tiny granite fingers. The sensation that the towel would slip, tangle around her feet, or maybe make an eye-catching fall past the ground-floor windows nearly overpowered her. She battled the urge to take her hands from the wall to hike up the maddening bit of cloth.

She ignored it and continued inching along till she reached the library window. It was still open.

A frisson of released tension and excitement raced up her spine. She grabbed the partly open window to steady herself. Her psyche immediately stabilized. She relaxed her body against the stone. She listened closely and heard voices speaking in German.

"I wanted…fully aware of the importance…timing. Gall is set for…August fifteenth."

Not surprisingly, the voice was Manfred Wagner's. Very distinctive, although he seemed to have his back to her so she missed some of his words.

"But it can only be a success if Detlev is able…exact

time of departure. Since he has assured us that this will be no problem, I am confident…carry out your instructions."

A slight silence, then another voice started speaking, as if someone had nodded to Wagner, then indicated the next man should begin.

"I feel confident we've anticipated and essentially contained any damage we might have sustained regarding the British coal plant."

Nova didn't recognize this voice.

"More incidents will, of course, keep questions fresh in the minds of the media, so we must continue vigilance," the voice continued. "Tomorrow morning's event, for example, is going to stir up the press hounds again."

Something special had been planned for the morning? Maybe she'd really stumbled on to something.

Another pause.

Then the same voice. "The faxes will go out tomorrow."

Faxes… Her mind started to chase off after that incredible word.

She yanked her sprinting thoughts into line: her job was to memorize every word, every sound. Speculation would come later.

"I can handle it." Same voice.

"Good."

It was a different voice. It sounded like Jean Paul's. But one word was too little, especially through drapes and a mere slit of open window.

"I took the liberty of asking you…I felt this was the perfect…we're all here in one place, to toast…successes." Wagner again.

Another pause. She shifted weight slightly back and forth, keeping her muscles loose. There was, after all, a trip back to the egg room.

She heard the unmistakable popping signature of a champagne cork. General murmurs, some rustling sounds. "Fellow visionaries." Wagner's voice again. "To the future. To bringing sanity and peace to our species at last. *Terra eterna!*"

Voices repeated together what sounded like a salute, their nuances' individuality masked in simultaneous utterance. Not fifteen or twenty men and not just three. More like four, five, or possibly six.

"I should return to my guests." It was Wagner, projecting his voice again.

"And I'm afraid I must leave. I have an early day tomorrow." Good. Another for-certain. That was Kleitman.

So she now had Wagner, Kleitman and at least two and maybe three voices not identified. She could tell they were all moving away, toward the library door.

Finally she heard the closing of the door's heavy latch.

She shifted onto the balls of her feet a couple of times. Keeping a tight grip with her right hand on the edge of the open window, with her left hand she hitched the towel up under her arms.

The minute she released the windowpane, insecurity grabbed and squeezed her chest like a vise. She took several slides left before realizing she wasn't breathing. "Breathe, woman," she whispered, "or you're going to provide this reception with some pretty X-rated entertainment."

At the block protrusion, as if determined to thwart her, the towel seemed to reach out and grab the granite's rough edge again.

She edged past the jutting protrusion and the towel slipped.

She hugged the wall. Her nipples shrank at sudden contact with the cool stone. The towel's plunge stopped at the level of her knees. Her palms were sweaty again.

She had to keep moving. The towel escaped over her knees to her ankles.

"Oh, God!" Her bare bottom was exposed for the world to see, and the sound of her thudding heart had to be audible at least fifty feet in every direction.

She hesitated. The wall began pushing.

She immediately stepped out of the towel, left foot, then right.

She finally reached the window and yanked open the panel. She squeezed back inside, her heart beating as though she'd run up Denali. She dropped her feet to the floor and poked her head out the window. The towel lay in open view, dark green terry cloth draped over dark green bushes. The angle from the downstairs' windows to the bushes was steep. From inside the first-floor rooms it shouldn't be visible.

No one would find it tonight. But what about tomorrow? With luck, Manfred Wagner's gardeners would never mention it to their boss. She picked up the panty hose, sat on the chair opposite her gown, and took a couple of deep breaths. Even if they did, how could Wagner connect her to a towel on a bush?

Joe felt Blair's hand on his arm. She squeezed hard. Her face was composed but her voice, though soft, vibrated with excitement. "Time to leave."

In the cab she said nothing and looked as cool as an ice princess, but she'd passed him a thumbs-up sign. The minute they were free of the cab she slipped her arm in the crook of his elbow. They sauntered away from her hotel's entrance. "So what have you got?" he asked.

"Wyczek told Jean Paul there would be a meeting in the library. I couldn't find you. I had to work fast. I located the library and figured out a way to listen from the ledge outside."

"What? How could you?" He took a step away from her and examined her dress. As untouched as virgin snow.

She shrugged. "I found something else to wear."

"And why? What about the tape recorder?"

"Jean Paul borrowed the pen. I don't think he suspects it's anything but a pen, but I couldn't get it back in time to plant it because when I looked for him, he'd disappeared. As I said, time was short."

"Mmm." Just what, he thought, did she mean by something else to wear? "So give me the rundown."

She started reciting, squinting in concentration while spinning out a word-for-word replay. He'd several times observed her debriefing with Cupid. Part-time spy status notwithstanding, Blair was astonishingly skilled at memorizing and regurgitating details. She guessed four to six men were involved. She fingered Wagner and Kleitman as two absolutely definite makes.

"And König?"

"A third man also spoke. A voice definitely different from Wagner's or Kleitman's. But I couldn't identify him. The person who simply said yes could have been that same man, but I have to say, my impression was that the person who said yes was Jean Paul."

"Let me think a minute." They kept up the slow walk. It was great, at last, to get something concrete to go on. He said, "Something called 'Gall' will happen on August fifteenth. That's a little less than a month. It's no doubt another 'punishment.' Any idea what was meant by 'this morning's event'?"

"None."

"Okay. The same voice then says 'The faxes will go out tomorrow.'"

He stopped walking and looked at her.

"Right," she said.

A thrill of discovery prickled the skin at the back of his neck. "These Earth Alliance bigwigs are concerned about their organization being blamed for the attack on the dam. All of them could be legitimately concerned about such blame and still be as innocent as nuns. And who knows what 'Gall' actually is? Could be another innocent thing. Maybe a fund-raising event. Though I have to say, the name Gall sure doesn't evoke in me the kind of positive feeling customarily used to separate people from their money. But faxes! The Fucker always sends faxes.

"You said Wagner opened champagne and offered the toast, and they all said...what?"

"A Latin phrase that means earth eternal. *Terra eterna.*"

"Sounds Latin. Maybe it's an Earth Alliance rallying cry. Cupid can check it out. You know," he said, his thoughts now racing, "so far Operation Jacaranda's been based on little more than a vague suggestion, though from a reliable agent, that somehow The Fucker was associated with Earth Alliance. But this is urgent stuff. I'll roust Davidson pronto. Can you get away from König and come with me?"

She shook her head. "I'll debrief tomorrow, as soon as Jean Paul leaves me."

He finished his thought. "We need more minds working on König and on Earth Alliance, and right now."

"Just what I was thinking," she said as they reached the hotel entrance.

Nova started to walk inside but he caught her arm. "You did a great job."

She gave him a smile, one that struck him as a little sad. "Thanks, Joe."

"I suppose if I told you I wish like hell you would get on a plane tomorrow and take a bunch of folks backpacking in Outer Mongolia you'd just give me that special icy look?"

"What look?"

"Nothing. Forget it." He turned back to find a cab. He was excited about Nova's discovery, but part of him still doubted whether the legendary Nova Blair could pull off this mission—alive. He'd do anything to make sure she did.

Nova undressed, wrapped herself in her robe, sat very deliberately in the large overstuffed chair in the corner of the lovely room she had shared with Jean Paul for many nights, tucked her legs under her and stared into space. Her thoughts turned dark. Human history seemed damned, endlessly revolving around deeds often done in the name of a just cause. Human life was trapped in this monstrous dominance-crazed world plagued by suffering and destruction. The Founder was no different, no matter how valid he thought his cause was. *I possess the truth. My way is the right way. I'll tell you how to live and think. Disagree, and I'll kill you. Refuse to submit, I'll kill those you love.*

Instead of soaring high on the thrill of discovery, she felt crushed by the weight of it. She didn't want to believe the implications of what she'd heard. Because, no matter what her instincts screamed, the evidence argued that Jean Paul was guilty. Guilty of so much pain and destruction.

She sat, paralyzed by her thoughts. When she snapped out of her reverie, she looked at the clock and realized Jean Paul could arrive at any moment. She braced herself for his arrival, reminding herself of the many innocent dead who were the reason why she was here, willing to dirty her hands.

He came in smiling, happy. She felt nauseated.

They made love. She felt as though a fairy godmother with a sadistic streak had let her sample for a time the wonderful intimate feelings normal people shared. *But you can have only a sample,* the bad fairy said with a cackle. *And you're not normal. So don't get impossible notions.*

Jean Paul flicked off the small light on the table by the bed, snuggled next to her spoon-fashion, his hand cupping her breast. She closed her eyes and thought about what she would tell Cupid tomorrow. Suddenly her stomach lurched, her eyes snapped open. *Terra eterna. Terratornis.*

She shuddered, then lay with muscles tensed, listening, afraid Jean Paul would notice. But his breathing remained slow and regular. He was asleep.

Terra eterna. Terratornis.

The pipeline employee had thought the terrorists had yelled a dinosaur name. A good guess, just not quite right. More like monster than dinosaur.

Earth Alliance had, in fact, embraced mass murder. And the man whose arm embraced her, to whom she'd hoped more dearly than she realized was innocent, was in fact a slick, handsome sociopath. And to make matters worse, somehow Jean Paul had found a weakness, a way to reach beyond the defenses she'd taken years to construct. Perhaps it was simply that the human heart, even hers, couldn't deny forever the need to love and be loved.

She lay beside him like a stone. Two convictions hardened. No matter what the cost, she must devise a scheme to put so much pressure on Jean Paul he simply could not refuse her request to go to Bavaria. And she would stop Gall. If fate gave her any breaks at all, there would be no more killings.

When she was certain Jean Paul was in deep sleep, she slipped from beneath the sheets, threw on her trench coat and, in the wee hours of the morning in the empty, quiet lobby, called Cupid. Then Joe.

He was pleased with her deduction, more like beside himself with fly-boy Cardone enthusiasm.

She started to hang up, but she heard his voice yelling her name. She put the phone back to her ear. "Did you say something?"

"You bet," he said in a very grave tone. "Please start being extra careful."

Chapter 18

Munich

Joe sat and dangled one leg over the edge of Ellen Nöe's desk. His stomach churned. He was sure this op would never work. Nova had insisted to Cupid that she must do something to win Jean Paul's unquestioning confidence. Cupid and Nova had agreed on this plan. In Joe's opinion, it was too dangerous, especially for Nova.

Ellen gave him a big smile and said, with utter lack of conviction, "I'll be in terrible trouble if Peter Grund finds you sitting on my desk."

He leaned close and whispered. "Grund is a prick."

She giggled and nodded.

Wyczek's little pig eyes never rested. The bull-necked guard with the Vandyke beard and billiard-ball head sat against the far wall, watching everyone who came in. And watching Joe charm Ellen. Joe shot her a medium-hot smile. "How about a drink after Nova and I get back from the photo shoot?"

The swinging glass door behind him made a whooshing sound. He turned. Nova strolled in. He set his jaw— the op was beginning. She was doubtless on time, so it was two-twenty on the dot. At two-thirty, plus or minus a minute, they must exit the building. It had been decided that midafternoon was best since there would be little foot or auto traffic. Timing of the individual elements was going to be tricky. He thought again that the whole scheme was not just tricky, it was dangerously nuts.

Nova was dressed for a photo shoot—or a rescue: khaki slacks, long-sleeved green silk blouse rolled to the elbows, loafers. "Hi, Ellen. Joe." She nodded to Wyczek.

Looking at Joe she said, "You look like you're making yourself right at home."

Peter Grund's door opened and the man stalked three paces into the room, already wearing his lightweight summer suit jacket. He snorted. "Let's go. I need to be back early. And get your butt off Ellen's desk, Cardone."

In the trade, a good sense of time was critical. Joe had learned to estimate time's passage under differing conditions: when bored, or excited, or scared shitless. Nova had taken the same training. He knew, and figured she did, too, that they were in the ballpark of three minutes too early. Even given the leeway built into the plan, they needed to stall.

Grund, unfortunately, was in high gear. He marched to König's door, thumped twice and opened it. "I'd like to leave. I must be back as early as possible."

König came out, shrugging into his suit coat. "Fine with me."

Wyczek stood. Nova caught Joe's eye. Unstated message: we have to stall. They all headed for the door. In the hallway, Wyczek touched the elevator button and its door sucked open.

"Nice earrings," Joe muttered to Nova for no good reason. Maybe it was to wish her good luck.

The men waited for Nova to enter, then crowded in after her. They descended. The elevator gave a little termination heave and made its sucking sound as the door opened. The men parted for Nova. Wyczek followed her out, his gaze darting into every corner. Between the elevator and the entrance, stores lined the ground level. They were still more than two minutes early. Grund and König stepped out, and Nova delivered the prearranged stall. "Jean Paul, I missed lunch today. Would you mind if I buy something at the gift shop?"

"Of course not."

Dithering a believable bit over her choice, she settled on a packet of candy-coated chocolates and paid at the cash register. Each time Joe had done a dry run of purchasing anything here, he'd felt like he was in line to buy Superbowl tickets. Unfortunately, Nova was relieved of her money in what had to be the place's all-time record speed.

He was deciding whether to use up time begging Nova for candy or do what the plan called for next and capture Grund's attention when Grund started to join König. "Herr Grund," Joe snapped, "have you had time to read the article I gave you?" The question worked. Grund slowed.

Wyczek was stuck like Velcro to his boss's right side. Nova moved quickly to Jean Paul's left side. Success required that she, König and Wyczek be the first to exit, and in exactly that configuration. He and Grund should exit behind them. But the clock in Joe's head said the operative assigned to distract Wyczek wouldn't be in place yet.

He was a millisecond from purposely tripping over his feet and flattening himself on the floor when candy-coated chocolates began raining on the marble entry, jumping and pinging and rolling. "Oh, dear!" Nova said as she held her hands out and looked surprised.

Joe grinned tightly, impressed with her improvisation. She dropped to one knee.

Grund grunted. "Leave the damn stuff."

König, reaching a hand down to Nova, said, "Let's just push it off to the side. Wyczek, buy another bag while we brush this out of the way."

The bodyguard frowned, so far his only known expression. For Wyczek to leave König's side in a public place was unthinkable.

Nova said, "I'll buy them."

Joe and the men played miniature soccer with the colored candies. When she rejoined them, the group headed for the door, everyone in proper position.

"So, did you have a look at the article?" Joe asked to distract Grund again. Grund took over the talking. For the moment Joe didn't have to think what to say. His eyes should be fixed on Wyczek but they kept flicking to Nova. God, he hated this whole setup. He hated working with this woman—because he hated being worried for her.

They walked out the door into a blast of warm sun. Along the block he counted only five pedestrians and, as expected, only light traffic.

Right on time, the agent appeared. Even knowing

she'd be there, Joe blinked in amazement. Blond-white hair punked in spikes, flaming red lipstick, a leather miniskirt tighter than a snake's skin and the billowing reek of cheap perfume.

König looked right, to where the limo was parked. Nova searched left, undoubtedly looking for the black BMW. The punk-looking agent stepped into Wyczek's path. In German, she said, "I really could use an ecu or two, sweetie. Have you something to spare?"

Joe followed Nova's gaze. There the BMW was, still on a proper course on the street. The car swerved slightly toward König. Wyczek saw it. He thrust his hand inside his coat. Hesitated. The BMW was definitely coming at the five of them.

Wyczek hauled his Sig-Sauer out of its holster. The spike-haired chick should stumble into him.

Done!

But Wyczek stepped right, his left hand forcing the woman down as he got off a shot.

An ear-stunning *kapow,* and the BMW's windshield shattered.

The spiky-haired agent headed for the nearest door.

Another shot at the BMW from Wyczek.

Joe's wildly thumping heart jumped into his throat. *Hell.* Their driver might have taken a hit. Sure enough, the BMW curved toward them too sharply.

"Jean Paul," Nova yelled.

She threw herself against König, shoving the politician backward several steps, out of harm's way. He fell. The car careened off the pavement, onto the walk, heading for Nova.

Joe knew he wouldn't reach her in time. The sidewalk felt like glue to his feet. He fought to take one sticky stride toward her and then another. The fender caught her right hip; he heard a sickening thump and the sound of her hand slapping against the hood.

The BMW jerkily angled back to the street. With a screeching crunch, it took off the limo's left rear taillight and sped away. Another step through glue. Nova whirled to her left, a missile aimed directly for the granite and plate-glass building front. One more step. God. Please. No!

Joe grabbed at her. Still she spun. The sound of ripping silk registered as one of her blouse's shoulder epaulets came off in his hand, but mercifully he'd stopped her forward motion.

Nova collapsed onto the street.

He fell down beside her. "Jesus, God, Nova." Her eyes were open but unfocused.

König scrambled to her other side. He snatched her hand and clutched it. He looked as dazed as she. "Nova?" His face was ashen.

The sonofabitch is going to faint.

"Nova?" König said again, choking out her name. He started to rock back and forth.

"I'm…okay." The words were spaced with a week between them.

With the speed of a hooker guarding her favorite corner, Peter Grund latched on to König. "We're in public, Jean Paul. Take hold of yourself."

Grund switched to German and yelled to Wyczek, who faced the street, pivoting with the gun as he repeatedly scanned left and right. Nova's eyes started to clear. Grund and Wyczek pulled König away from her. König fought to shake them off.

Grund pushed König farther from Nova, saying,

"Let Joe take care of her." Wyczek blocked König's attempts to throw Grund off as the campaign manager continued to mutter wise words of counsel in his candidate's ear.

Joe couldn't stop himself. "I told you—damn—I said this was crazy," he whispered.

Their dangerous escapade had gathered a small crowd. Joe searched their faces. "Could someone call an ambulance?"

Nova whispered, sounding angry, "You really think I'm crazy."

He didn't answer her. From behind him, a member of their op team, a chunky Bavarian matron, reassured him in English, "Someone's already called an ambulance."

God how fragile Nova looked.

The matron handed him her sweater. "For her head."

His hands shaking, he raised Nova's head just high enough to slide the sweater under.

"Jean Paul?" she asked.

"Fine. He's just fine. Grund and Wyczek are trying to calm him down. He was on his way to flipping out right here on the street."

And if Nova had been— With heart-stopping certainty he knew that if Nova had been seriously hurt, or worse, König wouldn't have been the only one to flip out. Maybe because she was unlike any woman he had ever known. A dove with the heart of a falcon.

She grasped his hand and squeezed it. "Thanks, Joe. That wall was coming up fast."

"Where do you hurt?" König had squirmed out of Wyczek's bear hug to kneel beside her. "You shouldn't move. There is an ambulance coming." He was pleading.

She shook her head. "I'm okay. Really."

Wyczek loomed over them. In a gruff voice he said, "It's not safe out here, Herr König. Come back inside."

"Leave me alone, Wyczek. Goddamn it. He's not going to come back for another try."

Nova moved, as though she was trying to sit up. She sucked in a breath and gingerly touched her hand to her hip.

König, moments ago looking as white as milk, now glowed as red as a tomato. "I insist, Nova. Don't move."

Joe couldn't have agreed more. He saw her bite her lower lip and rub her side where the car had hit her. It had to hurt like hell, but she didn't flinch.

Like figures in a Christmas tableau, they held their places for a minute or so. The ambulance arrived and a medical team in whites checked her out. They strapped on a neck brace and lifted her carefully onto a gurney, then moved her into the van.

König started to climb into the back. Grund grabbed his arm, protesting in English, low but firm, that he wanted König to avoid any appearance of entanglement with Nova.

König gave Grund a withering look and said, "You and Joe see to the dedication, Peter. Make my excuses."

With the ambulance's red light flashing, Nova and König were quickly gone, Wyczek with them.

Joe prayed Nova had no broken bones. Nothing inside busted up.

A policeman arrived and zeroed in on him and Grund. Questions followed.

Later, when he and Grund were in the limo, Grund, still pale, turned pensive. "If she hadn't seen the car and pushed him, Jean Paul could have been—well—I hate to think what could have been. She may well have saved his life."

"Yeah," Joe said.

"I certainly hope she'll be okay."

"Yeah," he repeated, a prize-winning understatement. "Me, too."

Chapter 19

Nova had noticed Cupid had a habit of rinsing his gold-rimmed banker's glasses and then wiping them with a handkerchief of purest white linen. He rose and disappeared into the hotel room's small bathroom. Over the sound of running water, Nova heard him say, "A number of research complexes in Germany work similarly."

While she and Joe waited for their chief of station's return, Joe said, "How's the hip today?"

"Better and better by the hour. It's sore, but even a deeply bruised and aching hip beats having a shattered elbow like the poor BMW driver."

She studied Joe's face as he tore a napkin in the process of creating a paper bird. He was quite good at origami. Was he as delighted as she was at the prospect of spending a week isolated in the Bavarian countryside with König and his cronies, a vacation scheduled to begin in two days? Precisely as she had planned, Peter Grund had relented, bowing to the hurricane force of Jean Paul's insistence that he wasn't going to leave her for a week and that her assistant must come, too. She'd won that battle.

Cupid reappeared, drying his glasses. "World-class outfits, like some of the Max Planck Institutes, are essentially small, contained communities. They provide work, housing and recreation for all their employees. By the way, everyone—employees and staff—call the core area of the place 'the Compound.'"

Helmut Hass was now highly suspect. Joe was convinced that Jean Paul König was The Founder, but Cupid remained neutral. He conceded only that Detlev Kleitman probably was not since Nova's description of the conspirators' conversation suggested Kleitman took orders rather than gave them.

Nova frowned. "I think it's bizarre, living holed-up like a baron in some Medieval fortress castle. And how did he get involved with pharmaceuticals? What are his credentials? You don't get fancy training in chemistry through home study."

Cupid readjusted his glasses over his ears, one slender gold arm and then the other. "Hass inherited this mega-pharmaceutical from his mother's side of the family. The father was a history professor. Heidelberg University. Some sort of political and ecological visionary. His writings explain Hass's strong environmental views. Hass senior dropped dead of a bad heart at forty-eight. Hass's uncle—his mother's brother—ran things before Hass took over. The two men had a nasty fight over lead-

ership. Hass took over when the uncle had a fatal—
somewhat suspicious—car accident."

At the phrase "Bavarian complex," Nova's mind, like
a determined hound, returned to sniff again at her prin-
ciple worry. The isolation. The core area of the property—the mansion, chemical plant and artificial
lake—occupied six hundred acres. An attractive brick
wall encircled the area. Outside the wall lay another
thousand-plus acres of undeveloped land all owned by
Hass: fields and small stands of forest. The lands had
few roads, and they and the wall were patrolled by
guards in vans—ostensibly because Hass frequently entertained prestigious houseguests who valued their privacy. She would also feel isolated because Hass had a
No Cell Phones rule and, assuming that their luggage
might be searched, they had agreed she and Joe would
go phoneless.

Hass Chemie's employees could eat breakfast and
lunch in a company dining hall, but they all resided off
the property, most in the small village of Turm, two
miles away. Compound security wasn't especially tight.
Anyone could come and go, but visitors had to secure
a pass at the gate. Joe asked, "Any luck getting someone on the grounds?"

Cupid steepled his finger over his generous belly.
"Sorry. We've tried everything we can without rousing
suspicion. The nontechnical positions are all filled by
people from Turm who've held them for years. There
are no openings of any kind for nonskilled workers.
And Hass doesn't hire foreign technicians."

Nova felt as though the Blair and Cardone team was
set to be launched into barracuda-infested waters in a
potentially leaky boat, lacking a life raft. Davidson had

a room in Turm, but Turm was two miles from the Compound. Nova would be with Joe at the Compound for the entire week—without immediate backup.

The Founder's Compound

With one final grunt, he maneuvered the half-life-size bronze of the naked girl on her knees, bent over and fully exposed, onto the cart. He patted her rear end, thinking again that "Invitation" was perhaps his greatest triumph. He stroked her buttocks, felt a warm sexual stirring, and grinned. He pushed the cart to the studio door, opened it, returned to the cart and pushed it into the brightly lit underground corridor.

Having decided yesterday where he'd place the statue—between "Agony" and "Terror"—he had already removed the piece that had formerly occupied the niche. The office door opened and he heard the rapid click of Braunwin's high heels. He decided to ignore her. Perhaps she would pass on by, leave him in peace.

"Jean Paul arrives in two days," she said. "I want him to be comfortable. I am amazed you said he could come with a woman. Still, they must have the best bungalow."

"I assure you, Jean Paul made it clear beyond questioning that he would not come at all if the woman and her partner could not come, too."

"He is playing with fire. If rumor leaks out about this affair, his career might well be finished. Certainly his image tarnished."

"By the end of the week it won't make any difference what he wants, will it? If you tell him then to ask the woman to leave, he will. You trouble yourself for nothing."

"Perhaps." She looked at the bronze. "You are sick,

Helmut. Your mother was sick and she created a sick son. Sometimes I feel sorry for you." She turned and left him.

His half sister was a first-class bitch. From the very beginning, their marriage had been one of convenience. Actually, more one of coercion. Shortly after their father's death, Braunwin had discovered his secret hobby. She had been repulsed. Still, she had given him a choice: marry her and give her heirs to his family's fortune or she would expose him.

Braunwin still baffled him. The child of their father's life-long mistress, she had grown up, as he had, listening to their father's visionary philosophy. But he did not understand her obsessive love for a man now long dead. She had given him Peter and Heinie, though. The boys almost made enduring her bearable.

He pulled his gloomy thoughts from Braunwin and settled them on Nova Blair. Attractive in an exotic way. He'd felt an earthy pull to her at once. The idea had floated in his mind for days that having her here would be interesting. When Jean Paul could no longer object, all sorts of possibilities would present themselves.

He patted the bronze bottom again and smiled.

Chapter 20

Five Days Before Gall

The Bavarian farmland didn't have the picture-perfect neatness of Switzerland, but in Joe's mind it came close. Late-summer countryside undulated outside the window of the Mercedes limo, punctuated with a barn, a field of stacked or rolled hay, a herd of brown-and-white Guernsey cows.

Wyczek made a left turn into Turm. In the limo's left back seat, Peter Grund stared out one window. Nova sat in the middle. König laughed quietly at something she'd said.

In only minutes, tiny Turm was behind them. They were on the final leg of the seventy-mile trip from Munich. König laughed again. Nova was telling him some cock-and-bull story about getting lost in the Brazilian jungle. She seemed eagerly willing to reveal to König more about her private life than the ridiculously meager tidbits he had pried out of her with numerous, well-crafted questions.

To the south, the Alps thrust out of the horizon, blue and gray and green. Fifteen minutes later the limo glided to a halt in front of a triple-barred gate bearing the letters HCI for Hass Chemie International. Wyczek flashed a pass. The single guard—armed, Joe noted, with a holstered Sig-Sauer that matched Wyczek's— waved them ahead.

A well-maintained, two-lane concrete road led straight south into the Compound's heart. Dead ahead, the ninety-acre artificial lake beckoned, indigo-blue and placid in the August heat. To her right, lined up on the lake's western shore in a two-story row, sat the chemical plant: four ultramodern, black-glass and white-concrete buildings.

The road curved left, skirting the lake's east side. The property's only elevated bit of topography loomed at the far end of the Compound, a hundred-foot-high, dome-shaped hill covered with heavy beech and oak forest. The hill lay within the Compound's walls. Nestled at the base of the hill were the Hass Chemie offices and dining hall.

The road divided. Wyczek banked sharply left, up a small rise leading to the mansion. In stark contrast to the ultramodern design of every other structure on the grounds, Hass's Tudor mansion was two stories of gray stone. To Nova this suggested a schizoid imbalance in the man's personality. The circular drive looped around the front of the house. Wyczek braked. Even before the bodyguard could open the rear door, Helmut Hass appeared at the head of four flagstone steps.

Hass spread his arms. "*Grus Gott*. Welcome to all. Please. Come in."

Wyczek leaned against the car to wait. With Grund and König, Nova accompanied Hass through the arched stone doorway. Joe followed a couple of paces behind. A butler closed the door and disappeared. The pink-and-blue eyes fixed on Nova. Again, Hass spoke in English. "It is a particular pleasure to have you, my dear." He took her hand but instead of shaking it smoothly delivered a hand kiss with practiced skill. She resisted the urge to snatch her hand from his.

The entry walls were paneled in dark wood. A door opposite the entry led to a dining room; doors left and right led to halls. Four lighted niches flanked the doorways. Displayed in each was a half-life-size bronze statue. The place was too heavy. Too dark.

A woman and two young boys appeared at a door. "Peter, you know Braunwin and my boys. But, Mr. Cardone, Miss Blair, allow me to introduce my wife and sons."

Braunwin was a striking, tall Nordic-looking blond, with intelligent blue eyes. Nova saw that her two young boys were also blond and good-looking.

Frau Hass's gaze immediately settled on Jean Paul. "Herr König," she said. She smiled with impressive warmth.

Was her interest sexual? Somehow Nova felt it wasn't. But it was clearly intense.

To Nova's surprise, Brawnwin Hass seemed particularly interested in her. The woman's intelligent eyes swept over her from crown to toe. Braunwin seemed to have zero interest in Joe, something Nova rarely saw when women met him.

When it was Frau Hass's turn to talk, her gaze flew back to rest on König's face. She really lit up. "My sons, Heinrich and Peter," she said with a thick but pleasant accent. It looked more and more as though English would be spoken through the week whenever she and Joe were present. "You must excuse the boys," Brawnwin continued, her eyes still on König. "They are due in the library for their English lessons."

The kids shook hands all around like grown-ups, then disappeared down the hallway.

"You have breathtakingly beautiful grounds," Nova said.

Frau Hass's gaze returned to Nova. Her eyes lost their warmth. "When the Compound was designed, we retained an excellent landscape architect. Come see the view from the dining room. It overlooks part of the lake."

Joe watched the two women stride purposefully through the opposite door. The bronzes in the niches caught his eye. He stepped close to the one nearest, a full-length piece of a young man in Greek toga. The label said Alexander the Great.

"Is Wyczek working out well?" he heard Hass ask.

"Superb," König answered. "I am finally becoming used to the lack of privacy, and as you know, I owe my life to him and Nova."

"Good. Very good."

Joe said, "This bronze is very powerful."

"Thank you, Mr. Cardone. The works are mine. I'm gratified when I find someone who appreciates them. The others are Napoleon, Mohammed and Shih Huang-ti."

So, a fascination with conquerors.

The women returned. Braunwin excused herself, then disappeared down the hall. Hass opened the heavy entry door again. Two golf carts had been lined up behind the Mercedes, and Wyczek was indicating which luggage should go into which cart.

Hass said, "The men will take you to your bungalows." He gave König a pointed look. "While you are in what I like to call the residence area, in my home and all of the guest bungalows, you may be confident of complete privacy. The maids and groundsmen have been with me for years. In other areas or the plant itself, however, you will meet plant employees. More discretion will be required. I would like to offer a tour of the facilities. As soon as you've settled in, if that's agreeable."

Jean Paul assured Hass a tour would be wonderful. Peter Grund begged off, saying that he'd been here several times and could pass on the science tour. Hass looked at his watch, then at König. "It's now one-thirty. I shall meet you at the main office at, say, two-thirty. Just follow the brick path to the south end of the property."

Joe picked the golf cart holding his soft-sider and laptop computer and climbed in the back seat while Grund plunked himself down alongside the driver. The little private taxi hummed down a wide brick path that joined the residence section of the complex, on the lake's eastern shore, to the plant and research areas to the south and west.

Joe began to play the new piece of information like a bobcat plays a field mouse. *How is Wyczek working out?* Hass had asked. His tone suggested more than idle inquiry. Perhaps Hass had recommended Wyczek to König. Perhaps at some time, Wyczek had worked for Hass?

With the unerring instinct of a politician, Jean Paul had determined their driver's name and that his family was from Munich before Nova finished an admiring survey of the landscaping. Rudy, their driver, deposited their bags in their quarters then disappeared, taking with him a generous tip. The trees, the lawns, the bricked walks, the flowers—all were beautiful. One wrong step, though, and she could be planted here as fertilizer for the lovely landscaping.

She stepped into Jean Paul's embrace and hugged him. "Everything is delightful."

Time pressed her brutally now. Even her extreme discomfort with the thought of being trapped in the Compound with a mad group of terrorists was sublimated to the obsession to stop Gall. Four days or less.

Jean Paul grasped her arm. "I expect to do more work than rest. But I'm glad you're with me." A slow, passionate kiss. His hand strayed to her breast. She pulled him toward the bed and he laughed.

"Oh, no, Ms. Blair. Have you forgotten we're committed to a royal tour?"

"There's time." She pulled him another step toward the bed.

He laughed again, but then grabbed her hair and twisted it at the back of her head. "God, I love you."

"Show me."

Another kiss, his tongue searching, probing deeply as if to make them one. He pressed close and she felt the hard signal of rising passion.

He let her go with a great show of looking at his

watch, pointing at the face and shaking his head. "If a thing's worth doing, it's worth doing well. But just look at the time!"

"Agreed." She put her hand against him and massaged. "But it seems a terrible waste."

Together they explored the suite. It was done in shades of mauve and gray. A large living room opened onto a covered, low-walled patio overlooking an expanse of lawn and farther on, a thick patch of woods. The friendly smell of baking bread scented the air, presumably coming from the Compound's kitchen. It seemed they would have complete privacy.

Jean Paul led her back into the living room, that possessive arm still around her. For more than a week she'd lived with the knowledge that Jean Paul was a man able to order the deaths of innocents, apparently without the slightest remorse. The morning's "event," to which the conspirators in Manfred Wagner's library had alluded, had turned out to be the bombing of a British Rolls-Royce auto factory. Forty had been injured, eighteen killed.

The bedroom opened onto the same patio. She said, "I can see us breakfasting here."

A small dining area and a kitchen with a sink, well-stocked bar and large refrigerator completed the suite. No stove.

"It's a small house," Jean Paul said with a smile. "We can pretend we're at home. An old married pair."

Marriage. Family. Kids. Impossible. To divert her thoughts, she checked her watch. "We're supposed to be at the office in ten minutes."

On the walk to the administration building, Jean Paul kept his arm firmly around her but removed it when they left the residential zone. Joe and Hass were already waiting.

Hass began the tour. Nova paid close attention to the layout. The administration offices, small library, dining hall and single-room clinic were all unexceptional.

Wyczek hadn't shown up. She understood there would be no need for him in the secure residential area, but what about this more public section?

"Did you tell Wyczek he didn't need to stay with you?" she said softly to Jean Paul.

"Helmut assures me that I needn't worry anywhere within the Compound. They check everyone who comes in or goes out. I told Wyczek he's more or less on his own for the week." Jean Paul gave her a heart-stopping smile, or a smile that would have stopped her heart had she been in love with him. "One of the major benefits of being with you here is that we'll not have to put up with a nosy Wyczek."

From the administration building, Hass set a brisk pace toward the chemical facilities. Joe peppered Hass with questions. She had by now watched him engage enough people, men as well as women, to have a profound respect for the way his seemingly boyish enthusiasm loosened tongues. Joe's mind was not nearly as young as she'd surmised or as he often let others think.

Green willows lined both sides of the lake. The grounds were brilliant with mature flowers and shrubs—golds, reds, blues. She smelled a hint of jasmine in the air. No feature of this idyllic scene hinted they were on their way to a chemical plant. Still, somehow the place felt oddly sterile.

Hass stopped at the entrance of the first of the four buildings. A green circle with Security—HCI printed in

German was stuck to the glass pane next to the door. Inside, they were shown two laboratories. Hass seemed particularly proud of a "scanning-tunneling microscope."

"What we do in this building," he said, "is quality testing and advanced research on compounds that have been long-term staples of Hass Chemie. Estrotonin, our birth control drug. Our wonderful Chondroil, for arthritis. The defoliant, Autumnox. Very popular with military organizations. Even our new male reproductive enhancer, Erectril."

They trekked, via a covered walkway connecting the second floors of all four structures, to the second building. This time they paused at the outer door. She noted another circular sign with Security—HCI in the center, this one yellow. A substantial lock secured the door. Hass pulled a pass from his pocket and inserted it into a slot in the lock. A green light flashed and he pulled the door open.

They descended a stairwell, Hass saying, "We are continually developing new products and do not wish to make life unduly easy for our competitors. Security at the gate helps. The building passes are added protection."

At the first door on their right, Hass paused again. "I have asked our chief scientist, Dr. Sanjiv Singh, to conduct the remainder of your tour as he is more knowledgeable than myself. Frankly, I know shamefully little chemistry."

Hass pushed the door open. Perched behind a chrome desk, a secretary smiled warmly. "He has been waiting," she said in English. Nova hadn't yet heard one word of German. Apparently everyone had been informed that the Americans were coming.

The secretary depressed an intercom button. "Herr Doktor Singh, Herr Hass and his guests are here."

"I shall be out at once." The thin voice had a pronounced Indian accent. The man who followed the sound into the room was thin and slightly stooped. The few remaining strands of his straight dark hair were slicked across his scalp. As everything else about him, his dusky lips were remarkably thin, almost to the point of nonexistent.

Hass made introductions, excused himself, then added, "Please do not forget that dinner will be in my home at eight this evening. Nothing formal."

He left. Nova didn't miss him. Something about Hass gave her the willies, especially when he turned those alien-pale eyes on her.

The second building extended deeper into the property, away from the lake, perhaps three times as much as the first building. "You will have noticed perhaps," the doctor said, "that for entrance to this building, a security card is required. That is because we manufacture our birth control pill here. In this particular building security precautions are due not so much to our concern for the research—our formula is patented—but because we have many times received threats. Not only to destroy the facilities, but personal death threats, as well. Fanatics are very frightening people."

How very true, Nova thought. And she was at this moment conducting an affair with one of the world's first-class ones.

The laboratories began to look pretty much the same. Even with people in the rooms, the buildings had the quiet feel of a library. Smaller rooms were dedicated to special functions, like the "centrifuge room." The phrase "scintillation counter" stuck in her mind, as did "reverse osmosis, spectrophotometer" and "separation gel." Only initiates could understand what it all meant, although the Indian scientist seemed to be doing his earnest best to get through to her.

Singh opened a door near the back two-thirds of the lower floor and she was hit with a familiar, musty smell. The vast room was very like a modern winery she'd once visited. The same gleaming stainless-steel vats, the musty smell that was at the same time clean.

"Here we grow the bacteria for our genetic work." Sanjiv Singh's voice sing-songed.

He explained how they "designed" molecules. "We then inject the prefabricated DNA into our bacteria and fool them into making the compound for us in large quantities. They are very efficient, our little friends. In our next building I shall show you the very sophisticated computer we use."

They marched rather quickly to the third building, this one wearing an orange security patch. As Singh let them inside, Joe said to him with typical eagerness, "You know, this is fascinating stuff. I'd really like to do an article on Hass Chemie, as a successful business willing to be environmentally sound." His voice was perfect innocence. "Could I get a security pass?"

The thin hands fluttered like a bat at dusk on the prowl. "I am not the one who can answer this question, Mr. Cardone."

"Please. Call me Joe."

The Indian winced at the brash American familiarity, but took it in stride. "Well, Joe, I am not the one you need to ask. I would imagine, however, that Herr Hass would look favorably on such an idea, but you must speak with him."

"No problem."

The hands calmed down again and disappeared into Singh's lab coat pockets, the thin lips stretching wide in what Nova assumed was a smile. "If the article gains Herr Hass's favor, I will do all I can to assist you." Singh halted in front of a door, then indicated they should follow him. They entered a laboratory full of smells. Fascinating smells. Every lab bench seemed to have a different scent. Mint. Then jasmine. Even sweaty socks. Then coffee.

First her mind jammed at the word, then the tips of her fingers tingled and her thoughts caught fire. The pipeline employee had mentioned the smell of coffee to Dr. Graywing. A coincidence? The CIA didn't believe in coincidences, and neither did she.

"The work we do in this and in the next building will lead to future products. I cannot say more than that. But I can say that the delivery of drugs can be accomplished in several ways. The most common and most desirable to date is orally—by mouth. But of course, some must be taken as suppositories, or intravenously, or injected intramuscularly. We are working on ways to allow the body to absorb drugs by inhalation. At present, this is only rarely possible because the vast majority of therapeutic drug molecules are too large to pass nasal and other membranes. But we are hopeful." Singh grinned. "As are several of our competitors. This is an area of very keen interest."

Nova's pulse thrummed in her throat. Interest? Or already a success?

Singh steered them back outside, past a door leading into the fourth building, saying there was nothing different to be seen in the fourth structure. She knew Joe had to be thinking what she was. *What's behind door number four?*

Chapter 21

After the royal tour, Joe returned to his bungalow and went straight to the phone. He dialed the admin office. The operator informed him that Hass's office was in the mansion, then she rang through. Hass answered immediately. *"Hass hier."*

Joe explained his idea for an article on Hass Chemie as a nonpolluting pharmaceutical. After assuring Hass that he would not slight his work on Jean Paul's campaign, Hass agreed that Joe could have a pass, even to the secure areas. "You may pick it up from the secretary in the administration building. As for interviews, limit them to me or Doctor Singh and only to those employees who have green and yellow clearances. In any case, those with orange clearances will not talk with you."

Joe thanked Hass and hung up. He strolled back to the chemical facility. From the north end of Research

Building No. 1—green security patch—he reentered the complex and walked down the central hall toward its southern exit. His hand was on the door to the outside when a red patch, plastered onto the wall just to the left of what appeared to be a stainless-steel, elevator door, caught his attention. Except for color, the patch was identical to the other security patches, but there was no slot beneath it. Instead, at waist height, a gray metal tube jutted a few inches out from the wall.

The tube made a forty-five degree upward bend, and set horizontally on it, like a rectangular plate, was a black-glass panel, about four-by-eight inches. The door resembled a stainless-steel elevator but it had no call button and nothing indicating floors.

Something definitely did not compute.

Once outside, something even more interesting became obvious. The steel door with the red security patch led, not into another building, but into the domed hill. He was sure the pass that Hass was arranging for him wouldn't include clearance into this red zone.

"Darf ich Ihnen hilfen?"

Joe nearly jumped clean out of his skin. He whirled around to find an armed guard in brown pants and a green shirt giving him the evil eye. On a leash at the guard's side was a German shepherd.

The dog's amber eyes stared intently at Joe, but suggested no hostility. Nor was the dog's tail stiff or his lip curled. Joe flashed a sincere smile. "I am Herr Hass's houseguest," he said quickly in English. "Just looking for the administration building to pick up a security pass." He repeated, "Administration building."

The man waved an arm with bulging biceps toward the administration building and said, "Administration."

Joe nodded and smiled again. *"Danke schön."*

From behind the counter inside the administration building, Hass's secretary slid the pass and a pen across to Joe. She pointed with her own pen. "Sign your name here."

"Sure. No problem."

He scanned instructions on the back of the pass and, finding no mention whatsoever of a red security zone, smiled. Scratching his signature, he said, "I just ran into one of your guards with a German shepherd. They make great guard dogs."

He finished the signature, his eyes met hers, and a nice rosy glow spread on her face. She straightened the collar of her blouse. "That would be Bruno," she said in a thick German accent. "He's not a guard dog. He's our sniffer. We've had bomb threats."

"My mistake. Next time I meet Bruno I'll give him a big pat."

He asked where there was a public phone. Using the phone in his bungalow was out of the question; he wouldn't be surprised if all the Compound's phones were tapped and the rooms bugged, as well. The public phone also posed some risk, but he and Nova had agreed with Cupid on a set of conversations that would allow them to report their general status.

He found the phone and punched in the number given to him. They were using the name, but not the number, of a Turm shop that carried electronic equipment and photographic supplies. He let the contact know they were personally okay and that some significant information had been uncovered and it would be put in the agreed-upon nightly drop.

On the way back to the bungalow, he saw a couple

jogging around the lake. The path turned out to be dirt and wood chips, ideal for running. He picked up speed, eager to change into sweats and charge up the old heart.

In his bones, he felt they were close to pay-off time. These experiments involved something that smelled like burned coffee, as John Wiley with the steel plate in his head had so aptly described it.

The jog did more to relax him than a double shot of Scotch. By ten to eight, he was dressed and on his way to the mansion.

A light, warm breeze stirred the leaves of the trees. A few low lights illuminated the brick path. At the point where the path emerged from trees and began a gentle climb to the mansion, he caught up to Nova and König. She looked as inviting as a Popsicle on a hot day, all cool in an icy-pink sleeveless dress. König wore a white, lightweight suit.

Joe couldn't help but wonder what made the bastard tick. He had it all. Intelligence, looks, power. Some of the man's pie-in-the-sky ideas even sounded good. Too radical, but going in the right direction. And Joe could see that if König was all that hot for the world to change, he was going to be highly frustrated. Things weren't going to happen as he wanted. König could persuade many, but he could never persuade enough.

He'd answered his own question. That's where the blackmail came in. Those who couldn't be persuaded had to be forced.

Hass greeted them and led them down the hall to a living room as darkly tapestried and paneled as the entry. With Nova and König, Joe made himself comfortable in the overstuffed chairs of one of four conversation areas. Hass served them cocktails.

Peter Grund lumbered in and dumped himself into a chair. Soon Braunwin Hass and the two boys joined them. As she had earlier in the day, Braunwin seemed allergic to Nova and devoted herself to König. The two boys hung close to the politician, young eyes bright with intense interest. To Joe's surprise, the dour butler escorted Dr. Singh through the wide door. Hass hadn't mentioned that the flighty scientist would be sharing their evening meal. Well, well, the cast of characters continued to enlarge.

"Come in, come in, Sanjiv," Hass murmured as Nova took another tiny sip of her gin and tonic. "Now we are all here. Your usual?"

Sanjiv Singh nodded. Hass poured him a glass of sherry.

Nova sipped her drink, studied the four men's faces. A looked had passed between them, a shared signal of being in at the beginning of something big. She took a moment to reconsider the possibility that The Founder was really a front name for a group of men—these men.

Joe and Grund conversed about soccer. Braunwin started an awkward exchange with Nova about painting; Nova listening with only half attention. After a few minutes, Nova experienced her "What's wrong with this picture?" feeling.

She gave herself a second and the discrepancy clarified. She would have expected König to be the focus of everyone's attention. Instead, while Singh seemed only interested in what Braunwin was saying to Nova, Grund and König deferred to Hass.

The butler announced dinner.

The aroma of fresh bread filled the spacious dining

room. Hass walked to the head of the table. He indicated that Nova should take the seat to his left, Joe to her left, König to his right. Braunwin stood behind the chair at the foot of the table. Grund took up a place opposite the boys and Dr. Singh moved opposite Joe.

Two young women appeared and began serving. Joe attacked the onion soup and warm bread with a fervor suggesting he could put away a ten-ounce steak. The butler poured wine with practiced smoothness.

Hass smiled. The White Praying Mantis seemed in remarkably good humor, as though he'd already been fed. "I decree we will not talk of politics tonight."

Peter Grund countered. "Please allow me only the luxury of saying I saw today the figures from our latest poll. We should eat heartily in the knowledge that Jean Paul is favored to win Bavaria. We can't let our guard down, of course, but perhaps the only man as popular in all of Germany is the chancellor."

"Marvelous news, indeed," Dr. Singh twittered, his glance going to Braunwin Hass.

"If we're not to talk politics," Nova said, addressing Hass as soup was replaced by salad, "perhaps you could tell us a little more about Hass Chemie. I understand your grandfather founded the company."

Hass shifted cold eyes to Nova. There was an eerie pause. Hass let his eyes rove over her face and breasts and she felt her skin crawl as though his glance were a physical touch. She glanced away and noticed that Joe was observing Hass, his lips compressed into a hard line. It wasn't the first time she'd seen a protective response from Joe. She noted Jean Paul appeared entirely oblivious.

She knew already that Jean Paul admired Hass. He

frequently called him a great man. But this was too much. Hass didn't feel like a great man to her. Hass felt—creepy.

Whatever Hass had been thinking while doing his mental undressing of her, it didn't affect an eager willingness to talk about the pharmaceutical company. By the time the main course of first-rate pork roast, rissole potatoes, asparagus tips and applesauce appeared, Hass switched to a monologue on his father.

Braunwin, who up to this point had been quiet, said with surprising animation, "He was a visionary, much underappreciated and misunderstood by his peers." Nova made a mental note to have Cupid look more deeply into Braunwin's past.

Joe nudged the topic to Earth Alliance. Grund, König and Hass did most of the talking. Singh sat like a timid mouse, his thin, fluttery hands busily bringing food to his thin, hard mouth. Braunwin ate more or less in regal silence.

Grund was expounding. "Our species is a growing cancer in the body of the earth," he intoned, then forked in another mouthful of pork. "Dr. Singh could explain far better than I. As a scientist he appreciates the similarities between the finite earth and its resources and the colonies of bacteria one might grow in a petri dish."

Grund looked at the scientist who smiled but appeared painfully unwilling to enter the conversation. To Nova's surprise, Braunwin stepped into the awkward silence

"That comparison is extremely apt. Human history has been like an inoculation of a few bacteria into a fresh clean dish full of nutrients. The bacteria multiply and spread, just as from Africa we have multiplied and spread to every corner of the planet. We have filled our petri dish. Eventually, though, nutrients run low, wastes accumulate. The bacteria begin to die. Finally in the dish there is no bacteria left alive."

Braunwin was interrupted as the main course settings were whisked away. Dessert was fresh fruit and cheese.

"And how close do you believe we've come to that ominous point?" Nova coaxed.

Braunwin hesitated. She seemed a bit flustered, as though she thought she'd made an error. Quickly she signaled to one of the waiting girls while she said, "Peter would have a better grasp of that than I would."

The girl bent over Braunwin's shoulder to listen to whispered instructions.

Peter Grund picked up the discussion. "Some resources we require, and especially many things we've treasured, are already scarce. But I'm convinced the dire problem isn't lack of resources. It's poor distribution. The difference is, of course, irrelevant if too many people are produced simultaneously. The end result is the same—death and war."

He waved his knife to signal he wanted more wine, but kept right on talking. His tone grew so sober the room seemed to hush. "A great dying off is already on us. But like any patient in the early stages of terminal illness, we cling to denial. We possess technology that could let us build a virtual utopia. Instead we have famines and diseases of epic proportions. The great celestial experiment of sapient beings on planet earth rushes toward a nasty conclusion."

Grund's knife clinked loudly in the quiet room as he laid it on his china plate. "Unless a leader emerges with the power to transform the hearts of millions, we're surely doomed. I believe Jean Paul is that leader. That is why I help him."

König's face lost color. His eyes were fixed on Grund. Everyone else at the table stared at König.

Braunwin broke the silence. "That is why we are honored to have you visit us, Jean Paul. Peter has simply stated forcefully why we feel your election now and your success in the future are so vitally important. You are our great hope."

König pulled his shoulders back slightly. "Thank you Peter, Frau Hass. I suppose I must thank you." He smiled a wry, almost sad smile. His eyes went to Nova. "No one man can do what you're wishing. But together, backed by Earth Alliance, I do believe we can alter the course of history in a positive way."

"Boys," Braunwin said, "it is time for you to be in bed." She stood and the boys followed her example. "Young men, say good evening to our guests."

After excusing themselves, Hass's wife and sons left. Nova accompanied Joe, Grund, Singh and König back to the living room. The men said yes to brandy. Nova passed; she asked for soda water.

After perhaps another hour of conversation, Singh excused himself. "I have a full schedule tomorrow."

Joe then said, "I'll be going, too. It's been a long day." He insisted to Hass he could find his own way out. Nova knew what he had in mind and approved, but still the room felt suddenly, disconcertingly, lonely.

Halfway to the door Joe met the butler who hightailed it ahead of him back to the door and opened it. "Good evening, sir," the butler said.

Singh wasn't very far down the path. Joe fiddled

with his jacket pockets as though he'd forgotten something. When the scientist reached the stand of trees and disappeared, Joe began walking fast. Time now to start filling in the blanks on Sanjiv Singh.

Singh passed the bungalows. He was striding toward the public buildings. At this late hour? Joe pursued, keeping far back.

Singh never broke stride. He made a beeline for Research Building No. 1, nestled into the shoulder of the dome-shaped hill.

When he entered and paused in front of the stainless-steel doors with the red patch, Joe was surprised—and not surprised. Here it was, almost eleven-thirty at night and Singh was seeking out the red zone. Joe's every instinct said that whatever was rotten here involved this red zone.

He suddenly realized that if the steel doors opened, he was at the wrong angle to see what lay behind them. He sprinted to a bush with a better view.

The scientist unbuttoned and rolled back the left sleeve of his shirt and laid the underside of his forearm over the horizontal black-glass panel to the left of the door. *Some kind of individual ID implanted under the skin?*

With a movement so sudden that Joe imagined he heard them swish, the doors parted.

There wasn't much to see inside, just more hallway. But one thing was certain: the steel doors didn't lead to an elevator to the basement. Hass had spent big money, when plenty of available flat land lay all around, to excavate into the side of a mountain.

Singh went in. The shiny doors enveloped him.

Joe returned to his bungalow, changed into sweats, set his alarm for one-thirty, put the travel clock under his pillow and fell into bed.

At one-thirty the muffled alarm jerked him awake. He silenced it and flicked on the bedside lamp. He started water running in the bathroom sink. The false-bottom compartment of his travel bag yielded to a light touch in the right spots and he fished out one of the many waterproof capsules.

He composed a note to Davidson, put it into the capsule and then put the capsule into a discarded cola can. He slipped out of the bungalow and, at the point where the brick compound wall came nearest to the residential bungalows, he threw the can over the wall. At three o'clock it would be picked up by a young man wearing black who was an excellent cross-country runner with a good eye for patrol vehicles.

Chapter 22

After quietly shutting their bungalow's bathroom door, Nova folded a towel on the closed toilet seat and sat. The Company felt, and she agreed, that Jean Paul shouldn't know how little she slept. Should he awaken, she would use a trip to the toilet as her excuse for being up.

She opened her new novel, then let the book drop to her lap. Since the night in the Wagner library, making love with Jean Paul had reverted properly to a strictly business thing. Since her stepfather, she'd lived for years with this kind of sexual numbness. But lying in the darkness, she felt empty, as if a great emotional tide of sweet possibilities had flooded and lifted her soul for a while, then ebbed, leaving in the sand only squiggly lines and popping bubbles.

She forced her attention to the book. The novella, *The*

Devil by Tolstoy, sucked her in. She lost contact with the Compound. With the mission.

The bathroom door opened. "What are you doing?"

Gooseflesh flashed across her chest. Did he sound angry? Suspicious? She checked the travel clock. It was nearly two in the morning.

"What are you doing up and about at this hour?"

"I—I'm reading."

"At two in the morning? In the bathroom?"

"Something at dinner must not have agreed with me," she explained to him.

Jean Paul's frown slowly dissolved. She rose, glided to him and took his hand. "I feel fine now. And I'm tired. I'm sure I'll sleep. Let's go back to bed."

"You should have awakened me."

She kissed his cheek. "No, sweet. You looked too peaceful to disturb." She threw off the dressing gown, slid between the sheets and beckoned. "Come hold me."

His body cupped hers and her pulse gradually quieted.

No more reading at night. She tried to conjure up the look she'd first seen on his face as he stood in the doorway. She couldn't shake the feeling that she'd sensed suspicion.

Four Days Before Gall

It was six-thirty and the morning was breezy. Nova watched the limbs of the willow trees sway like jellyfish tentacles. She and Joe were in sweats, walking fast on the jogging trail around the lake. When this little confab was over, a good run might help settle her nerves.

"I left Jean Paul taking his shower," she said. "I told him you and I were going to jog. He meets with Hass at eight. I'll follow him. Maybe I can plant a recorder. Did you wangle a pass for Building No. 4?"

He nodded. "But I've found something new, and I'd bet big money Building No. 4 isn't where the action is. They have another secure section built right into the big hump of mountain behind the admin building."

She didn't interrupt, just tossed him a questioning look.

He continued. "I called Hass to arrange for a pass. He agreed. Then I walked back through Number 1—the building with the green patch—and just inside the south entrance, I saw what looked like an elevator. Next to the door was a red patch. Want to make a guess about whether the pass I picked up from the secretary has clearance for a red zone or not?"

He was having fun. She smiled. "From the way you're talking, I'd say it didn't."

"And you'd be right. The stuff on the back of my pass explains all about green, yellow and orange zones. It doesn't even mention a red zone."

"It'll be hard enough to get into Building No. 4. How the heck could we penetrate anything built into that mountain?"

"That's what I should do today. Try to find a way in."

"First I want you to scout the Compound and the exterior grounds. We need better information than what we have from the photos."

"But I've got a feeling about this red zone."

"We can't go off half-cocked. While I keep an eye on Jean Paul, you do a thorough recon of the Compound. You know the routine. Where are the cars kept? What about Hass's private little airstrip? It's guarded, but by how many, and on what schedules, and do they have weapons in the two hangars? Also see if Hass's planes are still there."

"But, look—" His voice rose. "I'm nearly positive what we want is behind those steel doors. That's where we have to go."

"I'm not saying you're not right. Only that today we need to do recon. If you discover some lead on how to get into the hump, great. But first things first. We have to be careful and we have to be smart. We're in here alone."

For a second it looked as if he was going to dig in his heels, but he surprised her. "Okay. You got it." They walked a few seconds in silence, then he said, "Look, I have another gut feeling I want to try out on you. I think the big villain here is Helmut Hass, not Jean Paul."

She stopped. "What do you mean?"

Joe started walking again, explaining something about Hass asking Jean Paul if Wyczek was "working out okay," and then he gave her a mini-lecture on social deferral, saying that Jean Paul deferred to Hass, not vice versa.

In the end, she didn't buy it. "Jean Paul's the one with the mass following, Joe. Helmut Hass is only one step removed from a recluse. And he's weird."

"Sure he's weird. Maybe that's why he needs Jean Paul. He needs a charismatic front." Then he said heatedly, "There's no point in debating it now. Hell, we don't have a lick of proof that either one of them is anything other than St. Peter and St. Paul. But I'll bet you Hass is boss."

"How much?"

He laughed. "I'll pay for every cup of cappuccino we ever drink together."

There was no point arguing with Joe until they learned more. But it bothered her that he still didn't trust her one hundred percent, or follow her orders as leader of this mission. "Done."

"Another thing," he said. "What do you make of Braunwin?"

"She's very drawn to Jean Paul. She's been politely nice, though cold, to me. And she seems to have been very taken with Hass's father. We must have Cupid find out more about her."

"Agreed. I put that in the drop capsule."

"Well done," she said, trying not to sound patronizing and get into another pissing match.

They started a slow trot, then picked up speed. She thought she'd left enough time to shower and change before Jean Paul left the bungalow, but when she came in, he was already on his way out. He kissed her lightly and left.

She waited a moment, then followed. He headed toward the lab complex. She watched from behind covering bushes. When he reached the sidewalk, which put a line of trees between them, she sprinted after him again, now very exposed. She passed five people and breathed easier when no one turned to stare.

At the sidewalk, she slowed to a fast walk. Jean Paul had never looked back, and he was going into Building No. 1.

Through the glass panels of the entry doors she saw steel doors that fit Joe's description. Perhaps she shouldn't have been surprised, but she was, in fact, amazed when Jean Paul paused for a moment in front of the flat glass panel, blocking her view of it, and then the doors opened and he passed through them into the side of the hill. She wanted to stop and gawk, but forced her feet to keep moving.

So, Joe's hunch appeared to be right on the money. The real action probably was inside the mountain, about as secure a location as any bunch of snakes could wish for.

She returned to the bungalow and showered. During the remainder of the morning she did her own quick recon of the grounds. At one o'clock, Jean Paul met her at the bungalow just as the luncheon they'd ordered was delivered. Wurst and kraut, mustard and fresh hard rolls and beer.

After they ate, he invited her to go sailing. During their sail they worked together in a harmony that made her feel amazingly young. But when her feet again touched land, she had to swallow back tears.

Now that was unbelievable—Nova Blair getting tearful over a man!

By five they were back in the bungalow and he mixed cocktails. At a quarter to six she told him she was going to change to meet Joe for another run. He frowned. "Why should you run again? Stay with me."

"He's been working hard on the project all day. I've been slacking off." She ran a finger across his lips. "I won't be long. Dinner's not until eight. I'll be back soon."

She kissed his cheek and hurried out the door, leaving him no time to argue.

Four days until "Gall." She and Joe had to find a way into the mountain. They were close now. She could feel it. This time they had a fighting chance to prevent another deadly disaster.

Chapter 23

Four Days Before Gall

Nova greeted Joe for their second conference-disguised-as-a-jog by asking, "What did you find out?"

Joe gave her a succinct, thorough summary.

"What about the red zone?"

"I was saving that. I questioned Hass's secretary and several of the researchers. I came up more or less dry."

It was her turn. "I followed Jean Paul to see where he and Hass would meet. It will probably not surprise you that Jean Paul didn't go to the mansion. Guess where?"

Joe gave her a satisfied grin. "Into the mountain."

"Right. I was too far behind to see what he used. His body blocked my view. He doesn't have any scars on his arms. I know that. Perhaps that scanner can also read card keys or fingerprints. Or maybe someone on the inside opened the door for him. Or maybe there is some other kind of device and you missed it."

"I didn't. There is only the glass plate."

"If that scanner reads only some kind of individualized ID implanted under the skin or fingerprints, we'll have a devil of a time bypassing it. The place can't be self-contained, though. They have to breathe. They have to bring supplies in and haul trash out."

"After dinner I'll reconnoiter every square foot of the damned hill. If I find a way in, I'll tell Cupid in tonight's drop what we intend to do and how."

"If we'll need special equipment, tell him you'll pick it up tomorrow. By tomorrow night for sure, Joe. We have to get in there. There's not much sand left in the hourglass."

She thought of something else. "Tell Cupid to include a couple of automatics in the package. And ask for a radio."

Joe stooped to pick up a fist-size flat stone. He skipped it into the lake surface. "What about my idea that Hass is running the show?"

She shrugged. "You included that in last night's drop, of course. As a speculation."

"Sure."

"I'm still skeptical." She wished she could help scout the mountain. For now, she had to wait for her determined partner to find them a way in.

An hour later she and Jean Paul stepped onto the path to the mansion. Nova pulled a light wool shawl over her shoulders. She'd picked a backless, emerald-and-white cotton sheath. Jean Paul's arm was warm around her shoulders.

He said, "If Helmut Hass weren't such a very important man—" He stopped walking and put both arms around her. "How long have I known you? Only weeks. What I feel doesn't make sense, I know that. There's simply no way I could show you how much I love you. Right now I want to take you straight back to the bungalow and the dinner be damned."

He pulled her onto the balls of her feet. His kiss searched her mouth, his hands drifted upward under the shawl and stroked her back. She thought, How is Hass important, Jean Paul? Important because he serves you? Or because you serve him?

He let her go and when she had her heels on the ground again, she took his hand and tugged him toward the mansion.

Jean Paul sighed. "But he is important. So let's get dinner over with so we can hurry back to being alone."

The dinner party included the same characters as the previous evening, except that Hass told them his wife had taken the boys to visit her mother in Heidelberg. Hass shot an odd glance at Singh, and for some reason, Nova had the distinct feeling Hass had lied. She couldn't imagine why Hass would lie about his wife.

The dinner conversation, too, was similar. A lot of talk about politics and ecology.

Jean Paul said, "Helmut is trying to convince me that if I'm elected, he feels I should set my sights right away on the chancellorship. I've promised to let him know my answer this week." He gave Nova a look that seemed both apology and an acknowledgment that he should have told her he was considering such a move.

She smiled. "I hope you decide yes."

"Very good, Miss Blair," Grund said. "I think all of us in this room have the same vision for Jean Paul."

Joe asked Hass how he saw the changes that were necessary happening quickly enough to do any good. Grund interrupted and argued that force would be necessary in order to rid the world of the entrenched power. Hass countered forcefully. A strange look of intense cunning passed over his pale face. She saw the Mantis at the very moment it is going to strike its prey, clamp bristled pincers to the body and devour it head first. Singh's nervous hands fluttered to his glass of sherry.

"Force is not necessary," Hass said slowly, "if one can sufficiently persuade the mind and ensure that key leaders work in unity toward the desired goal. And, my dear, social transformation can occur with breathtaking speed. Aborigines have been brought from the Stone Age to the Space Age in one generation. Mankind can be brought quickly from the Space Age to the final Golden Age of Human Fulfillment once the collective minds of our leaders have been altered." He gave her a pink smile. "Do not despair, my dear Nova. We all will witness the change. And Jean Paul will be at its heart."

Having Hass call her "my dear" made her want to puke. She forced her mind back to business. Was Hass simply a rabid convert? Or was he using Jean Paul? Perhaps to raise money. Or even more likely, as a magnet to attract followers—men whom Hass could subvert to ecoterrorism.

During the after-dinner sherry, Joe asked to use a car to drive into Turm the next day and was told it would be no problem. The butler appeared and glided to Hass's side. "It's Herr Maurus," he said in smooth low tones. "He begs to speak with you, sir. Urgently."

Hass stood and murmured regrets. "This could be important."

Nova felt, when he left, as if something alien and brooding had scuttled away. He never returned.

Later, as she and Jean Paul returned to the bungalow, Jean Paul said, "Why are you so cold to Helmut?" His voice was stiff with controlled anger.

The hair raised at the back of her neck. "I don't understand what you mean."

"Nova, this is me." He took her hand. Afraid her suddenly sweating flesh would betray her, she fought the instinct to jerk it away. "I've learned to read you. Why don't you like Helmut?"

A tremor shimmied up her spine. She'd made him quite angry. And he claimed he could read her. What else had he managed to sense? The golden rule to avoid tripping up was to avoid outright lies. And keep it simple. "He's strange."

"Helmut and his wife have supported me for years, even in lean times. He believes in our cause and he puts his money behind his beliefs. I admire him. And look at this chemical plant. It's a model of enlightened business."

"Of course. I shouldn't let his appearance prejudice me. I'll try to be more open-minded."

"I would sincerely appreciate your making an effort."

During a night that seemed an endless torture, she lay beside him, listening to his light snoring, trying to second guess if she'd triggered his suspicions sufficiently to compromise the mission. And creating pictures in her mind of Joe on the mountain—getting caught.

6:30 a.m.
Three Days Before Gall

Joe watched as Nova jogged across lawn to meet him
on the lakeside trail, her ponytail swinging. He knew she
considered him a kid. Sort of like a pesky younger
brother.

A fierce urge to ferret out the critical missing piece
of the Nova Blair puzzle hit him again. How in the name
of God had she come to the place where she'd take
these kinds of risks for her country? But the moment he
turned any conversation personal, she gave him a ver-
bal stiff-arm there was no getting past.

They started walking fast, side by side. "I couldn't find
any door into the hump except the one in the lab building,"
he informed her. "They either bring everything through
that building or a tunnel connects the mountain's inside
with some other Compound location. Maybe a basement
in one of the research buildings. Or maybe even someplace
outside the wall. And except for a single loop of jogging
trail around its base, there are no indications of traffic, light
or heavy, on any other part of the mountain itself."

"So there's no way in but those steel doors?"

"Didn't say that." He let his satisfaction put a bit of
swagger in his voice. "On the back side and top I found
openings to three ventilation shafts."

This won him a big smile. "And?"

"The openings are large enough for us. Can't guar-
antee how far we'll get. I'll pick up what we need from
Cupid today."

"So you will pick it all up today? And hide it?"

"Roger."

"We should settle on when to meet."

"There's no moon till one o'clock. How soon after dark can you get away?"

"I can take care of Jean Paul sometime between nine and ten. When I'm ready I'll let your phone ring once. I may need help."

"Roger, again."

"One more thing." She hesitated. He waited.

"Jean Paul was angry with me last night. He's figured out I detest Hass."

Joe felt his jaw involuntarily harden. "He can't expect you to like every person you meet," he said sharply. "Don't worry about it."

"I'm not worried. Exactly. But you need to know I'm not feeling iron-clad sure about our cover."

"It's too late to worry about that now."

Chapter 24

Nova returned to the bungalow as Jean Paul stepped out of the shower. Water streaked down his skin. With both hands he palmed strands of wet blond hair backward from his forehead. "Breakfast will be here in twenty minutes," he said. "And I've arranged for us to go riding. I need exercise."

Her gut felt an unpleasant jolt: a sudden craving for exercise was quite out of character. "Then we will exercise."

When she came out of the shower he caught her and held her close. His hands moved over her buttocks, dug in tight. His tongue took her mouth possessively. In spite of everything, she felt a warmth spread deep inside her. Then, before he let her go he said, "Never, ever, doubt that I love you."

Nova loved horses and had ridden since childhood, but the stables were outside the Compound's west wall.

They would be completely isolated. Five horses stood in the paddock, two already saddled. A black gelding with white stockings reminded her of the pony her father had given her and she strolled toward it.

"Not that one, miss," the lone stable hand called after her in urgent, awkward English. Lean, maybe eighteen, the boy was dressed American Western, in cowboy boots, Levi's and hat. He rushed to her. "Mittenacht hates women. You ride Mädchen."

"I'm an experienced rider."

He shook his head. "You ride Mädchen."

She looked to Jean Paul, expecting him to support her on her choice of a mount.

"We ought to do as he suggests," he said. "He works here."

She doubted either of them rode much better than she, but making a scene was pointless so she strolled to Sweetheart's left side. The stable boy gave her a hand up.

Jean Paul mounted the misogynist Midnight. While adjusting their stirrups, the boy gave them general directions. "You can't get lost. Just look at the mountain."

They rode the horses at a walk across the meadow that stretched northward from the Compound wall to the first stand of sycamore, oak and beech trees. The blue sky lifted the spirit, the pristine-seeming landscape seduced the eye.

She patted Sweetheart, a leggy chestnut. A shallow, rock-strewn stream curled down the meadow's middle. They crossed, their horses shod hoofs crunching and clinking on the rocks. On the other side Jean Paul said, "We can run here. Want to?"

"Let's do it."

Jean Paul led. She tightened her knees and her grip

on the reins and kicked Sweetheart twice. The filly took off, eager to let out her muscles. They cantered the distance from the stream to the stand of trees and passed into the forest, Jean Paul still leading on the ten-foot-wide trail.

Nova's saddle slipped a few inches left. Her horrified thought: the boy hadn't properly tightened the cinch.

On purpose?

Panicked, she leaned forward, clutched Sweetheart's mane. The horse took it as a signal to redouble her efforts. The saddle turned farther, slipped down the horse's side.

"Jean Paul," she yelled.

The boy had insisted that she ride Sweetheart. Jean Paul had agreed.

The saddle slipped again. Her right foot twisted in the stirrup. She caught a glimpse of Jean Paul looking back over his shoulder just before she upended, her right foot still caught. Pain slashed through her ankle, her head hit the ground and she curled her belly and wrapped her arms around her face as the filly continued her run.

Blinding pain streaked between her temples. *He's going to kill me and make it look an accident!*

Sweetheart slowed but didn't stop. Nova's hands flailed. Trees flashed by in an upside-down world. She tightened the muscles in her abdomen to pull herself up to grab the saddle. Again breath-stealing pain shot through her ankle. She let go, hung down the horse's side, hands protecting her head.

Suddenly, Sweetheart jerked to a stop and four black-stockinged legs danced in front of Nova's eyes. "Halt! Halt!" Jean Paul kept saying as Sweetheart reared.

Nova dangled helplessly.

"Hang on," Jean Paul shouted.

He ran around Sweetheart's head and Nova glimpsed his hands. Would he have a weapon? He didn't.

He slid his arms under her armpits and lifted her. Her weight came off her ankle. She twisted free of the stirrup and Sweetheart reared again.

The second Nova's feet hit the ground she whirled and threw a punch at Jean Paul's larynx. Her ankle gave. Shuddering, she collapsed, unable to rise, her blow having harmlessly hit his chest. Jean Paul fell on his knees beside her and at the same moment Nova saw the filly's front hoofs descending.

"*Nein,*" Jean Paul yelled, throwing himself over Nova. "Aa-hh" he exhaled as a hoof grazed his shoulder.

The filly moved off.

"*Liebchen,*" Jean Paul whispered.

She gasped for air. "I thought— I thought…you—" She shuddered, horrified by what she'd thought.

A warm, strong hand stroked her cheek. "What, *liebchen?*"

She shook her head. Then, as her shudder subsided, whispered, "I thought you would leave me."

His arms tightened around her again. With her head pressed to his chest she could feel his warmth, hear his thudding heart. "Never, *liebchen.* Never. How could you think such a thing? Leave you?"

She remembered his shouted no. Saw him throw his body over hers.

In a great rising wave, certitude floated her off the ground. Pain vanished. Doubt disintegrated. She was certain of Jean Paul's love.

Wherever his fingers touched, her skin responded

with fire. "You saved me," she whispered to him. For the first time in so many years she could hold nothing back. Cracks in a great wall of ice around her heart opened and widened, and then the wall crumbled. Past and future melted, too. There was just now and this rush of freedom.

She responded to his caresses with a tender kiss. There was nothing to feign now. No desire to keep control. Or play. Or lie. Or protect herself. This was not Candido. Not a man who wanted to use her. From the beginning, Jean Paul had asked nothing from her but that she love him and let him love her. He would never hurt her.

But as they began the return ride to the Compound, reality hit her. With chest-crushing force. She was completely compromised.

She couldn't even begin to sort out let alone face the moral implications of falling in love with Jean Paul. But the practical implications were horrendous. Joe depended on her. Innocent lives depended on her. Could she trust herself to do "whatever, absolutely whatever, is necessary?"

Nova and Jean Paul approached the Compound's front entrance. Nova listened to Sweetheart's hoofs clopping a steady rhythm. Her thoughts were a hopeless jumble. *I've completely lost control.* She should tell Joe how shook up she was, shouldn't she? Cupid would expect to be informed. Gall loomed only three days away.

A gauntlet of six protesters stood just outside the gate, three on each side of the road. *Weird.*

The activists called out in German. Jean Paul trans-

lated. "'Stop producing chemical defoliants. Stop killing children.'" In spite of their yelling, they smiled
cheerfully enough at him. The moment's irony struck
her: crusaders resolved to fight evil smiled agreeably
when real evil passed by them.

Jean Paul was evil, wasn't he? God. She couldn't
think one straight thought.

The stable boy's apology was profuse. He begged
Jean Paul not to report him. "It's my fault," the boy
said. "They told me Sweetheart hates a tight cinch and
holds her breath. You have to make her blow out before
you tighten it. I forgot. If you report me, I'll lose the job."

"What do you want to do?" Jean Paul asked Nova.

She didn't believe the boy. But whatever had happened, for whatever reason, it didn't matter since nothing could be done about it. "There's no permanent
damage. Only a sprained ankle and bump on the head.
Let's just drop it."

By four-thirty she and Jean Paul sat soaking in the
tub. A hoof-shaped bruise flamed on his shoulder. Her
ankle was propped on the rim and packed in ice, a gin
and tonic was in her hand. Her heart was in much worse
shape than her leg. *I could love him. But I could never
have him. I would destroy him.*

Even if he weren't a monster. Even if he were the passionate leader and visionary he seemed to be. Her murder conviction would make her a crippling liability for
any great leader, if the truth were discovered.

But it didn't matter—he *was* a monster.

At six, he ordered dinner, to be delivered at seven-
thirty. By seven-fifteen she'd changed into her green
robe, he into the black terry, and dinner arrived. The
strain of waiting to do what she had to was shredding

her nerves. She wanted to hurry through the salad, hurry through the roast, hurry through the fruit and cheese. Hurry and get it over.

At last, it was time for her cappuccino. Her ankle felt better. She made sure she beat Jean Paul to the coffee machine. "Let's watch TV," she said. "See if you can find something that's mostly action so I don't need to understand the words."

Her imagination was clamoring now to see what lay behind the steel doors into the mountain. With a steady hand she added the knockout drops to Jean Paul's cup. Smith, in Technical, had assured her Jean Paul would have no telltale morning-after hangover, and that if she put him in bed, it would be easy to convince him he'd gone there himself. She knew from personal experience the drops left no after-effects, but she'd have to take Smith's word that she could convince Jean Paul he'd spent a perfectly normal evening with her.

She curled up next to him on the sofa and handed him the cappuccino.

He said, "It's an old Charles Bronson movie. *Telepfon.*"

"Perfect. I've seen it. I forget how it ends, but I'll be able to follow the story."

Charles Bronson was clueing Lee Remick in on how evil mind-manipulators had programmed people to go out and kill on command. The dubbed German voice doing Bronson was all wrong: too gruff and macho, no trace of his soft sibilants. In no time at all, Jean Paul's head fell back against the couch. His breathing deepened.

She hurried to the phone, rang Joe once and hung up. In less then half a minute she heard a single light knock. Together they wrangled Jean Paul out of his robe.

They agreed to leave him nude since that was the way

he usually slept after making love to her. Joe grasped Jean Paul under the arms and, using a fireman's lift, hauled him to the bed, scowling.

She covered Jean Paul to his waist and checked his breathing. Joe tossed her a pillow-size brown package he'd set next to the door. He had told her he'd bring slacks, shirt and shoes for the search. Always conscious of bugs, he handed her a note.

Put on some jogging stuff. We'll change into these when we get to where I've stashed supplies.

She threw on a dark jogging outfit, racing against time to find out what Hass was hiding in his mountain.

Chapter 25

An almost supernatural darkness cloaked the Compound. The moon wouldn't rise for hours, and since on the hump's far side the Compound lights were hidden, nothing eased the blackness surrounding Joe. Nevertheless, tiny flashlight in hand, he readily led Nova to the packages wrapped in plastic and stuffed under a ground-hugging bush.

Five trips he'd made from the Mercedes to this hiding place, carrying one or two items at a time under his jogging suit—climbing equipment, radio and guns. To look as though he were just out for strenuous exercise, he made a circuit around the lake each time before heading up and around the hump.

"How's the ankle holding up?" he asked.

"Hurts. But it's not slowing me down."

They changed clothes and he tried to avoid any glimpses of Nova who was changing right next to him. She appeared completely oblivious to him. Then again, she had a lot on her mind and sex sure wasn't likely one of them.

"By the way," he said, "I forgot to tell you something Cupid said today. I'm not sure why he hadn't mentioned it before. It's weird, as if things here could be any weirder. Braunwin Hass is not only Hass's wife, she's his half sister. Same father. Her mother was the father's mistress."

"Why doesn't it even surprise me?"

Cupid had packed two 9 mm Sig-Sauers with shoulder holsters. He and Nova loaded, shrugged into the holsters and stuck an extra clip each into one of their clothing's many pockets. He showed her how to attach her headband to the tiny but powerful light that would illuminate their spelunking through the ventilation ducts.

"Which shaft?" she asked.

"I picked one that's horizontal. With luck, we may be able to reach a corridor without having to do a vertical climb."

The shaft's entrance lay roughly three-fifths the way down the hump's backside. He'd brought three sockets for the special wrench. His first choice fit snugly. Two minutes later he wrestled the cover off. Blood pounded in his ears as he stared into a black hole that looked like the gullet of eternity.

After securing her knee pads and checking that the Sig-Sauer had a bullet in the chamber, Nova motioned to Joe and said, "I'll go first."

"I will, if you want."

"No," she insisted. She was team leader, she'd put herself at risk first. "I'll go first."

Joe paused, then said, "Fine. I'll bring a line along in case we find a place where we need to go vertical."

Nova crawled headfirst into the hump and Joe followed close behind. Her light wagged up and down, back and forth on the narrow wall in front of her. Their soft clothes made a swishing sound along the metal duct. She wished they were making no sound at all; to her ears, their slight noises sounded like water running over a tin roof.

After roughly a hundred feet, she stopped. She turned off her headlamp and Joe quickly doused his. Light from a corridor rose through a metal ventilation cover. She plastered her back against the smooth metal of the shaft ceiling and dug into a breast pocket for the gadget that unscrewed things from the inside. In less than a minute she'd unscrewed the ventilation cover, let it down slightly while holding it with a magnet, then twisted and fished it into the shaft with them. They would replace it when they came out.

Next she removed her headlamp and the elbow and kneepads. After setting them aside, she edged her face through the opening. Nothing. She pulled back in. "It's clear," she whispered. "And I don't see any security camera, either, but keep an eye out."

She crawled over the hole, backed her legs through, eased down as far as her waist, then dropped to the floor, her hands catching the edge of the hole to break her fall. Joe was quickly beside her.

It was eleven-twenty at night and the corridor was fully lit. She felt like a black beetle plunked down in-

side some scientist's off-white maze. They were
screwed if the scientist showed up. The great liar Br'er
Rabbit himself couldn't think up a plausible explanation
for their being here. Her ears burned with the effort to
pick up sounds.

"I don't like the light," she said. "We stay together.
Either this conservation organization isn't really very
conservation-minded or there are people in here."

The corridor looked like those in the other four research buildings except for the absence of windows and
the fact that the floors were of brushed concrete, not tile.
She began to construct a mental map of their position.
They were on the west side of the hump, headed due east.

The slit between the door and the floor of the first
room they encountered was dark. She pressed her ear
to listen, then nodded. Her heart hammered against her
ribs as it had when she'd checked under her bed for
monsters as a child. She closed her eyes and took a
deep, silent breath, then turned the knob.

Darkness. The unmistakable stink of urine. Soft skit-
tering sounds. She fumbled along the wall, found a
switch, flicked on the light. Rows of small-animal cages
filled the room and a hurried survey revealed mostly
mice, some guinea pigs, some rabbits.

A storage room came next: paper towels, soap, plastic Baggies, test tubes. The darkness in the third room
was humming. Light revealed ventilation machinery
and switches, junction boxes and circuit breakers, all
neatly labeled for the laboratories' electronics, lights,
sprinklers and phones. She moved with Joe deeper into
the maze, her eyes darting back and forth.

The passage intersected a north-south corridor. It ran
a short sixty feet or so before ending in a stainless-steel

double door. Beside the door were a solid-red security patch and an identification-scan panel. The corridor section leading south was so long and featureless it had the look of a lighted tunnel. "Still no security cameras," she said. "It's a good sign that the slimeballs feel totally secure inside their mini-fortress."

"Maybe. Let's go straight ahead. Cover all the east/west rooms first."

She nodded and pointed to a painted, six-inch blue stripe a foot above the floor that ran the length of the north-south corridor, then pointed to a brown stripe running down the east-west hall. Without windows, orientation in the hallways was probably a problem.

When they glanced into the next room, she had to catch her breath from surprise. "There's enough explosive stored in here to blow up the Empire State Building," she said as they retreated into the hall.

The next door stood open and led into a fully lit room. Automatically she and Joe plastered themselves against the wall outside the room. A flush of adrenaline tightened the skin over her shoulders and throat. Tomb-like silence, that was all she could hear.

She bent low and slipped around the jamb and into the room. Within seconds she found something that brought a grim smile to her lips.

She returned to Joe. "No one's home. Come take a look."

Joe followed Nova into the large lab. He noticed two free-standing lab benches running toward the room's opposite end—each maybe fifty feet long—that sat parallel to each other. A six-foot aisle stretched between them and similar-size aisles between the benches and the walls. Cluttered wall counters held exotic-looking instruments and glass-fronted cases attached to the walls were filled with glassware and reagent bottles. The ceiling rose an impressive twenty-five feet, and hanging suspended halfway down from the ceiling, above the center of each lab counter, were long fluorescent fixtures. A three-shelf, see-through partition stretched down the midsection of each lab counter. The shelves held beakers, racks of test tubes, reagent bottles and other stuff he couldn't identify.

Nova led Joe straight down the center aisle and stopped where the counters did in the middle of the room. Built against one wall smack in the center of the lab was a small cubicle about the size of her kitchen. Beyond the cubicle, the lab's other half was a duplicate of this end. The cubicle was peculiar not only because of its odd position—against one wall and square in the center of the lab—but because it had a double entry. You entered through one door, passed through a space of about three feet, then through another door.

"What do you make of that?" she asked, her voice low.

Following her gaze, he saw six gas masks dangled on a series of pegs beside the outer door.

"Well, well, well," he said.

"Not exactly a smoking gun, but sure interesting, aren't they?" She gave him a tight grin.

Before he could agree, she heard footsteps in the hall. Joe raised his gun, and she did likewise.

The lab had two doors, both open: the one he and Nova had entered from the brown corridor and a similar one at the room's other end that exited into the north-south blue corridor. For some odd reason, maybe because they were underground, he couldn't tell where the sounds were coming from.

Joe looked at her, the question, "Which way?" clear in his eyes.

She shook her head as if thinking hard and fast.

Joe visually combed the lab, looking for a place to hide, praying the footsteps would pass by. Unfortunately, anyone who walked the length of the lab would easily see them. They could gamble: pick one end or the other and hide behind a bench and pray, or pick one door or the other and hope to get away clean. But they might pick wrong.

The steps came closer and at a rapid clip. *Hell*, he thought.

They had to choose, and right now. He grabbed Nova's arm and shoved her toward the opposite end of the room but she dug in her feet and pointed up.

His eyes followed the line of her finger. She was pointing to the lights. He shook his head hard. She wanted them to crawl up onto the light housings. The idea was nuts.

"Do it!" she snapped so softly he barely heard her.

She wrenched her arm free and shifted her gun to her left hand, then climbed onto the bench to their right and scooted aside a few bottles on the reagent shelf.

Hell.

He started climbing onto the other bench. When she straightened and stood upright on the top of the reagent shelving, he was already halfway up his own ad hoc stairway. The damn metal hood over the light was warm even through his gloves. Without the gloves, gripping the metal for any period of time would be impossible.

So, just ignore the heat.

And damn if it wasn't easy, from the top shelf, to ease his body onto the fixture. He stretched himself flat along the metal housing being careful not to let the metal of the gun clink against the lamp; mentally he tried to make his body a small, small thing.

He looked at Nova. She stared back and gave him a weak smile. She was probably realizing how rash this idea was. Had she considered, for example, how long the fixtures could bear a man's weight?

He recognized Singh's voice coming from the direction of the door he and Nova had used. If he'd just grabbed her and shoved her out the other door, like he'd wanted to, they'd have been out of here. The old doubt about her competence raised its head.

"I assure you, as I have before, if it takes, the treatment is irreversible. We shape the mind, we bend it permanently." Singh continued to jabber in English as he walked into the lab. Joe had already noted that Singh spoke better English than German.

Joe's biceps and thighs had the quivers. He wanted to move his head to see who Singh was talking to, but couldn't afford the risk.

"I have studied Jean Paul carefully. He is not only grateful for our support, he admires Helmut deeply. Make no mistake, the Loyalty Inducer will work on him. I have no more doubts. We can proceed with the dedication early tomorrow."

Joe looked again at Nova. She, too, lay tightly bunched, arms tucked, shoulders scrunched, head cocked.

"You know how critical König is," said a new voice. Deep. Confident. "If we use the Inducer and he isn't primed for the imprinting, he'll know something irregular is going on. He'll be alarmed, maybe lost to the cause. We can't lose König. He's unique."

"I am very sure of him." Singh's voice oozed assurance. "He is ours. And consider this. The man is an idealist. Should he gain any hint of what we are about, his current strong positive feelings for Helmut will shift. Then we absolutely will have lost him. It's risky to wait any longer."

Singh and friend now stood practically underneath the spot where he and Nova hung like captive flies in a spider's web. Joe couldn't imagine that one of the men wouldn't look up. His palms were slimy inside his gloves. His belly and thighs were heating up.

"It's settled then. He'll be dedicated. Tomorrow," said Singh's companion.

"You won't be disappointed. Jean Paul will never know that from that moment forward, our slightest wish, as they say, will be his command." The slight Indian laughed. It was a nasty giggle.

"Gall is on schedule for the fifteenth," said the deep voice.

"Good, good," Singh chuckled. "All the things we have planned for so long are advancing now with increasing speed. I have asked you here tonight, Maurus, because I have arranged a little after-hours demonstration. I have perfected the Rage Inducer."

Joe looked at Nova. She was alarmingly pale and her eyes were riveted on the two men standing directly below him. He wondered what she was thinking. Obviously, König was a dupe. Did that make her feel good since she'd always said her gut feeling was that she sensed no evil in him? Or did she feel bad? Because somehow Nova had definitely gotten her wires crossed on who had been in Manfred Wagner's library. Jean Paul couldn't possibly have been there.

Again footsteps in the hall. Just wonderful. That's all they needed, a goddam party.

"Here they are now," Singh said cheerily. "The demonstration can begin."

11:45 p.m.

Terrible danger. The words flooded Nova's mind and set her stomach to rolling. *Jean Paul is in terrible danger.*

Her finger squeezed hard against the gun's trigger guard. She thought of killing. Right now. Just blast Singh and the man with the grotesque, half-dead face. Clean up some ugly pus. A sure means to save Jean Paul from this filth.

But what about Gall? Her hand remained clenched. What was Gall? Whatever it was, Gall was going down in three—no, it was nearly the thirteenth now. Only two days.

God only knew how many other notables had been guests at this Compound. The solution here couldn't be as simple as letting her instincts flow out through the barrel of a gun. The Company had to know who else might have been ensnared.

Her stomach rolled with cramps. She forced her eyes open. Singh and colleague gazed expectantly toward the door. She heard what sounded like the wobbling wheel of a rolling cart. It came into view and she saw that it held two large-animal cages. Only their tops were visible to her, but she heard toenails clicking against the metal bottoms of the cages. And Wyczek was pushing the cart.

Her astonishment was huge but quickly absorbed. Of course. It made perfect sense. Somehow Hass had arranged for Wyczek to guard Jean Paul, the better to spy on him.

Her mind leaped off track. How had she gone so wrong at Manfred Wagner's? Wyczek had passed her in the hall and gone into the bird room and said, "There will be a meeting in the library in fifteen minutes." But Jean Paul was clearly not one of the conspirators. Then she remembered. Hass, too, had been in the bird room. Wyczek must have been speaking to Hass.

"Put them both in the room," the white-coated scientist said to Wyczek. "And put on a mask."

Nova's mind snapped back to the present. Wyczek opened the door of one cage and yanked a golden retriever out by its collar. He led the dog toward the small room.

Singh scurried toward a counter. "Let me show you what I've done with the ampoules." He motioned for the scary-looking man to follow. Two gas masks lay on the countertop. Singh handed one to Dead Face. "Maurus," Singh had called him. "There is very little likelihood of an ampoule breaking accidentally, but just to be sure."

The two men donned the masks. A prickle of alarm rushed over her scalp. She and Joe had no masks. Leaning over the counter, Singh grasped a handle, pushed down slightly. With a soft click, a section of the countertop slid back to reveal a two-foot square, white storage area. Lined up in rows, resting in miniature cradles, were small glass vials. She made a quick estimate—about fifty.

"I've color coded them," Singh continued.

Even behind his mask she could hear boyish pride in his voice, a grown man flaunting his fondest possession.

From her perch, Nova could just barely make out that the necks of the vials had colored bands around them.

The singsong voice continued cheerily. "The Sleep Inducer is green. Loyalty Inducer, yellow. Fight Inducer, brown. Tranquillity Inducer, orange. And this new Rage Inducer is marked in red." Singh pointed to one of the rows. "These purple ampoules are the Pacification Inducer. I'm sure you recall the demonstration. The subject immediately and permanently loses all will." Singh's voice came to her muffled through the mask, as if he were talking under water. "They are not merely calmed," he continued. "Under the influence of the Pacification Inducer, they do not voluntarily want or do anything. There is no drive. No ambition. Not even emotions like love and hate. And like most of these drugs, the effect is irreversible."

"Right," said Maurus. "The lobotomy vegetable thing."

Nova's loathing for Singh went ballistic. She envisioned a living human vegetable. She envisioned herself a living vegetable. Next to the horror of a painful, lingering death, her greatest fear was of losing control, of becoming a thing, of losing the grasp of one's destiny and dignity. She had suffered that feeling over and over as a child and had killed to escape it. And the sick scientist had consciously designed a drug to produce that result.

Singh's colleague made his own comment. "I can see many situations where we might wish to pacify. But the value of reducing subjects to vegetables escapes me."

"But, Maurus, just think! As long as the authorities do not know what to look for, they will find no trace. Within ten minutes of contacting air, the transmembrane carrier changes form and loses its characteristic coffee odor. The drug can be used surreptitiously to eliminate enemies. They will be physically alive but mentally dead, without any explanation. Or we might eventually openly describe the drug and threaten its use. A mindless existence is a terrifying prospect to any person. The drug becomes a tool for blackmail. And a very easy-to-use one."

Nova was looking at the back of Singh's head. A renewed urge to use the automatic tightened her finger on the trigger guard.

Wyczek had removed the two golden retrievers from their transport cages and, though she couldn't see the chamber, she presumed he'd moved them, as directed, into the small cubicle. Now, wearing a mask, he leaned against the bench directly beneath her. The top of his shiny head wasn't more than eight or nine feet away. Her imagination screamed that the bodyguard was so close he might be able to hear her breathe. Certainly he must hear the heartbeat that was a pounding throb in her ears.

She looked at Joe. The angle from Wyczek's head to Joe's stretched-out body was such that Wyczek's peripheral vision couldn't help but catch Joe's slightest body movement.

"Ah. We're ready," Singh said. He took one of the vials, a red-banded one. A "Rage Inducer," he'd called it. He crossed under her fluorescent hiding place, out of her line of vision. Her neck felt as stiff as the barrel of her gun. She probably couldn't move even if she dared.

"Golden retrievers are especially appropriate subjects for this testing. The breed is normally quite docile. In addition, these two are littermates. They have been caged together and never fight." Singh's minilecture settled it. She simply had to see what happened. She had to risk moving at least a little.

Watching Wyczek, still slouched against the bench, Nova slowly rotated her head. She honestly thought she could hear her neck creaking.

The lamp housing blocked her view of the cubicle's two doors, but she could clearly see its interior. The retrievers sat watching Singh through the glass, one with his tongue lolled out and both with happy, slobbery grins and trusting brown eyes.

Singh placed the red-banded ampoule into a tube built into the cubicle's glass wall. He twisted a knob. The ampoule slid down the tube into a small cup inside the room. Earlier she'd noticed thick rubber gloves also built into the glass wall. Singh thrust his hands into the gloves, picked up the vial and snapped its stem. "It will take approximately five seconds," he said.

She couldn't think of anything but the dogs—and John Wiley's burning coffee. Fury, wordless and incoherent, welled deep in her chest. Her throat tightened. Her vision wavered. *Stay cool, stay cool.*

The drug kicked in. Both dogs stood, went momentarily rigid, then their lips curled. And then biting, thrashing, lunging and ripping began. Blood was drawn at once when the retriever with a slight reddish cast to his coat gashed the muzzle of his companion.

Through the glass, she could even hear, faintly, the guttural sounds of their rage. A strip of bloody fur flapped back and forth on the shoulder of one. Other wounds soon appeared on both dogs. White teeth in a foaming mouth ripped off an ear of the other. Whatever had been their dominance relationship before, neither signaled surrender now, neither gave way, neither gave quarter.

The dog with the reddish coat sliced a gash down its companion's hind leg. Nova expected the wounded animal to howl, cower, surrender. Dragging its leg, it continued to attack. She pinched her eyes closed and squeezed the lamp housing tightly.

Stop it! her mind screamed. She flushed hot all over with her own "induced" rage.

"My God." Maurus's deep voice.

"Impressive, no?" The scientist said.

"I think they're getting tired. Will they stop?" Maurus again.

"Watch."

Nova forced her eyes open. The dogs formed one lump of thrashing fur on the floor. Tiring, they had dug their teeth into each other and were pummeling with their feet. Great steaks of blood fanned out around them on the floor and more was being added every second. Again she squeezed her eyes shut. *You loveless piece of shit, Singh!*

"Ah," Singh sighed. "We've hit a jugular. Now watch this. Because the drug's effect is irreversible, the winner will continue to tear at the dead animal until total exhaustion downs it. See." Singh's voice fairly burbled with the pleasure of creation. "When the subject recovers from exhaustion, it begins the attack again."

The man with the droopy face stepped into Nova's line of view and leaned close to the glass partition. If he looked up and she and Joe were discovered, she'd have no alternative but to kill them.

Maurus put a hand on the scientist's arm. "I've seen enough." The men turned from the window and removed their masks. "But this is good work. Exciting. A valuable weapon for our arsenal. You deserve every reward I've ever supplied you."

"Thank you," Singh said, giving one of his froglike smiles. "As ever, I serve the cause."

Dead Face headed for the door, disappeared.

Singh looked at Wyczek. "Kill the one that's still alive and clean up." He removed his lab coat and hung it on a peg beside the cubicle door. "I will want their brains for tests, so put their bodies in the freezer."

"Yes, Herr Doktor Singh."

"And don't forget to either wait ten minutes or purge the chamber before you enter."

"Yes, Herr Doktor."

Singh left. Wyczek disappeared, presumably waiting beside the small cubicle's outer door. After maybe a minute he entered and walked to where she could see him. He must have somehow activated a purging system rather than wait ten minutes. He held a knife. He grasped the head of the exhausted but still snapping retriever and slit its throat. A vivid red arc sprayed across the glass and Wyczek dropped the dog's head to the floor like so much garbage.

Bile burned its way to her mouth. She swallowed hard. Inside her gloves her hands swam in sweat. She looked at Joe. His lips were set in a thin hard line, his eyebrows drawn together tightly.

Wyczek seemed to take forever to clean up, having to hose down the walls and floor. When he left, he turned out the lab light and the room fell into twilight from the hall illumination. She and Joe waited on their slowly cooling perches. After perhaps ten minutes, when she climbed down, it was with difficulty: her muscles still shook, a letdown from tension, fatigue and anger.

"You okay?" Joe asked.

"Are you?"

He smiled—a warm, tender smile she'd not seen before. "Not really."

"Looks like I'm the one who's going to be buying the cappuccino in the future. You were dead right about Hass. And who do you think the guy with the scary face is?"

"One of the Alyeska pipeline terrorists. No idea. I got only a quick glimpse, but I knew I'd seen his face before. He was in the Anchorage airport. What's obvious, though, is that König doesn't have a clue about what's going on here."

"I have to tell him, Joe. As soon as we return to the bungalows." In fact, her feet wanted to take her to Jean Paul this instant. "We have to stop this 'dedication' thing."

Joe frowned. "You've always liked the guy, but we can't risk telling him. He definitely admires Hass. He might take what you say to Hass. We can't risk it. We're not through till we find out what Gall is and, most importantly, we have to have hard proof that Helmut Hass is The Founder."

Chapter 26

Nova was relieved to the depth of her soul that Jean Paul was innocent in this deadly game. Joe had no way to know the true quality of her feelings for Jean Paul, and now wasn't the time for long explanations. But she couldn't let Jean Paul be sacrificed.

"We have to contact the Company," she said resolutely. "We have to tell Jean Paul."

Joe's frown deepened. "We can't blow this entire mission for him."

Nova clenched one fist. "Let me be very, very clear. I know what's at stake." She locked gazes with Joe. His dark eyes were glittering with anger. "I've done terrible things in my life. I've killed. I've done prison time. I've done things for the CIA you'll never know about. But I will *not* let Jean Paul be destroyed by this monster. I'll not let this 'dedication' happen."

A rock-hard stare from her partner continued as he absorbed her challenge. For a brief moment she envisioned dropping to her knees and begging Joe to do this one thing for her. Agent Cardone, though, would never compromise Operation Jacaranda to save one man. But she knew Jean Paul could be trusted. He didn't have to be turned into a walking zombie.

Joe looked at her a moment, as if searching for a reason to trust his life to her. He glanced at his watch. "It's already two forty-five. Jean Paul and everyone else is sleeping. Let's search this friggin' place down to the cracks in the walls. Let's find what we need. Then we go back to the bungalows, pick up König and take him with us, willingly or not, and go into Turm. The Company can take it from there, and you won't have to decide whether we risk telling him or not."

Her mind did battle with her heart. Jean Paul wouldn't wake for hours. Joe was right that it would be foolish to abandon their search now. But he'd agreed to save Jean Paul. She'd won the battle, but she couldn't help but feel she still had to win the war with Joe.

They picked up their search where they'd left off. Apparently all three men had cleared out. The corridor lights were still on but the halls had taken on a deathly quiet. The complex was surprisingly large. Searching went slow. In a research section, they found other animal rooms and labs. Drawers, cupboards, desks and filing cabinets had to be checked without leaving evidence of violation.

The smell of garlic hovered in a small kitchen. An adjacent room had bunks, as if people sometimes worked round-the-clock schedules. It was late, nearly five in the morning, when in the southeast section they found a communications room and, next to it, a computer room. She stared at the computer terminal. "When we met, your cover was IBM representative. So exactly how much do you actually know about computers, Mr. IBM Man?"

He grinned and flexed his fingers. "Some."

"I think Gall will be in here."

"There's a possibility we'll find only scientific stuff. This is a big mother, though. Japanese. This thing could handle anything scientific and keep track of Hass's little terrorist actions without breaking into even a light sweat. The whole hump's secure. There seems to be no reason for Hass not to use it."

"We have to be away from here before first light." She checked her watch. "Twenty, twenty-five minutes max. Hustle."

Joe fiddled some, then said, "Hot damn. No log on, no passwords required. These creeps feel real secure."

She thought about Singh's Loyalty Inducer—soon to be used on Jean Paul. Perhaps only irreversibly "dedicated" personnel were allowed into the hump, personnel so loyal Singh hadn't protected his computer files. If that was the explanation for this security lapse, and if what she and Joe wanted was in this computer, Singh's reliance on his drug's efficacy was going to prove to be his downfall. She would relish the irony.

Joe tapped several more keys and a menu, in German, appeared on the screen.

She began translating words and acronyms. Joe kept clicking the mouse. Finally he turned and smiled. "The system's definitely not connected outside. I'll bet you one cup of the many cups of cappuccino you owe me that the files won't be coded. Just named. I bet their networking with the outside world is done from the mainframe in Building No. 3 and they bring copies of things in here." He grinned widely. "The best security possible—unless of course someone brilliant breaches their mountain fortress."

They found a menu for a long list of scientific software. Then a mammoth directory in which a few files had somewhat recognizable names—Blood Brain Barrier was one.

Her concentration drifted from the computer screen as something to their left caught her eye. She said, "There's another door into here."

The keyboard console occupied the center of the forty-by-forty-foot room; the computer sat in sections along the walls. And there was a break in the pattern. She strode to the door. Joe followed. The door was the color of the room's ceiling and walls. It wasn't hidden, but it wasn't obvious, either. Easy to overlook.

She said, "Where do you think it goes?"

He shrugged. They stepped into the corridor. The adjacent room was for storage, but there had to be something—a narrow passage or elevator—between them. He said, "My guess is, the door leads outside somewhere."

She tugged him back to the computer. "Let's get what we came for and get out."

So far it was all Singh's stuff. She began to doubt, and time was racing by. Joe explored some more and they came up with a directory that included "German Homeland Party."

Two clicks and the screen projected a German Homeland subdirectory.

Joe clicked as Nova read through the files. The first file was finances. Nothing suggested a terrorist operation.

Two files later she got excited. She put her finger to the screen. "Try this one, Joe. It means Earth's Warriors."

The Earth's Warrior subdirectory immediately delivered something they wanted. Under the title "Members" they found a list of names. Brief biographies were listed under three categories. Warriors, where they found Wyczek. Supporters—Manfred Wagner was included—and Tools—politicians, judges, even movie stars. She recognized more than half of the names, including Peter Grund's, Jean Paul's and Senator Legnett's.

"We should have been out of here over forty minutes ago." Joe checked his watch. "We're running way behind schedule."

"This one says 'Dedications,' Joe."

The list of names under Dedications was arranged by date. She caught her breath. She pointed to Jean Paul's name and beside it was today's date. She pulled her hand back and tucked it under her arm. Clearly, unless she did something, and soon, Jean Paul would soon become a permanent Hass fan.

Other names followed Jean Paul's, including hers, but not Joe's. Next to Nova's name the space for the dedication date remained blank.

Then they hit gold. "Operations," she said. The actions had the usual clever nicknames, among them Calling Card, the Tahiti air crash; Roadrunner, the Glen Canyon dam attempt; Viper, the Alaskan pipeline; Wormwood, the Rolls factory; and Gall. Joe opened the Gall file and Nova began translating it out loud. The target was a hotel in Munich. Clearly, Hass intended to blow up the whole of one side of the building. But was it the building or someone in the building he was after?

Nova stopped reading. "Let's copy it. All of it. Then

figure it out. I want that copy in my hands. This is all we need to convince the Company and to nail these slime."

They were now way past the time they had planned to be back at the bungalows. Most unfortunately, Jean Paul would likely have been up for quite a while, wondering where the heck she was.

While the computer copied, she started reading the screen to Joe again, then clarity hit her. "I can't believe it," she said. "It's not just the hotel. God in heaven. It's the German chancellor, Joe. They're going to assassinate Chancellor Gottfried. I saw on the news that he's been in Munich for a couple of days now."

Joe handed her the copied disk and returned the screen to the prompt. They had a little less than forty-eight hours, but still plenty of time to deliver the goods to Cupid and to stop Gall.

Nova felt rather than heard a whoosh from the direction of the second door behind them and to the left. "How did you get in here?" Singh's singsong voice demanded.

Joe stiffened. Nova whirled. He noted that she hid the disk behind her by slipping it under her shirt and into her waistband. Joe reached under his arm for the Sig but Wyczek's familiar voice bellowed, "*Hande hoch!* Stand up and turn around." He did as directed. There stood Singh and Wyczek. Behind them, in the doorway was König.

Had König been dedicated already? So soon? Joe supposed it was possible.

Only Wyczek was armed—with a 9 mm Beretta. The very model of Beretta, Joe knew, whose great flaw was that if you could just get your hand over the slide, the gun couldn't be fired. His mind clicked off the distance between his right hand and the Beretta's barrel.

"Both of you. Remove your guns slowly, with two fingers," Wyczek demanded. "Place them on the floor." He nodded. "Kick them over there. In the corner."

Joe complied even though he thought he should take Wyczek now.

Singh backed out the door, looked down the hall, and yelled, "Stephan, Fritz."

Wyczek's weapon wavered slightly in Nova's direction. Joe charged, his hand stretching out in hope for the slide. First shot—wild. Second shot—a hot branding iron slammed into his shoulder. He crashed into Wyczek. They toppled. They rolled right. Wyczek ended up on top.

Singh screamed. "Stop her, Jean Paul!"

Another gunshot, painfully loud and close to Joe's head.

He tried to raise his right arm. Useless. Wyczek's fist slammed into his chin and Joe bit his tongue. He clamped his left hand on Wyczek's throat and, as the sound of running feet grew louder, squeezed hard.

Wyczek rammed both beefy arms upward, easily stripping Joe's hand away. He grabbed Joe's dangling right arm, pulled on it and twisted. A fiery agony ripped up his arm and across his shoulders. Black soup swam in front of Joe's eyes.

Wyczek flipped him; Joe flopped like a beached porpoise onto his stomach. Another man rammed a knee in the center of his back and his breath whooshed out. Grimly, Joe wondered, Could this be the delightful Stephan or Fritz joining us?

Together, the new guy and Wyczek tied his hands. They

rolled him onto his back and the white-hot branding iron again poked its scalding way through his shoulder.

A second man, stocky and blond with a nose that had been broken at least once, held a gun on Nova. He glared at her and was nursing a bleeding wrist. Apparently the third shot had been a hit by Nova.

Singh was so pale he could have passed for Hass's brother. And Jean Paul stood with his back against the door frame. He was dazed and looking as though he hadn't moved the width of a cat's whisker. Not good.

Wyczek barked something in German to Singh. Wyczek had figured out the obvious: Singh's mind seemed momentarily out of commission. After a second, Singh said, "Yes." To the broken-nosed blond, Wyczek rattled off something else and nodded toward Nova. Then while Wyczek babbled into a wall intercom, the husky blond used a length of computer cable to tie Nova as Joe was tied, hands behind her back.

Wyczek finished at the intercom. He gestured to the blond who hauled on the cord around Joe's wrist to lift Joe to his feet. The fire in his shoulder flared again, followed by the momentary darkness and a spinning sensation. Their entourage trouped down the hall, he and Nova leading, each with a gun at their back. Singh and Jean Paul brought up the rear. The parade marched north, turned left and ended up at the security door that Joe had earlier guessed led into Building No. 1. They descended a flight of stairs, exited the stairwell and stood in front of an identical door.

Singh pushed his lab coat sleeve up and placed the lower side of his forearm over the detector. Slick as a whistle, the doors opened, revealing another corridor, even wider. *Probably runs under the research buildings.*

Two electric carts hugged one wall. The seven of them clambered aboard, Joe being shoved onto the back seat of one and Nova the back seat of the other, a guard each glued to their sides. It occurred to him that no one other than himself seemed the least interested in how much blood he might be losing.

Singh and Wyczek took the steering wheels. Jean Paul was acting peculiar as hell. He'd said nothing. Now he sat ramrod stiff next to Singh.

The two carts hummed down the corridor passing four steel doors at distances corresponding to one door for each of the four research buildings. They angled right briefly, then went north again. They had to be heading for the mansion.

Heartsick, Nova studied Jean Paul. The look on his face, a lost-child look, made her long to hold him. He kept touching a white gauze patch on his forearm. This was a nightmare. It couldn't be real.

She clenched her fists, tightening the bonds on her wrists, which dug painfully into her skin. She relaxed her hands and ran her fingers over the upholstered cart seat. They would search her. If she could get rid of the disk, she and Joe could try to deny knowing anything of substance. The crease between the seat and back pads felt almost deep enough. From the corner of her eye she gauged her captor's attention: she didn't think he'd notice—if she moved slowly. She slid her hand inside her waistband, fingered the disk up and out, slipped the disk into the crease, pushed it down, then ran the tips of her fingers over the spot. Maybe an eighth of an inch, no more, of disk stuck out. With luck, no one would see it.

Singh and Wyczek stopped the carts. The two guards,

Stephan and Fritz, yanked her and Joe to their feet, marched them into what appeared to be a large, subterranean office, and shoved them onto metal, straight-backed chairs.

Happily, she'd gotten off one shot—Broken Nose was nursing a bleeding wrist—but the other man had piled onto her like a leech hopping a blood meal. Wyczek spoke to the taller, dark-haired thug, a big man with a slight limp. "Go to the studio and find something to tie them to the chairs."

In a time all too brief, Limper was back and wrapping a quarter-inch nylon cord several times around her chest, binding her to the chair's seat back. He gave Joe—whose bloodied arm looked useless—the same treatment. Joe's jaw muscles worked furiously during the whole procedure. She didn't want to imagine how his arm felt, and she prayed his wound was superficial. Blood drenched his sleeve. She saw droplets on the floor.

In a corner, still avoiding her gaze, Jean Paul hunched in a wing-backed chair. Singh paced in front of a large desk. He'd finally stopped jabbering to Wyczek and Jean Paul about how angry the man named Maurus was going to be.

A bronze statue behind the desk caught her eye. It was grotesque. The figure—a man—was cutting the skin from his own body. She spied another statue on a corner pedestal. The female form had her mouth open in a silent scream as she held her severed fingers. A violent shiver shook Nova and left her muscles quivering. What kind of sick mind would create such monstrosities?

Silent minutes dragged by. Then Maurus arrived. He glanced around the room, then spoke in German. "Sorry you've been subjected to this mess, Jean Paul. It seems this woman isn't what she appears to be. She and her friend intend to sabotage your campaign. I have to find out who they represent."

To her surprise Jean Paul finally spoke. "Yes," he said simply.

She could scarcely credit her ears; he sounded like a zombie.

"I think you should leave. Would you like to leave?" Maurus said to Jean Paul.

"No."

Maurus looked to Singh. "Should he leave?"

The scientist was toying with items on the desk. "It will make no difference one way or the other, except that he is going to be privy to more than we originally planned. He's in shock now. Something I've not seen before. I believe because of a conflict between the conditioning to our cause and his exceptionally strong feelings for the woman. But the shock will pass. I am certain he will be functional soon. A day or two at most."

Maurus looked at Joe. Switching to English, he said, "Who the fuck are you?"

Joe said nothing. Maurus signaled Wyczek. Using his gun butt, the bodyguard struck Joe on the side of the head. Blood spurted from Joe's cheek. She felt the blow in the center of her chest.

"How did you gain entry to the mountain?"

Again silence. Again a blow to Joe's face.

Her underarms were sweaty, her fisted hands moist and hot. The muscle in her left calf began to quiver. She promised herself that if he hit Joe again, she'd kill Wyczek.

Maurus turned to Singh and reverted to German. "Clearly we're under suspicion. But that isn't proof. If they still haven't delivered proof to their bosses, we're safe. We'll just delay Gall—"

"Yes," Singh interrupted, "but shouldn't we assume they know everything? I have been thinking. Shouldn't we leave here at once?"

Maurus gave the twitching scientist a brutal stare. "Don't be a fool. If they had proof or had passed proof on, do you think they'd still be here? It's much more likely we've caught them in time. But we do have to know for sure. My guess is they're CIA." He shook his head. "I have no time for this."

He walked behind the desk, opened the top center drawer, took out a pair of shears, handed them across the desk to Wyczek and said in German, "Cut off their shirts. Fritz, you take some of the clothing to Bruno. Have him sniff every square inch of the Compound. I want to know every place these two have set a foot."

Wyczek cut up the belly, under the ropes and through the neck of Joe's lightweight cotton sweater, then out the arms. Like a hunter stripping the skin from a kill, he peeled the shirt off Joe's body. When he came to her, Wyczek skewered her with his eyes, smiling an oily leer. He began to cut, rubbed his rough hands slowly across her belly and then over her breasts.

Maurus snapped, "Don't waste time."

When Wyczek finished, he gave the clothing to Fritz, the Limper, who raced out to take them to the Compound's German shepherd sniffer.

After ordering Singh to return to the computer to find out whether she and Joe had damaged it or the files, their tormentor smiled at Jean Paul and, in German, told him, "Go with Herr Doktor Singh. I want you to stay with him until he knows if the computer and its programs are secure. Then I want you to come with him to report to me."

Singh hurried toward the door. Nova watched as Jean Paul rose from the chair like an old, old man. The handsome features drooped. The lost-and-fearful-child look was gone now. His eyes were simply dull. Her heart wept as he followed Singh out the door like an obedient slave. Jean Paul was gone.

Maurus turned to Stephan. "We can't change our command center in the middle of the operation. But we have to tighten security. Do it."

Stephan left, leaving only four of them in the office. To Wyczek, Maurus said, "We have to know what they know, who they represent, how much they may have told anyone, and most important, if they've found or passed any proof. Find out however you can, as fast as you can. I'll be in Communications."

Giving Joe a final look of burning disgust, the man with the flaccid face left her and Joe in Wyczek's hands.

"So what the hell is going on?" Joe asked Wyczek. "I can see why Hass is pissed with our snooping around for his formula, but what's with all the violence? We didn't find anything. Wouldn't throwing us off the grounds be sufficient punishment?"

Wyczek snorted a chuckle. "Industrial espionage? We're not into fairy tales, Cardone."

The bodyguard—or whatever he really was—circled behind the desk, sat and propped his feet up. With eyes as cold as a meat locker and just as dead as its contents, he silently studied them. Finally he put his feet on the floor. "I think this'll work best if we start with you, Cardone."

The door opened and in walked Hass. The White

Praying Mantis had arrived. Scowling, he snapped in German, "Get out of that chair."

Wyczek obeyed and came out from behind the desk.

"I was told they were here," Hass continued in German. "I want the woman."

"Maurus told me to interrogate them."

"You can have the man," the White Mantis said, "but I want the woman."

Tendrils of fear that had been writhing in her stomach became coiling spirals that made it hard for her to breathe.

A smile, full of acid, curled Hass's lips.

He stared pointedly at her breasts, cupped in a black bra. A thin White Mantis digit reached forward and caressed the tip of one nipple. An electric wave of revulsion flashed over her entire body. In English he said, "We shall spend some time together, you and I. Indeed, we will get to know each other quite—intimately."

Chapter 27

10:20 a.m.

Hass marched Nova down a short corridor, still headed north away from the mountain. They turned right and marched maybe another hundred feet. Hass, having taken her gun from Wyczek, repeatedly jabbed the muzzle into her spine. Apprehension—better not to call it panic—constricted her throat. She tried to but couldn't ignore the niches along the corridor holding more bronze monstrosities.

You can survive. You know you can.

Several steps before they reached a door, Hass commanded, "Stop." He stepped around her and pushed open the door. Beyond lay cosmic darkness. An acid smile twisted his pink lips. "After you, my dear."

The wave of panic flushed up again and on its crest,

fear of the dark unknown. *Don't give him the satisfaction of seeing weakness.*

Hass followed behind her and flipped on the light. The large room was a sculptor's studio. In one corner stood a four-poster bed, handcuffs attached to each post.

"What have you done to Jean Paul?" she asked.

"Jean Paul will soon be elected Bavarian representative. Then he will run for the chancellorship. What has happened to him in no way hurts him. It simply makes him loyal, permanently."

That explained why they were going to kill Chancellor Gottfried. To ensure that Jean Paul would be elected. Gottfried was deeply respected, a man actually philosophically akin to Jean Paul. Doubtless the only man who might have a chance to defeat Jean Paul. "You're going to kill me, aren't you?"

"Not yet."

He waved the gun toward another uncomfortable-looking, straight-backed, metal chair. "Sit!" he commanded.

She forced down another surge of panic. If Hass meant what he said and made the mistake of not killing her at once, she still had hope.

"You are feeling uncomfortable, are you not?"

She refused to play.

He ignored her pointed silence and went on. "It is a terrible thing to lack control of oneself. I personally can think of nothing worse than the humiliation it involves. A great deal of the distress you are feeling stems from knowing you are no longer in charge of your life—and never will be again. You know I control it."

The mass in her stomach exploded and shivers swept over her skin in waves. There wasn't any point calling this anxiety. This was galloping fear, and Hass had named its exact source.

"Psychiatrists say the happiest people are ones who feel they command their destiny." He was almost crooning to her. "This is true regardless of whether, in fact, anyone can actually guide their fate. To achieve happiness, it is enough for people to merely feel they are in control. We will have time to talk about destiny."

As quick as the flash of a strobe, she understood him. Hass was an ultimate control freak. Not just of his own life, a compulsion they shared. No, Hass needed to control others, body and soul. She wondered what in his past might have so twisted his spirit—and as a result, left her helpless now in an insane man's clutches.

He smiled again, a sly, knowing smile. "I am now in charge of your fate. I imagine it would surprise you to know that I plan to make you immortal."

Wyczek grinned at Joe. "I gotta piss. Then we get down to business." He chuckled, the first time Joe had ever heard Wyczek make any sound of pleasure. The bodyguard stood, walked to the door and said, "I'll be back." He stepped out and closed the door.

Hell. The creep even sounded like Arnold Schwartzenegger in *The Terminator.* Same accent.

Joe squirmed against the metal chair. His arms were bound behind it and his chest was tied to it, but his legs were free. He tried to wiggle down and out. No go. The rope was way too tight.

He was pretty sure he was still bleeding, but more slowly, thank God. For maybe twenty minutes his arm had been more or less numb. He hopped the chair once toward the door. Sparklers shot through his head. If he could crash the chair into the door when Wyczek came through, maybe he could throw the guard off balance.

He hopped the chair again. And again. Ignoring the hot flashes of pain, he made it to the door. If he positioned the chair too close to the door, he couldn't hit Wyczek with much force. He'd only make the sonofabitch mad. Too far back and he might miss altogether and topple harmlessly backward.

He heard footsteps and the door opened. Automatically, he slammed his feet against the floor and thrust backward.

With a resounding *wham,* the chair back struck the door and the door bounded backward and cracked Wyczek in the forehead. *"Sheist!"* Wyczek yelled. He lurched forward and bumped into the door again, then fell onto one knee.

Joe kicked backward at the door. It rebounded again from the bodyguard's head. Wyczek tilted forward, put a hand out to break his momentum. Joe whipped the same leg sideways. His foot connected with the side of Wyczek's head. He was clearly dazed. The door hit the chair then swung backward and closed. The chair toppled and Joe crashed to the floor on his right side.

"I didn't like how you touched Nova," Joe muttered, kicking again: the arch of his foot connected with the bridge of Wyczek's nose. Through his shoe, he felt the nose give. Blood gushed. Wyczek collapsed sideways and rolled onto his back.

With his arm in fiery agony, Joe twisted and wriggled to a better angle. He lifted his foot, then smashed the back of his shoe's curved heel onto the man's bleeding nose. The crunch this time was sickening.

Shaking from exertion, he took in a deep breath.

Wyczek's eyes were wide open and lifeless.

Joe's arm burned as though someone had lit gasoline on it. "Bloody mess." With his right leg he pushed against the floor and twisted his shoulders and tipped the solid chair so his back was against the floor. Pain lanced through his hands, which were still tied behind his back, and he rolled again so that he was lying on his left side where, at least, the overall agony was less.

He needed to stand. He rolled facedown onto his knees. The damn chair made him crouch into a bent-over position and he couldn't straighten his legs to rise. He just kept scooting backward.

This was ridiculous; he was on the floor and hog-tied to a chair. He glared at the door's shiny brass knob, unreachable, four feet above his head. Nova was out there somewhere with Hass. Possibilities of what was happening to her kept flashing through his mind. He clenched his fists. He was useless.

Struggling to control his anger, Helmut Hass moved the spotlights. He needed a better angle on the chair in which Nova Blair sat. Later he would move the lights back to their usual place in front of the bed.

He flicked them on. She blinked several times. Using his left hand, his gun still fixed on her, he placed new tapes into the video recorders and started recording.

From the moment he'd received Maurus's call, he'd been infuriated. Jean Paul had led informers into the heart of their operation. If not controlled, his rage could confound his judgment.

Perhaps they would be required to flee—a contingency he'd never believed they would have to use. But Maurus seemed to think not. So until Maurus said otherwise, Hass would proceed as he had done with all the others.

He addressed her. "You should not be thinking immortal in the sense of living forever, of course." His lips felt dry. He licked them. "Perhaps that will be the brilliant Dr. Singh's next project for Hass Chemie. But, no. I mean, immortal in the artistic sense." He spoke slowly, for emphasis. "I intend to make you the subject of my next sculpture. Perhaps you noticed some of my work along the hall."

He watched her face closely. She had remarkable poise. Only the close-up camera would catch the tiny twitch at the corner of the eyes, a tiny blink. There was no swallowing, no blanching, to hint that she understood, but she did. She'd seen his statues and she was afraid. "What do you think of that prospect?"

He waited, but she said nothing. Not surprising. Remaining silent was probably what she'd been trained to do.

"Since my having you is so unexpected, I have, naturally, no theme yet for your piece. But I can share with you the general subject on which my thoughts have concentrated of late. The obedience relationship of the controlled and the controller. My first pieces were inspired by Dante's *Inferno,* but I have begun to add some of my own punishments. Are you familiar with Dante?"

Again he paused. She was still doing a heroic job of revealing little, but her breathing was a bit more shallow, her nostrils slightly flared. She was afraid but also angry. Defiant. *Superb.* Of course she must be of tempered steel to be in such a business. Their obedience conflict would be a great test of wills. This strong woman might well inspire him to his greatest work.

"As I'm sure you know, Dante was a writer who described with remarkable imagination the eternal punishments which would befall individuals who would not submit to divine authority. You and I are going to have a test of wills, and you will learn to bend yours to mine. And when you do not, I, like the omnipotent God, will deliver a proper punishment."

She'd begun blinking more frequently. Wonderful!

"Have you wondered about my sculpting methods?" He removed the cattle prod, the carton razor and a roll of tape from the drawer and placed them on the center table where she could study them. Her control was good, but her eyes widened in the way that always excited him. "I use live models, Nova. It's what gives the pieces such realism and power." He picked up the cattle prod. "We will begin with something simple."

Until she was bound to the chair, he must be very careful. He mustn't get into a position where she could disarm him.

"This is my first command. Kneel and then lie down on your belly."

She didn't move and he felt the beginnings of arousal. He let his mind linger on the sensation a moment.

He nodded at the prod in his hand and explained in a patient tone. "This is a cattle prod, intended to stun a misbehaving animal. A negative reinforcer, the psychologists call it. It has three settings and will cause you a great deal of pain at any of the settings. I will repeat myself only one time, Nova. Lie down on your belly."

She looked at him, and he had to fight a flicker of anger. What he saw was disgust.

He touched her arm with the prod. She stiffened, but did not cry out.

"Do as I ordered," he repeated softly.

He waited.

He touched her again with the prod at the same spot, and again she bit back a cry of pain, but she dropped out of the chair and onto her knees in front of it. A tiny drop of blood appeared on her lower lip.

"Lie on your belly." He waited again.

Her head was bowed, as if she were praying. He had never possessed a subject this physically intriguing, man or woman. Somehow her exotic beauty would have to be incorporated into her punishment. Perhaps its defacement.

He touched her with the prod again. She jerked even more forcefully and then collapsed face first onto the floor. But she did not cry out. Her jaw muscles strained. Her back rose and fell with labored breathing.

I'll be okay. He said he won't kill me. Whatever happens, I'll be okay.

The voice in Nova's head sounded twelve years old. What was happening to her?

A sense of residual electricity at the prod's point of contact had her nerves squirting paroxysms of neural alarms and her muscles cramping in mass confusion. Her flesh, where the prod had touched, seemed on fire. Candido had used candle wax.

Remember, said the child in her mind, *the pain goes away.*

She heard Hass set the prod down. He stepped close. From the corner of her eye, she could see the razor in one hand and the gun in the other. An icy wave of alarm ripped through her. He knelt beside her thigh, ran the muzzle of the gun down the center of her back and said, "I'm going to cut your hands free, but do not move when they are loose or you may never move again. Do you understand?" He prodded the gun muzzle against the base of her spine.

She nodded, revolted at how eager she was to obey. *I always did exactly what Candido asked.* The spasms in her arms seemed to shake her whole body.

He placed the tape beside her, then cut the ropes with the razor and quickly moved in front of her. "Get up, slowly, and pick up the tape and sit in the chair again."

She complied, her knees wobbly. Submission was the way she'd always responded—and she'd loathed herself. Right up to the moment she'd plunged the knife into Candido's side, she'd loathed herself. Her trial shrink had said, "Killing Candido saved your sister Star. You did what you had to." But the thought of her body coupled with Candido's still triggered panicky feelings of loathing and shame and guilt. Feelings that made her want to curl into a ball in a dark corner and never uncurl again.

Because sometimes you enjoyed what he did.

No. No. No. No!

She felt her mind tiptoeing away to hide. Some truths were unbearable.

"Take the tape and bind your right leg to the right leg of the chair."

She plucked at the edge of the tape, pulled a few inches free. She bent down toward her right leg.

"That's right," he said.

She started to wrap the tape around her pant leg.

"No," he snapped. "Pull up your pant leg. I want you to tape your bare leg to the chair. As soon as you are secure, I will remove those slacks."

He's an amateur. She wanted to believe that. Only a sickly, pale copy of Candido. *I prevailed then. I will again.* But her heart said Candido's brutality had been, in comparison, merely average lust. Helmut Hass's was a practiced, systematic evil.

She tried to think of a way out of this new nightmare as she did a reasonably efficient job of securing her leg.

"Now the left leg."

Her fingers were trembling. Even his videotapes would see her fingers shaking.

"Now use your right hand and tape down your left forearm."

She darted her gaze around the room, looking for another door, as though there were some possibility she might be able to leap up and run out.

"I have asked you to do something once, Nova. Do it, or I shall be forced to use the prod again."

She looked at him, narrowed her eyes. *Obey, Nova, and you will be utterly in his power. Do you remember your own words, Never again?* She dropped the tape in her lap. "I'm not going to tie my hands for you or any man, you piece of shit."

The prod produced a click as he advanced the setting a notch. He touched it to her belly. She couldn't stop the scream. Her hands flew to the arms of the chair, clenched them so hard her knuckles seemed to melt into the metal. She slumped forward and gasped for breath.

"Do what I asked."

"Never."

"You must do what I ask or the pain will come again."

He waited a few moments.

She couldn't think.

"Nova! Do what I ask."

"Never," she managed to whisper.

* * *

Nova's hair hid her face. Hass worried that she might be sufficiently stressed that if he used the prod again she could very well pass out. "Throw the tape to me."

With shaking fingers, he watched as she took it from her lap and threw it into the far corner.

"That was childish." He walked to the drawer, took out another roll of tape, unwound several inches of it and walked to her right side. "Put your arms onto the chair."

She crossed her arms over her chest.

If he wanted to secure her, he had to risk putting down the gun. He dropped the gun to the floor and leaped to her. He grabbed her right arm, pulled it down, wound the tape twice around, binding her arm to the chair. A burning sensation raked his face.

He straightened, struck her back-handed, and stepped in front of her. She thrust fingers of her free hand toward his eyes. He grabbed her flailing left arm and taped it down. Bitch! he wanted to scream at her, but he didn't because the videotape was running. The intercom buzzed three times. Singh's buzz.

He flipped the wall switch. "Hass *hier*," he snapped.

Singh spoke in excited German. "Have you seen Maurus? I must find him at once, Helmut. Our target will leave Munich a day early. We must cancel."

"When did you receive the message?"

"Only moments ago."

"Maurus assures me we are still secure. In which case you need only advance the operation by a day." He checked the clock on the workbench. Apparently, if they were going to run the operation at all, Gall would have to go in less than twenty-three hours. Only Maurus would know if that were possible. "I will try to find him. He can take the helicopter and easily go to Munich and return in time if necessary. I suggest you begin what preparations you can to advance the action."

"Are you…?"

"Do not argue. Just do it." He switched the intercom off.

He walked to the Blair woman and caught a fistful of her hair. She tried to twist away. He slid a finger inside her bra and rubbed hard round the nipple, to hurt her. "You are mine, bitch. But it seems we are to be interrupted. That's the way of things sometimes, is it not? Plans become disrupted. You, for example, are not having the day you planned. Well, I must find out if our latest project can be completed. If so, in a few hours, in less than a day to be precise, I will share with you the good news of our success."

He withdrew his finger. "Until then, I trust you will wait for me here."

When he'd left her, Hass had shut off all the room's lights. The silence and darkness were absolute. Nova sat in a tomb.

She'd worn herself out thrashing and twisting. Her arms and legs burned. Now she rested. The exertion had helped distract her thoughts from Jean Paul, from the monstrous statues, from the White Mantis and his plans for her. But as she sat still in the darkness, nightmare visions uncoiled again. All the living models for Hass's monstrosities had been here before her. Their pain cried out from the walls.

She forced her thoughts to Cupid. When their next scheduled message wasn't found in the cola-can drop, he'd know something was wrong. But without proof, there would be nothing Cupid could or would do while she was within the Compound.

And Joe. It was good she and Joe had found "The Fucker," as Joe so enthusiastically persisted in calling him. She and Joe together. They were a good team. Better than a team. She remembered him being brutally beaten and a tear slipped down her cheek. She was still alive, so maybe he was.

When she and Joe turned up missing, the Company wouldn't sit idle. Hass had to know he was under intense suspicion. But he wasn't running. It didn't make sense.

Then a stunning thought hit. Was Hass's confidence in his "dedicated" assets in positions of power so great he believed he might succeed with his warped plans?

As time passed, she lost track of time. She had been up for hours and exhaustion and letdown were settling in, and the utter darkness, silence and lack of even the tactile brush of a breath of air put her into a deep sleep.

Chapter 28

12:30 p.m.

The Hass Chemie helicopter touched down at the private airport in a southern suburb of Munich. Maurus climbed out of the passenger seat, swiveled and fetched out a duffel bag. Stooping slightly, he ran toward the Hass Chemie hangar, hair and clothing whipping against his body. The pilot settled in to await his return.

Maurus had adequate time to get the delivery van packed with explosives to Kariango, the man assigned to detonate them, and still return to the Compound. But he didn't want to press his luck. He would move swiftly. The final delivery itself had been planned, timed and practiced to perfection. From that schedule, there would be no deviation. Except, of course, for the fact that Kariango would set it all off a day early.

The van was crammed full of enough plastique to demolish anything within three hundred feet of it. It was painted to match exactly those of the company that brought fresh bakery goods to the Hotel Daimler somewhere around three every morning. The team he had assigned to make sure the real truck did not show up was already in motion. Maurus would deliver the truck to Kariango and then fly back to the Compound.

The Founder's intelligence had, days ago, pinpointed the location of the chancellor's suite. When parked, the truck would be one hundred and twenty feet from where the chancellor now slept. And when Kariango set off the plastique, Wilhelm Gottfried would become a name for history books.

The door opened and Nova snapped awake and fully alert. A shaft of light burst in from the corridor. Oh, God. The metallic taste of fear filled her mouth. The studio lights went on. She blinked once against the sudden brightness.

"Nova?"

Jean Paul stood in the doorway. She blinked several times. With oddly uncoordinated movements, he closed the door and then walked toward her. Relief washed her with a warm flood, but fast on its heels came a cold slap of suspicion. Why was he here? He knelt and touched her cheek and asked, "What has he done to you?"

"I'm okay, Jean Paul. I just want to be freed." She had no choice but to trust him. She nodded toward the carton razor. "Use that. Please cut the tape."

Would he cut her free or cut her throat?

He slit through the tape on one arm, then the other. Relief left her momentarily light-headed as he cut her legs free. Stiffly, like a recording, he said, "You must get away from here at once, Nova."

Flee? Perhaps Hass was using Jean Paul to somehow set her up. "Jean Paul, do you know where Joe is?"

"Joe?"

She couldn't comprehend the change in him. He sounded as if he'd never heard of Joe. "Yes, Joe. Do you know where he is?"

"No. But I know you must get away from here."

"I have to look for Joe first." She stood. "What time is it?"

"Nearly midnight. Everyone is sleeping, I think. They left me alone. Do you want my shirt?"

Midnight! How could she have slept so many hours? She touched his cheek and immediately regretted having done so. This tenderness made her weak, unfocused. Any weakness now could mean death.

"Thank you," she said, taking the shirt. She buttoned it and tucked it in. While Jean Paul stood flat-footed, watching, she put the carton razor in a pant pocket then checked Hass's desk drawers and side cabinets for a gun. No luck.

"Come." She opened the door a crack and checked the corridor. Nothing but concrete silence. She eased the door closed behind them.

Mutely, Jean Paul followed her. Both electric carts were gone and unfortunately with them the disk she'd hidden in the cushions. She returned to the first office. Joe was there, alive but tied to a chair. She felt like raining kisses on his silly, relieved-looking grin. "You're supposed to be dead," she said.

He said flatly, "That pleasure went to Wyczek."

The guard's face was a mess. She didn't ask for an explanation.

The razor made short work of Joe's bonds. She shoved Wyczek's Beretta into her waistband at the small of her back. She frisked Wyczek's body, found a knife in a sheath on his leg and strapped it to her leg.

"Don't I get anything?" Joe asked.

She looked pointedly at his useless right arm. "How good a shot are you with your left hand?"

"Fair."

"And left-handed with a knife?"

"Lousy."

"So that answers your question." She handed him the razor. "For close-up work."

He nodded and slipped the razor into his left hip pocket.

Jean Paul broke his unnatural silence. "You must leave the Compound, Nova." Arms that had hung limply at Jean Paul's sides raised slowly and he embraced her tightly, as if afraid she might vanish.

Joe frowned. "I think he's all screwed up between his conditioning for loyalty to Hass and wanting to help you."

She stepped back from Jean Paul, holding on to both of his forearms. "I agree, Jean Paul, that we have to find a way out of here, and we need a telephone."

Joe nodded toward the door. "Let's try the steel doors opposite this room. They don't have a security patch, just a regular-looking call button. I think it's an elevator to the mansion. The only problem is, if we come out inside the mansion, we may find ourselves face-to-face with Hass."

She shook her head. "I don't think so. I'll tell you why in a minute." She hurried across the hall, pressed the button. The door slid open. It was indeed an elevator. "Listen, Joe," she said, fishing out the Beretta, "things have changed and not for the better." As the elevator rose she told Joe half of the conversation between Hass and Singh. The elevator stopped.

The door slid open. Step by cautious step, she preceded Joe and Jean Paul into a large, unoccupied paneled den. She scanned for a phone, still explaining. "It's midnight now. Hass said something that made me think if they do advance the assassination, it'll go down in about three hours. He said he'd send Maurus by helicopter. That had to be hours ago. So if they don't cancel, we probably have only a little over two or three hours to warn the chancellor. Or stop Hass from okaying the attempt."

Joe's eyes rounded with disbelief. "Two to three hours?"

"Correct." She spotted the phone. "There," she said, pointing to a table next to a wing-backed chair.

Joe beat her to it. "You have the gun," he said. "I'll call. You watch for bad guys."

Using his left hand, Joe cradled the phone between left shoulder and chin, then dialed. A pause. "Super," he muttered. "I think the damn thing's dead. Tell me again how you dial outside."

"A seven, then just dial normally."

"That's what I did. Nothing happened."

He tried again, shook his head. "It's definitely dead."

"Dial the switchboard. Ask if she can place a call."

Joe was already dialing. He talked, then listened. "No kidding," he said. "No, no. That's all right. It's not urgent. It can wait."

"So?"

"The outside phones are dead. Security thinks the tree-huggers did it."

The ironic absurdity nearly took Nova's breath away. "Well isn't that just marvelous."

Joe strode to one of the den's draped windows. "Let's get out of this house. This way." The window was large, climbing through it easy for her and Joe, but Jean Paul clambered through with the stiffness of a bear coming out of hibernation.

Her arm linked with Jean Paul's and Joe leading, they crept downhill toward Hass's private tennis court, passed it, then stopped. In a small grove of oaks, she and Joe squatted beside bushes. She yanked Jean Paul down beside her.

She needed to make some fast decisions. "The radio you stashed may be our last chance to stop the assassination."

"Agreed," Joe said. "What happened to the disk?"

"I hid it on one of the carts, which is probably sitting back in the tunnel at the door to the hump. We don't have time to hunt for it, though, if we're going to stop the assassination. One of us has to get to the radio ASAP. If their dog sniffed our clothing, though, then that same person will have to get into Turm. By then it'll probably be too late to save the chancellor, but we have to try."

Joe frowned. "Why do you say, 'that person'? I don't like the sound of where you're going with this."

"One of us has to go back into the red zone. If our radio was discovered, the only way to stop the assassination may be from this end. And we need that disk."

Joe's whisper exploded as if someone had goosed him. "This place will be armed to the teeth now, especially the red zone."

They heard footsteps. A guard carrying an Uzi was headed their way. She put her finger to her lips, signaling Jean Paul to remain silent. When the guard drew opposite to the bushes where they were crouched, she rushed forward and tackled him. Joe used her Beretta to knock him out. He went down like a felled tree, and Nova passed the Uzi to Joe. He slung it over his good shoulder. Together they dragged the guard off the trail, then Joe reached toward the pocket where he'd put the carton razor.

"No," she said. "We tie and gag him. No one'll find him before morning."

They stashed the guard under a bush, and as they huddled again with Jean Paul she said firmly, "Look, we don't have time to debate. How's your arm?"

"You know damn well it's useless."

"Exactly. That means you go for the radio and into Turm if necessary, and I go for Hass and the disk in the red zone."

"That's insane, Nova. For one thing, there's no way to get in now." It was dark, but she imagined she saw Joe's face glowing red with anger. "They'll have figured how we got in. And even if you could get in, how far do you think you'll get before they catch you?"

"We'll find out."

"I won't let you do it. At least come with me to try the radio first?"

"Please, Nova. Listen to Joe."

Her throat tightened. To see Jean Paul so maimed was hideous. No matter what Singh had said, she had to believe there was some way to reverse the process.

"You can't go into the mountain," Jean Paul continued. "I beg you. Leave. Go away from here."

She squeezed Jean Paul's hand gently. "Both of you listen. I'm not going to repeat myself. We're wasting critical time. Joe, you know I'm right. We don't have the luxury of trying the radio first. We have to split up and hope at least one of us is successful in stopping the assassination. And one of us also has to try to find the disk." She gave him a smile. "I can handle it."

"Handle it." He shook his head. "How will you get in?"

"I'll figure something. More important, if the dog found our radio, how will you go into Turm?"

He clamped his mouth into a firm line, tightened his jaw. "I can't leave you here."

"You can. You will."

They both knew what her chances were.

Just as she decided she'd simply have to order him, he blew out a breath of air he'd been holding in and said, "I don't think with one arm I would be able to drive a car past the guards at the front gate. They'll be heavily armed. I think I'd do better stealing a plane than crashing the front gate in a car."

"How well do you ride? The stable's three times closer to where we hid the equipment than the airport."

He nodded. "I'll keep it in mind." He nodded toward Jean Paul. "What about him?" He spoke as though Jean Paul were a child.

"Jean Paul stays with me. He'd slow you down."

The time had come to part. Their hands reached out at the same moment. His left-handed grasp was awkward, but very firm. Then he grabbed and one-armed hugged her so hard it knocked the breath out of her. "Take damn good care."

"And you bring the cavalry back pronto."

Chapter 29

12:30 a.m.

Joe hadn't been out of her sight more than twenty seconds before Nova realized she'd have no trouble at all getting inside the mountain. She sucked in a shaky breath. "Jean Paul, I need your help. Will you help me?"

"Yes."

She squeezed his hand. "Good. Follow me. Walk exactly like I do."

By a miracle they reached Research Building No. 1 without being seen by guards.

"We're going straight to the Communications room," she said. "We must be very cautious and quiet."

"We shouldn't go here."

"Just do as I ask. Please."

She took Jean Paul's forearm and pulled away the

gauze patch. The tiny incision, halfway between his elbow and wrist, was less than half an inch long. "Hold it over the detector." He did. The steel doors sucked open. The corridor, leading directly south, was empty. She laid the gauze back over his incision and refastened the bandage.

"Follow me. Do just what I do."

Fifty feet inside, they came to the first cross-corridor. They'd almost reached the door to Singh's demonstration laboratory when two figures rounded the corner at the far end of the long hallway. She grabbed Jean Paul's arm and yanked him into the lab, hoping the men hadn't seen them.

Lights were on in the small central cubicle and at the lab's other end. She hurried Jean Paul past the cubicle and they were ten feet from the far door when, right in front of her, Singh walked in. He was five steps inside before he looked over his left shoulder. He spun to face her. "You. How can you be—"

Singh's gaze flicked to her right and she followed its trajectory to the door and an intercom. Jean Paul was three feet from the intercom, his body blocking her from it. Singh edged back toward the door. He was going for the intercom. Her mind flashed the image of the two ravaged golden retrievers.

Singh whirled. From the counter behind him he snatched an iron ring stand. She raised her leg and palmed the knife from the leg sheath.

His voice quivering, Singh shouted, "Do nothing further to help her, Jean Paul."

Singh rushed for the intercom and Nova shoved Jean Paul aside. The scientist swung the base of the stand at her head. She threw up her left arm. Pain like exploding shards of glass rammed into her armpit. Singh stumbled against her. She put the knife just below his rib cage. Shoved. Hard. Upward. Singh gasped, then sagged to the floor.

She knelt and gagged. She swallowed several times, forced down stomach acid, brushed her hand across her forehead. *Not now!*

She stood, but didn't bother pulling the knife out of Singh's body.

Jean Paul hadn't lifted a finger. She ran to the wall and turned off the light. The room crashed into near darkness, the only illumination coming from the hallways. In the corridor, she heard the sound of male laughter. She ran to Jean Paul and put her arm around him and checked his face to reassure herself he wouldn't call to them.

"*Are* you trying to harm Helmut?" he asked intently. She put a finger over his lips.

The men passed by the door through which she and Jean Paul had entered. She waited, listening. The voices turned south and walked past the second door. She heard the sound of another door opening and closing, and risked a peek into the hall.

"Stay here," she whispered firmly, praying he'd do what she asked. "Will you stay here and do nothing?"

"Yes."

The door the men had entered said Water Closet. She pulled out the Beretta, opened the door, found them with their hands to their flies. She commanded in German that they lie down. They hesitated, obviously wondering if they could jump her before she shot them. Apparently deciding it wasn't worth the risk, both got down flat on their bellies. Using the Beretta, she knocked out one and then the other, and then bound them.

"Nova?"

She nearly leaped out of her skin. There stood Jean Paul, more animated now. Why hadn't he done as she asked!

With three men down, the odds of stopping Hass felt better. Jean Paul again followed her down the hallway. She kept checking her rear. The computer room was dark but the Communications room was lit and discharging human voices. Hass might be here.

Jean Paul walked to one side and slightly behind her. She put a warning finger to her lips. They moved near the door. She slowed, then sprinted the last ten feet and flattened against the wall next to the opening. Jean Paul copied her.

She listened several seconds. One man complained about something. Then she heard a wheezy voice say, "You'll get no argument from me. I told him to fetch The Founder."

Wheezy Voice had been speaking in German. When he'd said, "The Founder," he'd used the feminine form of the noun. *Die gründerin*, not *der gründer*. It was as if— But that didn't make any sense.

She grasped the butt of the gun with both hands, spun around the door jamb into the room and barked in German, "Don't anybody move." Five men swiveled to face her; their jaws dropped open. One was Maurus. He grabbed for his gun.

She fired three times with the Beretta.

Maurus fell dead to the floor like a telephone pole crashing onto concrete. Communications equipment shattered and blacked out. She had the horrid thought she might have just destroyed her only way to contact Cupid. She yelled, "Get on your knees!" She could feel

Jean Paul slightly behind and to her right. "Remove your weapons. Slowly. Put them on the floor in front of you." The remaining men obeyed. "Push them away. Gently!"

Again they obeyed.

"Jean Paul, pick up their guns and put them in the trash can!"

Jean Paul picked up the first and second weapon, but instead of going behind her to reach the third, he crossed in front. Another man lunged for his gun. Two more quick shots from her Beretta. In a kind of balletic slow motion, the man collapsed.

At the sound of another gunshot, she felt a sudden pain and spun right. A third guy had nicked her right biceps.

Her Beretta spat twice again, and her aim was better than his. *Bloody mess!*

Hass would come quickly now, probably with reinforcements. She stepped to the remaining man, cowering on the floor and, using the Beretta's butt, whacked him.

From behind her a woman's voice yelled in commanding tones, "Kill her, Jean Paul. She will destroy everything."

Nova straightened and pivoted. Hass stood in the doorway, his lips contorted, his skin a bright pink, his eyes rimmed with red. But behind him stood Braunwin. Dressed in a dramatic scarlet suit, Braunwin radiated power.

The meaning of Wheezy Voice's use of the feminine form of Founder exploded into surety. Braunwin was The Founder, not the sicko White Praying Mantis. Hass was a front, Braunwin the fanatic visionary. Braunwin the one determined to make their father's dreams reality. Joe, Cupid, even Nova, they had all been thoroughly duped.

Hass screeched, "Kill her, Jean Paul!"

Nova looked at Jean Paul. His face was a mask of confused agony. A gun was in his hand. It pointed right at her heart.

"This is necessary, Jean Paul," Hass again screeched in German. "Do what I say. Kill her!"

Braunwin turned, ran down the hall, fetching reinforcements or escaping.

Jean Paul stood between Nova and the door. Their guns were barrel-to-barrel, four feet apart. "Put the gun down, Jean Paul. You would never hurt me."

He put his left hand to his temple. His eyes were glazed and their edges pinched. One corner of his mouth turned up, the other down, and his jaw muscles clenched and unclenched. Disbelief paralyzed her. He was actually going to obey Hass.

From her right she heard a loud scuffling noise. Jean Paul heard it, too. His gaze shifted toward the noise. Hass straightened, a gun from the wastebasket now in his hand, its barrel pointed at Nova.

Facing Hass and shouting, "No!" Jean Paul stepped between Nova and the albino.

The sound of a gunshot exploded once more. Jean Paul went rigid, fell to his knees and then sideways to the floor.

"No, no, no," she heard herself screaming as she switched her aim to Hass and pulled the Beretta's trigger. Hass crashed facedown to the floor, the back of his head a bloody red hole against white hair and skin.

Jean Paul lay on his side. Nova dropped down beside him. His image swam in front of her, and she couldn't hear clearly because the world seemed suddenly muffled in cotton padding. Nothing appeared to be moving or real.

She set her gun on the floor, noting dispassionately that it was covered with her blood: she'd only been nicked, but she was bleeding freely. Some part of her said it was wrong, terribly wrong, to put her gun down, but the voice was dim. She lifted Jean Paul's head and rested it against her thighs. He rolled onto his back. She laid the palm of one hand against his cheek, felt his warmth, the shaved stubble of his beard.

He smiled. "This way is better." Like everything else, he, too, sounded far away and muffled. "There is…" He stopped, coughed.

A different voice, in her head, intruded. *You've discovered The Founder, and The Founder may be escaping!*

"There is something wrong with my mind."

Blood oozed from a wound in his chest, though mercifully not fast like an artery. He might bleed to death on this floor. She felt icy-cold. He might die because she had used him: she had brought him here rather than send him away. And he had stepped in front of her and taken the bullet meant for her.

She said, "It doesn't make any difference now what they did to you. I heard them, Jean Paul. The conditioning was only to The Founder. If The Founder is dead, your mind will be okay. I promise. You'll have yourself back. You must hang on."

The insistent voice in her head said, *If Braunwin Hass escapes, others will continue to die.*

Jean Paul lifted his hand. She clutched it. "You do love me, don't you?" he said.

She kissed his palm. She laid his palm against her cheek. "Oh, God, Jean Paul. I do love you so very much."

She's escaping! yelled the voice in Nova's head. "I have to stop Braunwin."

He tried to squeeze her hand, but had lost his strength. "Do it then."

She kissed him. "You hang on for me, love. I'll come back for you."

He nodded.

She let his head slip down her thighs to the floor, picked up her gun and ran into the hall, down the corridor in the direction Braunwin Hass had taken, toward the computer room. Its door was open, the lights on. The screen was up—but blank. Nova would stop Braunwin. Then she would go back to Communications and call Cupid. If the equipment was still functional.

Braunwin was fleeing and would want to erase Singh's work, to keep the secrets for herself. That would explain why the computer screen was on but blank. Somewhere, though, there would be backup disks. Nova dashed into the hall, guessing that Braunwin might go to the area with the unique security code. Halfway there another thought yanked her to a halt. She released the Beretta's magazine and found one lousy bullet.

Why hadn't she snatched another gun!

At the far end of the corridor, Braunwin stepped into the hallway. Their stares locked. The Founder held a square silver case in one hand, a gun in her other. She fired four shots. All wild. She ran, disappearing northward into the long corridor that led to the exit into Research Building No. 1.

Backup disks had to be in that case.

Nova sprinted down the hall.

She careened around the corner and peered down the long corridor. Braunwin was three-quarters of the way to the security door. Nova pulled to a halt. Her traumatized right arm trembled like a struck piano wire.

She switched the Beretta to her left hand—just like Joe, she was lousy with her left hand—took aim at Braunwin's back, inhaled a breath, held it, fired.

Missed.

Braunwin had dodged right at the last second, into the big lab. At this moment, Braunwin would be stumbling over Singh's body.

Expecting that Braunwin would escape through the lab's north door, Nova dashed past the first door, grabbed the wall to help her round the corner, half expecting to crash into the fleeing woman. But Braunwin was still in the lab.

Nova barged into the darkened room. Three more shots exploded, glass shattered, metal pinged. She didn't see where the shots had come from, but all had missed. Nova crouched beside a wall counter.

When Nova had been framed in the doorway, she'd made a beautiful backlit target. But Braunwin Hass was clearly no marksman and she was expending too many bullets too fast. Already she'd used seven. How many did her gun's magazine hold? Seven? Ten? More?

Nova needed a weapon. Fast!

She listened. Nothing. Braunwin was probably still at the room's far end. Nova rose to a crouch, ran forward ten feet. Three shots, three flashes of white.

Got her! Braunwin was cornered. One way or the other, she would have to pass Nova to make either door. But Nova still needed to get her to use up her ammo.

Nova scuttled across the aisle between the counter and the closest lab bench. Three more shots rang out. Good! Thirteen she said to herself. Then she noticed pain as her left leg buckled. The Queen Mantis had made a lucky hit, right through one of the four knee-level holes spaced along the lab bench's length. Nova fingered where she'd been hit, low in the calf.

"Put your gun down and come out, Braunwin. I have both doors covered. There's no way past me."

Though Braunwin was taller and outweighed Nova by many pounds, Nova was a trained fighter. But she now had an injured right arm and left leg. Even Braunwin could probably thrash her senseless. There was the knife, buried in Singh at the other end of the lab. But to reach it she'd have to move from this spot and leave the lab's north door uncovered.

Singh had used a ring stand. Nova squinted into the near darkness. Nothing looked like a ring stand. Only glassware or equipment too heavy to lift or too flimsy to be of use.

The vials! She looked behind her to the location of the small compartment. Unfortunately no mask sat on the counter, but four masks did hang outside the door to the cubicle. If she could corner Braunwin in the cubicle....

It wouldn't be long before Braunwin decided to make a move. Like a lopsided crab, Nova scuttled back to the counter. Half crouched, her head below the counter, she reached an arm over the edge and felt for the knob. She twisted it and slid the lid back. Blindly she reached in. *Remember,* she coached as her fingers curled around a small, cool cylinder, *you don't want to break this thing till you mean to.* She pulled out a vial and tucked it into her bra.

To use the drug on Braunwin, Nova must somehow maneuver Braunwin into the cubicle. Fortunately, both its outer and inner door stood open. She snatched a beaker from the counter and dumped its contents—goo reeking of sauerkraut. Nova eyed the counter, rolled the beaker along its length. At the spot right where she wanted, the beaker hit the wall and shattered.

Two shots from Braunwin's gun.

Then a soft click.

Ha! Braunwin had to run now. And she did, exactly as Nova hoped, to the right. Just outside the cubicle's outer door, Nova grabbed Braunwin's arm and yanked the case from her hand. She limped past Braunwin, entered the outer door and threw the case inside the inner chamber.

"Bitch," Braunwin screamed. "Filthy bitch! You don't know what you're doing."

Braunwin dashed past Nova into the inner chamber. Nova, her leg on fire, turned, stumbled, limped back toward the outer door. Braunwin scooped up the case, whirled and started back out. Nova yanked a gas mask from a peg and looped its straps over her left arm. But at the inner door, before she could fetch the vial from her bra, Braunwin caught up to her.

"You stupid woman," Braunwin screeched. "You're interfering with greatness."

Nova smashed her palm against the woman's chest, aiming to push Braunwin back inside, but Braunwin's fingers caught Nova's shirt pocket. She heard a ripping sound, but her pocket didn't come completely free.

Braunwin slammed her arm across Nova's chest, tried to slither past and through the outer door. Nova grabbed Braunwin's arm, but her fingers slipped. Panicked, she threw herself against the larger woman. "You're not great. You're crazy!"

They grappled, scuffled, twisted halfway around in the inner doorway. The mask flew off Nova's arm and rolled into the inner chamber's far corner. Braunwin was wriggling free! With the sound of her blood pounding deafeningly in her ears, Nova piled her full weight against Braunwin and wrapped her arms and legs around Braunwin's body.

Together they fell into the chamber, then rolled left in a frantic embrace.

This was all wrong! Nova wasn't supposed to be in here. She couldn't use the ampoule's drug now. And what kind was it? She hadn't looked. She balled her fist, looked for a chance to smash Braunwin's larynx.

Hot breath brushed her face. Braunwin's hands were all over the place, pushing, clawing. Braunwin's weight pressed onto Nova's injured calf. In Nova's head a dizzying black cloud mushroomed.

Braunwin grabbed Nova's arm directly over her wound. Wave after wave of pain rushed up and outward from the contact point. Braunwin squeezed. Another surge of darkness hit. Nova twisted her left wrist free. Whatever the vial held—oh, God—whatever it held, she had to use it. She snatched the vial from her bra.

She sucked in air, lifted the vial to bring it down against the floor. At the same moment, she and Braunwin both saw that the colored band at the neck was purple.

Braunwin, her eyes full of horror, grabbed Nova's wrist.

Nova wavered, the horror in her soul a mirror of Braunwin's terror. What if she inhaled? She couldn't do it to herself. To die would be better.

Braunwin lifted them both halfway off the floor. Her right arm came free of Nova's grip. She grabbed the hand in which Nova held the ampoule. *Do it. Do it!* Nova's mind screamed. *There is no other way!*

She sucked in a breath. Another. Braunwin guessed her intention. Frantically pushing upward against Nova's arm, Braunwin, too, sucked in a breath. One last breath and Nova rotated her arm, wrenched it from Braunwin's hand, brought the vial's neck to the floor.

The soft sound of a click of breaking glass and the Pacification Inducer began to flood the chamber— Singh's proud equivalent of a prefrontal lobotomy.

Braunwin released Nova, clawed frantically toward the corner and the mask. Nova clung to her. Braunwin dragged both of them across the floor. *Don't breathe, don't breathe, don't breathe, don't breathe.* Again, Braunwin squeezed Nova's wound. A searing fire raced through Nova's chest, exploded in her head.

The Founder's lower body thrashed in frenzy, fighting to break the python-like grip of Nova's legs. The prospect of being dead while alive clearly terrified Braunwin as much as it did Nova. Nova tightened her predatory hug.

God, how she wanted to breathe!

Braunwin stiffened. Nova looked up at the beautiful face—now swollen, flushed, eyes bulging, hate-contorted. In a great wheezing gasp, through a lipstick-smeared mouth, Braunwin sucked in air.

Nova kicked away, rolled to the mask, slapped it against her face, purged it of residual air, frantically sucked in a breath. And another. And another.

Her hands trembled; she pressed the mask harder against her face. Did she smell coffee? No. That was good! Quaking from head to foot, she sent her mind in search of pain. If she could feel pain, wouldn't that mean the drug hadn't reached her? Her arm and leg stung as though someone had stabbed her with white-hot pokers, and relief poured through her.

Braunwin lay still, face calm now, blue eyes utterly blank.

Nova sat rigid. She didn't dare move—not the slightest move—lest gas leaked around the edges of the mask and the blank look on Braunwin's face happened to her. The Queen Mantis lay motionless, staring sightlessly at the ceiling. From now on, others would be running life for this control freak.

Singh had told Wyczek to either purge the cubicle or to wait ten minutes. Nova glanced at a wall clock. She had no idea how to purge the cubicle. She must force herself to wait. Then she must try to reach Cupid. And then see to Jean Paul.

The aluminum case caught her attention. Listening to the mask's amplified sounds of her slowing breathing, she stared at the case, trying to decide. What was the right thing to do? Destroy or save Singh's work? If she destroyed it, this dreadful means of controlling minds might never be rediscovered.

Provided she was very thorough. Again she checked the clock. Six minutes to wait.

The backup disks, the labs, anything that might reveal any details would have to go. Fortunately, the disk Joe had copied held nothing scientific. If she could find the electric cart, she'd at least have that disk to give to Cupid.

What you're thinking is illegal. In its way, unethical. The Company pays you. You've never cheated on them before.

And the Company expected her to tell all. And unless she was both very clever and very lucky, during debriefing they would catch her. Was she willing to pay the price?

In human affairs, knowledge had displaced brawn as the base of power: a few smart bombs were superior competitors to any second-rate army. Beyond question,

Singh's drugs constituted a terrible power. It was often said, and she believed it, that men had never invented a weapon someone didn't eventually use.

Finally the waiting time was over. And she'd made her decision. She rose, stepped past the dazed Braunwin, and headed for the Communications room.

Chapter 30

At one fifty-three in the morning, Joe fell off a winded horse in front of the pension in Turm. He stumbled up the single flight of stairs to Cupid's room. Cupid's first call was to station head in Berlin. Another agent—Johann—did a fair job of cleaning Joe's wounded arm and rigging a sling while Joe thumbnailed The Founder's assassination scheme. Word went quickly from Berlin to the chancellor's security team.

A second call rounded up the cavalry: in little more than an hour, he was on his way back to the Compound with Cupid, German soldiers and five helicopters. Halfway there, Cupid took a call from the chancellor's security detail. The chancellor was safe, a bomb planted in a delivery truck was being defused.

Shortly before three, hovering over the Compound, Joe

peered through binoculars. His gut was rolling. The scene was bizarre. All the lab buildings had lights on inside.

His chopper came in closer and he scanned the grounds. Finally he saw Nova, sitting on the grass well away from the mountain, not far from the lake.

Relief momentarily doused his guilt for having left her.

König lay with his head on Nova's lap. Braunwin Hass sat beside Nova. Joe blinked several times and squinted. Yup. Definitely Braunwin Hass.

Clouds of steam or smoke from the hump's air vent openings billowed into the night. Not far from Nova, König and Braunwin, a couple of handfuls of the Compound's armed guards stood gaping at the helicopters and the mountain. The helicopter lowered and touched down. The German soldiers began rounding up the Hass Chemie employees.

With Cupid, Joe raced to Nova. Braunwin Hass looked as though she was in a trance. König was bleeding from the chest and unconscious. Nova, too, looked dazed.

He saw blood on her hand and a wound high on her arm. On shaky legs, he knelt beside her. "We brought stuff to blow the security door. Your arm?"

She shook her head. "It's nothing. And you don't need to blow the door. In fact, keep everyone away. It's dangerous. Braunwin set the place on fire."

Braunwin?

Nova looked at Davidson. "We must get Jean Paul to a hospital at once."

Davidson squatted in front of Nova. "Where is Hass? Where is The Founder?"

She said, "Hass wasn't The Founder. I'll explain everything to you only when I see Jean Paul on his way to a hospital."

Two soldiers ran up. They started to lift König but Nova bent over and kissed the man on the cheek, whispered something into his ear. Then she let the soldiers take him.

"What do you mean, Hass wasn't The Founder?" Davidson asked.

Watching as the soldiers put König into the helicopter, she said, "Braunwin Hass is The Founder."

Dumbfounded, Joe looked at Hass's strangely tranquil wife.

Davidson said, "I don't understand."

"Hass was a demented front man." Nova proceeded to tell a wild tale. She had overheard men talking. One had said, "die gründerin," not "der gründer." Shots were fired. Hass was killed. Jean Paul was wounded saving her. The communications equipment had been destroyed. "Before I caught up to Braunwin, she'd started fires in several of the labs. The place is full of chemicals and explosives."

The word "explosive" had barely left Nova's lips when the backside of the mountain blew. Trees, dirt, rocks—all lifted skyward accompanied by a ground-shaking, bone-rattling boom.

All activity on the lawn froze. Some soldiers crouched or threw arms over their heads. Joe flinched and then just watched the rising mass of earth and stone. Within moments debris rained around them, smaller bits of pulverized rock and vegetation.

When it seemed that no further eruptions would occur, Davidson nodded toward Braunwin and said to Nova, "What's the matter with her?"

Hass's wife—apparently The Fucker—still sat calmly, her knees up, staring at nothing in particular. She seemed scarcely to have noticed the explosion.

Nova shook her head. "What about Willy Gottfried?"

"He's okay," Davidson said. "And they caught a Nigerian who showed up with a truckful of explosives. But what's wrong with Hass's wife?"

"Her own damn drug. The only way I could think to stop her was by breaking open a vial." She looked at Joe. "And neither of us had gas masks when we started struggling. We were already fighting when I realize it was the Pacification Inducer."

In a flash of frightening detail, Joe saw their struggle—blond Braunwin, dark Nova—in an embrace that meant living death for one or both of them. He searched her green eyes. No wonder she seemed dazed. There sat Braunwin Hass: deflated, defeated, dependent on others for the rest of her bodily existence. To take a gamble that big took guts. Or maybe just Nova's own brand of insanity.

Nova looked to Davidson. "It makes you a vegetable."

Davidson shook his head. "When will she snap out of it so we can question her?"

"Never," Joe answered. "The drug's effects are permanent."

Davidson recoiled. "Never?" He glanced back at the entry to the red zone, then at Nova. "Singh, then. Where is he?"

"Inside. Dead. Also Maurus." Joe watched as Nova pulled a computer disk from her shirt pocket. "This details the structure of the Hass organization."

Davidson stood, whipped off his glasses, his eyes narrowed in agitation. "But what about the drugs? The research? You do have samples."

"No. Braunwin erased the memory of the computer. When I caught up to her, she was making off with what were probably the only backup files and they got burned."

Joe suddenly noticed blood on Nova's left pant leg. "Nova, your leg's also hurt!" He put a hand to the wound and Nova flinched. He looked up at Davidson. "She needs a medic."

The chief of station's cherubic face had hardened to stone. "What about the backup files?"

"I went back for the files, but fire from the next room had broken through the wall. The case had already burned. Sprinklers never did come on. I got Braunwin out, and then I found an equipment cart and packed out Jean Paul and the three other men who were still alive."

"Three men?"

"You'll find three men hog-tied in a storeroom in Building No. 1. I told the guards out here that Singh shot Jean Paul accidentally. They also think the fire's an accident, in case you want to leave them with that impression. When Peter Grund finally came down from the house and saw Jean Paul wounded and I told him there was no way to call out for help, he started screaming. When he stopped, he ran back toward the mansion. Said he was going to drive into Turm for a doctor."

Nova brushed her hair away from her face, leaving a streak of blood. Joe fought an intense urge to wipe it away. She looked at him, gave him a crooked, shaky smile. She said, "It was only a few minutes before you showed up with the cavalry."

Joe had reached a point way beyond astonishment. But Davidson wasn't thinking along the same lines. His voice projected all the warmth of a lender telling you the mortgage is overdue and he's selling your family home. "Are you saying this place is on fire and you have no evidence of any kind of what was going on inside? Specifically, no data on Singh's project?"

Joe scowled. "That's what she said. And she's hurt. Let one of the choppers take her to a hospital. We can debrief later."

For the first time, Nova tried to stand. An intense grimace flashed on her face.

"You don't look so good, partner," he said. He gave her a shaky smile. "No earrings." That won him a small smile. "Here," he said. "Let me help."

Joe envisioned Nova lying on the Fairbanks hospital floor. He remembered how he had doubted her ability to lead or her ability to fight. The thug in Fairbanks had been doped up on one of Singh's drugs, doubtless something more powerful than PCP. And he guessed she'd just single-handedly blown up the bad guys' lair. He knew she wouldn't risk letting Singh's sick drug formulas fall into anyone's hands—not even the CIA's—and he didn't blame her. In fact, a profound feeling of respect and admiration for Nova filled him. He'd been a fool to think she wasn't one of the toughest and bravest agents working for the CIA.

With his good left arm, he lifted Nova gently onto her right leg. She gulped in a pained breath but made no comment. He wasn't surprised—not anymore. She wrapped her arm around his neck and together they hobbled to the nearest helicopter.

Chapter 31

August 16

"Nothing about it will touch you adversely, Jean Paul." Peter Grund grinned and poked a finger toward Jean Paul to emphasize his point.

Grund reminded Nova of a gleeful, mischievous child who had lied to the school principal and gotten away with it. The press had bought his fabricated explanation that Jean Paul had been injured in a disastrous accidental explosion in Bavaria, the same explosion that had killed gazillionaire Helmut Hass, his wife and several of his staff.

Jean Paul smiled at Grund, then turned to look at her. Nova's gut suffered a painful twist. She clasped her hands together tightly in her lap. Lying on this hospital bed in front of her was a man who loved her and offered her the stuff of dreams. Love. Children. Happiness.

Peter Grund lifted himself out of the chair he had taken beside the bed. A surge of panic prickled the skin at the back of Nova's neck. The moment had come.

Grund said, "We should leave. We've exceeded our half hour."

Joe had been leaning against the wall with arms crossed, patiently listening while she and Peter Grund and Jean Paul had chatted. Joe straightened and walked toward Jean Paul's bed, then, leaning down, took hold of Nova's hand and squeezed it gently.

She glanced up at him and felt the intensity of his compassion wrap itself around her like a soft down comforter. He was a good friend, a solid man, a wild and free spirit like herself. He knew what she did and he accepted her just as she was, without reservations. It suddenly struck her that she could trust Joe every bit as much as she had learned to trust Jean Paul. And in a way, sharing this dilemma with Joe had given her the strength to do what she had to do now.

She looked back at Jean Paul. Knowing him had profoundly changed her. Despite what she had believed for years, despite a past so twisted she could never share it with anyone, she could now trust a man, and trust enough to accept love and return it. Jean Paul had given her this precious gift.

Her mind and heart waged war with each other as she watched Joe bend over the bed to shake Jean Paul's hand. They were two amazing yet vastly different men who had touched her life briefly and altered it forever.

Jean Paul said, "Let me say again, Joe, I am most deeply grateful."

Her partner's smile was warm, generous and as big as all Texas. "No thanks necessary. Accomplish half the things you want to, and I'll have the thanks I need."

Grund and Joe turned toward the door and Jean Paul said, "Nova, wait a minute," just as she said, "I'll be out in a second, Joe."

The moment the door closed behind the two men, Jean Paul held out a hand toward her. "Nova, how I've missed you. Why did you take so long to come? It's been four days."

She stepped to the bed. He took her hand. "The doctors said only family and close friends. And I don't fit into that category."

"Nonsense. You could have gotten Peter to make up some excuse." He placed her hand against his chest.

"I didn't think it was wise."

"Wise? Nova, I needed to see you."

She pulled her hand away.

He looked at her hand, then back to her eyes. He frowned. "What's wrong?"

"I am so grateful that you're alive. That you're going to be okay."

"Nova." His voice held more force now. "What's wrong?"

My God, this was so hard. And because she couldn't tell him the whole truth, he would probably never understand.

"I think it's best that we don't see each other again."

He moved to sit up but instead grimaced and fell back. She continued, certain she had to get it all out now or never. "Please know that I love you. Not seeing you again will be hard for me. But you don't really know me."

He stared at the sheet covering him a moment, then

fixed her gaze with those startling blue eyes. "Of course I know you. I love you. I've told you I want to divorce my wife and marry you." He started to protest further. She quickly put a finger to his lips. He put his hand over hers.

After a moment she pulled away. "No, Jean Paul. You barely know the real me. And you know nothing significant about my past. There are things I have told no one. Ugly things."

"I don't believe it. And I don't care about your past."

"One of us has to. You have a destiny to fulfill. Like it or not, you belong to the world. You know this is true. And the world just came frighteningly close to losing you. The truth is…you'll have to trust me about this… I'm the wrong woman for you."

A sudden dark cloud of anger passed over his face. "That isn't so, Nova. I need you. I love you." He tried to sit up, winced and clutched the bandage over his chest wound as he sank back again. "I want to marry you."

Nova Blair would be nothing to Jean Paul König but a scandalous, destructive liability. And slowly her feelings for Jean Paul would change as time passed.

She was truly an independent woman, and needed control over her life—control she would surely lose as a politician's wife. She'd won that control as a fifteen-year-old in a most brutally hard way and hadn't this mission only cemented how much she valued that independence?

Jean Paul waited, his eyes willing her to love him, to share his life with him.

But what if she was all wrong? What if true happiness required giving up some of that control. She inhaled a steadying breath. "I'm simply not willing to take that ride to fame and power with you."

He frowned. She rushed ahead, desperate now to get away. She felt dizzy. Nauseated. She must say something convincing. Something he could understand. "I don't want the publicity. I don't want the pressure. I don't want the worry. And I would never ask you to give up what you are meant to do. If I did that, and if you quit, then I couldn't live with either of us."

He shook his head. "I don't believe any of what you are saying."

She looked at the floor, swallowed, looked at him again straight-on. Jean Paul had no idea what kind of life she was accustomed to. "Believe me," she said firmly.

Using both hands, he pushed himself past his pain until he was fully upright. He reached a hand toward her.

She didn't take it. "When I leave," she said, "you won't be able to contact me." Her voice sounded hard in her ears. Did it sound hard to him?

She backed away a step. "I want very much to kiss you. On the cheek. Will you let me? And then let me go?"

His eyes held her gaze, but he said nothing.

She stepped to the bed, bent to him and kissed his cheek.

He touched her lips. Stunned, she realized that something had happened. The chemistry, the magic, had changed. It was over and she would never look back.

She stepped away, turned and walked to the door.

Outside, she leaned against the wall. As he'd promised, Joe was waiting.

"You okay?" he asked.

She nodded.

They turned and headed together down the corridor toward the entrance. Joe said, "You know, partner, you may have convinced Davidson and the others, but I'm never going to believe that all that damage to the hump and to Singh's research was caused by Braunwin Hass setting some room on fire."

She made no comment. He knew her better than she'd realized and, in turn, she knew he expected no answer.

She had worked hard during debriefing to convince her interrogators that there had been nothing she could do to save the data on Singh's drugs. She had easily fooled the lie detector test.

Although, at the end, one of her agents had let it slip that word had actually come from Washington, through the office of the DDO—Claiton Price himself—that her debriefing should be considered over. She might never know exactly what they would put in her file concerning her loyalty or truthfulness, but her conscience was clear. No fear that someone might ever use Singh's drugs would haunt her.

"Why do you do it?" Joe asked. His voice had taken on a different tone. Gentle as well as puzzled. "Why did you ever start working for the Company?"

They arrived at the waiting room near the entrance and stopped. "I do it because I'm good at it."

"It's dangerous. The people are stinging hornets or sucking leeches. You don't need this."

"Why do you do it, Joe? Why does anyone do it?" She looked into his eyes and felt an inexorable pull of a whirlpool dragging her under into dark places where she didn't want to go. He said nothing, waiting for her to answer.

"Maybe I do it," she said haltingly, searching for words, "to make up for things I've done that I prefer to forget." Heat rose to her face. She'd said too much. "Let's just leave it there."

Joe touched her arm, his hand strong but tender.

She imagined—was it possible?—that her face grew still hotter. Once again she thought how, unlike Jean Paul, Joe was the opposite of tame.

Joe pulled his hand away, jabbed it into his jacket pocket and retrieved a small purple box. Her first impression, because of the box's small size and shape and the gold lettering she couldn't read, was that it might hold an engagement ring. *What an odd thought.*

He held the box out and said, "I saw these yesterday." He grinned. "I've noted that you could desperately use some jewelry. So I thought—well, I saw these and of course right away thought of you."

She opened the lid and inside, on a bed of white cotton, lay a pair of dangly earrings. Each was a silver dove with wings spread, their eyes tiny emeralds.

She lifted the earrings, felt the message they actually conveyed. He, too, had enjoyed their partnership.

"They're beautiful, Joe." She handed him the box, removed the silver moon-sliver earrings she was wearing and exchanged them for the doves. She tilted her head.

He said, "They look great."

She closed the box lid and slipped the box into her jacket pocket.

They turned and Joe linked arms with her. Their steps in perfectly matched stride as they walked through the door and into a beautiful, sunny day, Nova said with a new air of confidence, "Agent Cardone, I think we make a great team."

ATHENA FORCE

Chosen for their talents.
Trained to be the best.

Expected to change the world.

The women of Athena Academy
share an unforgettable experience
and an unbreakable bond—until
one of their own is murdered.

The adventure begins with these six books:

PROOF by Justine Davis, July 2004

ALIAS by Amy J. Fetzer, August 2004

EXPOSED by Katherine Garbera,
September 2004

DOUBLE-CROSS by Meredith Fletcher,
October 2004

PURSUED by Catherine Mann, November 2004

JUSTICE by Debra Webb, December 2004

**And look for six more Athena Force stories
January to June 2005.**

Available at your favorite retail outlet.

HARLEQUIN®
INTRIGUE®

No cover charge.
No I.D. required.
Secrecy guaranteed.

CLUB UNDERCOVER

You're on
the guest list
for the hottest
romantic-suspense
series from

PATRICIA ROSEMOOR

A team of outcast specialists with their own dark secrets has banded together at Chicago's hottest nightclub to defend the innocent…and find love and redemption along the way.

 VELVET ROPES
July 2004

 ON THE LIST
August 2004

Look for them wherever Harlequin books are sold!

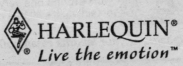

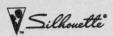

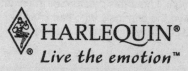

COMING NEXT MONTH

#5 KISS OF THE BLUE DRAGON—Julie Beard
Angel Baker wasn't your typical twenty-second-century girl—she was trying to rid the world of crime and have a life. Then her mother was kidnapped and Angel was forced to rely on powers she didn't know she possessed, and was drawn to the one sexy detective she shouldn't be....

#6 ALIAS—Amy J. Fetzer
An Athena Force Adventure
Darcy Steele was once the kind of woman friends counted on, until her bad marriage forced her to live in hiding. But when a killer threatened the lives of her former schoolmates, she had to help, even if it meant risking her life—and her heart—again.

#7 A.K.A. GODDESS—Evelyn Vaughan
The Grail Keepers
Modern-day grail keeper Maggie Sanger was on a quest, charged with recovering the lost chalices of female power. But when her research was stolen and suspicion fell on her ex-lover, Maggie was challenged to uncover the truth about the legacy she'd been born into—and the man she once loved.

#8 URBAN LEGEND—Erica Orloff
Tessa Van Doren owned the hottest nightclub in all of Manhattan, but rumors swirled around that she was a vampire. Little did anyone know this creature of the night had a cause to down the criminals who had killed her lover. Not even rugged cop Tony Flynn, who stalked her night after night....

SBCNM0704